FIRESIDE

Book 2 of The Path of Ashes

a post-apocalyptic series by
Brian Parker

This is a work of fiction. Names, characters, places and incidents are the product of the author's imagination or are used fictitiously. Any resemblance to actual events, locales, or persons, living or dead, is purely coincidental.

Notice: The views expressed herein are NOT endorsed by the United States Government, Department of Defense or Department of the Army.

Fireside
Book 2 of The Path of Ashes

PROLOGUE

The ringing of the family's alarm bell woke Aiden from a fitful sleep. He'd gone to bed late last night after telling the story of Aeric Traxx, the family's patriarch, to his grandchildren. The old man had a restless night as he dreamt of the past and the destruction of the city of San Angelo when he was a boy.

He peered around his bedroom, scanning for a threat, half-expecting to be attacked by someone in the darkness. The ink-black night outside his windows told him that it was still likely hours before dawn. The sturdy, old grandfather clock down in the foyer was the only timepiece that they had in the house, so he couldn't be sure of the time. If it had been the alarm, he needed to respond, regardless of the time of night, it was his duty.

He listened intently. The sound of the clock's swinging pendulum permeated the darkness, causing him to question his old ears. *Had I imagined it, possibly another nightmare?* he wondered. Aiden began to relax and lay back. The alarm no longer rang outside the house, so it was entirely possible that it had been a dream.

The scrape of boots against the concrete sidewalk made him sit up again. *Was that movement outside?* That wasn't right. At this hour, there shouldn't have been anyone awake except the sentries on the perimeter walls. No one should have been out in the courtyard unless the alarm had gone off and they were responding to it.

Regardless of his body's protests, Aiden chose to listen to the little voice telling him that something was wrong. He swung his legs over the side of the bed and walked quickly over to the armchair in the corner and sat down. He slid his legs into the ancient denim jeans. They'd been produced before the destruction of the old world almost eighty years ago and were then scavenged from an abandoned store in the former Republic of Texas.

"What is it, dear?" Aiden's wife asked.

"The alarms," he answered, grunting as he pulled his boots on. "They woke me up."

He saw the outline of her jaw in the moonlight as she tilted her head to listen. "I don't hear anything. Maybe you were dreaming?"

Aiden exhaled loudly and said, "I don't think so. I have to wake Blake and tell him what I thought I heard."

"Just come back to bed, you old fool! There's nothing out there but the wind. We're safe here."

He stood up and grabbed his sword with another sigh. She'd become complacent behind the Homestead's fence. Almost ten years younger than he was, she didn't remember the horror of San Angelo as almost four thousand people perished in less than a week. Anna was only an infant when her grandfather Tyler had led the survivors to safety. She'd been a toddler while the group struggled through the wastelands, fighting against mutated creatures and raiders as they looked for a permanent home and she was a young child when the Homestead was founded. Anna's childhood had been drastically different than Aiden's, who'd watched a madman behead his grandfather while he hid in a field, too afraid to intervene.

No, Anna had come of age in a simpler world. She didn't understand the true level of depravity in the new world.

"I'm going out to check the perimeter," he stated gruffly. "Then I'll come back to bed. It will only be a few minutes."

His wife harrumphed and turned over on the threadbare mattress that had been a permanent part of their lives for as long as either could remember. Aiden shook his head and padded slowly across the floor to their door, opening it cautiously and stepping out into the hallway. A shadow at the bottom of the stairs startled him.

"Blake?" Aiden called into the darkness.

"Yeah, it's me, Dad. You heard them too?"

Aiden's knees popped as he eased himself down the stairs. "The alarms?" he asked once he made it to the landing.

"They rang for just a moment and then stopped," Blake stated as he shrugged into his greatcoat and strapped the sword belt around his waist. He also stuffed an antique pistol into his pocket.

"I thought I'd dreamt it," Aiden said, putting on his own coat. "You sure that gun will even work anymore?" Guns were unreliable at best these days, usually more deadly to the user than their target since the years of intermittent ash and acid rain had wreaked havoc on most metals.

"Yes, sir. I've kept it clean and oiled like you taught me. I figured we might need the additional range if something did make it past the perimeter."

"If something made it past our guards then that little pistol isn't going to be able to stop it," the old man muttered. He patted his grandfather's sword on his hip. "This is all that matters now."

They went out through their front door into the Homestead's central courtyard where they maintained picnic tables and a communal fire pit for cooking animals too large for the fireplaces inside their individual homes. Aiden glanced wistfully at his old chair pulled near the pit's low brick wall. He was too old to be sneaking around in the darkness looking for intruders. Over the course of the night, the fire in the pit had burned down to small embers.

The night before, he'd sat in his chair and told his grandchildren about Aeric and Tyler's exploits in the beginning, at the end of the old world. As they stalked toward the wall's gate, he wondered if he'd ever have the chance to complete the story. His world was so different than it had been as a child, and his grandfather used to tell him how different *this* world was from the one *he'd* grown up in, before the nuclear missiles had irrevocably changed the landscape.

It seemed quiet outside, so what had caused the alarms to ring? Even more disconcerting for Aiden was the question of where the other residents were, or at the very least, where were the Traxx men? The noise should have caused the courtyard to be filled with men and the women who were not pregnant or not assigned the task of guarding the young. He looked around at the darkened buildings in disbelief. They'd trained for this scenario, where was everyone?

Blake had noticed the lack of response as well. "Why is no one else awake?" he whispered. "The alarm only came from the west. The other two guards didn't answer the sound with one of their own."

Aiden shook his head in confusion. "Something isn't right here, Blake."

The pistol glinted in the moonlight as the younger Traxx pulled the weapon from his pocket. They began heading for the western section of the perimeter fence when the scream of a woman broke the night's stillness. It had come from inside Luke's house.

The old man reacted slower than his son, who'd also pulled his sword from its sheath as he raced toward his brother's house. He slammed through the front door and tumbled into the entryway. Blake had expected the door to be locked, but the door had been ajar, not latched, and caught him off guard.

Aiden's sword felt comfortable in his hand as he took the porch steps two at a time. Adrenaline surged through him, causing the aches and pains of his old body to be temporarily forgotten. He arrived in time to see Blake sprinting up the stairs to the family's sleeping quarters, so he turned, heading into the family room to clear the bottom floor.

He wrinkled his nose at the metallic scent of blood and the acrid stench of loosened bowels. Aiden followed the odor toward his brother's room. His younger brother, Alex, had moved out of his home when his wife Mary died and now lived with Aiden's oldest son, Luke.

The smell got stronger and more pronounced the deeper into the home that Aiden walked. The clash of steel on steel drifted from the stairwell, startling him. Blake had found someone upstairs and fought with them. He wasn't worried for Blake; every member of the Traxx family was trained to fight from the day they could walk. Whatever he'd encountered upstairs would soon be nothing more than a quivering mass of flesh.

He took a deep breath to steady his nerves and walked several steps towards the room where his brother stayed. There was a strange sound coming from around the corner. It was something that he'd heard before. He couldn't quite put his finger on what it reminded him of, though. There was a wet, sucking sound and then... *Is that chewing*?

Aiden rushed around the corner with his sword held low. The darkness helped to hide the creature as it shrieked at him and charged. He had less than a second to lift the tip of his weapon, preparing to defend himself when the hilt jammed hard against his knuckles and knocked him backwards. The animal had run into the blade, heedless of its own safety, and skewered itself on the hardened steel.

It wasn't difficult to identify the creature, even in the darkness. It was one of the nightmares of the new world. The patchwork of black and gray fur mixed with hardened bone outcroppings made his bladder weak and the claws that flashed like wickedly curved daggers in the moonlight promised a swift and painful death to anyone who encountered the animal. It was a demonbroc. Long ago, before the radiation had changed them into the terrifying predator that they were today, the thing's ancestors had been called badgers. Somewhere along the line, someone who'd known that the Old English word for badger was "broc" had named the new, twisted creatures "demonbrocs," and it had stuck.

A lot of wild animals in the area had died out once the vegetation began to die. Not the badgers; they were omnivores and could eat almost anything to stay alive. They'd survived the devastation of those first few years after the war and over the years, their bodies had mutated to adapt to the harsh conditions of the wastelands. Besides the wandering human tribes, they were the largest threat to humanity in the wastes, at least that he knew of.

Aiden's mind reeled. Somehow the beast had gotten into the home without breaking down the door. Had it came in behind the person that Blake fought upstairs? What were the odds of an intruder *and* a demonbroc attack on the same night? He was reminded of old Huerta and his foolish breeding program in San Angelo.

The broc shuddered against his blade. Too late, Aiden stepped back away from it as its talons sliced through his coat and deep into his forearm. He screamed in pain at the creature's white-hot touch. A lifetime of weapons training was the only reason he didn't drop the sword as his body rebelled against his mind to turn and run away. He knew that if he let go and allowed the creature to maneuver, he'd be dead in seconds.

The broc jerked hard to the side, seemingly oblivious to the blade that had entered its chest and exited along its back. Aiden grunted as the damned thing pushed him hard into the wall and grabbed a handful of his coat. The thing pulled itself closer, jaws open wide to tear away the flesh on his face. The broc's mouth snapped shut on the empty space only inches from his nose.

He pushed the sword outward, using the crossguard to provide leverage against the creature's chest. The demonbroc dragged itself backwards several inches and the tip of his sword disappeared inside the creature. It was trying to pull itself off of his blade so it could get around his defenses and attack.

Aiden laughed bitterly. All his efforts were simply delaying the inevitable. Besides man, demonbrocs were the deadliest creatures that he knew of. He pushed forward, trying to reestablish control with the sword, and the broc yelped. The creature's back legs collapsed and it turned its head to snap at its backside. It couldn't determine a threat from behind, so it turned back to him, slashing once again with the daggers on its forefeet.

The knifelike claws jarred hard against the bone in Aiden's forearm. This time, his body ignored his training and dropped the sword. He was able to keep his wits about him and staggered back from the abomination. The demonbroc used its front legs to pull its unresponsive body forward toward him.

He allowed himself a moment's hope. When he'd thrust the sword in a second time, it must have severed the broc's spine. He rushed backward across the living room to the kitchen where Luke's wife, Skye, had an old world set of knives in an original chopping block. He pulled the meat cleaver from the top slot and turned in time to see the demonbroc scrabbling across the tile.

His left arm was virtually useless, so he swung the cleaver hard with his right across the front of the broc's snout. The blade buried halfway through the side of its muzzle and it screamed like a woman as it fell to the ground, trying to claw the cleaver out of its face. In its desperation, it inadvertently stabbed itself through the eye with one of its eight-inch claws and bellowed in rage. The gelatinous substance inside the destroyed orb oozed through the wound.

Aiden grabbed another knife and stabbed down through the demonbroc's ear into its brain. It shuddered once and died. He slid down against the cabinets and stared at his arm. The blood poured freely from multiple lacerations. The second cut was much deeper than the first, which had been blunted by the old man's greatcoat. The broc's second attack had gone all the way down to the bone.

He examined the wound with detached interest. His skin gaped wide as if it had been stretched across his arm too tight and the cut allowed it to spread open. A thin layer of round, pink fat cells lined the injury, just under the layer of skin and his forearm muscles vibrated uncontrollably. Blood pooled inside the wound so he tilted his arm to let the dark fluid pour out. For half a second, he could see the light-colored bone inside, then the blood filled in again.

Aiden didn't know how long he sat in the kitchen. He was dimly aware of wetness under his ass, unsure whether it was from the blood that he'd lost or if he'd pissed himself; it didn't really matter which. He knew that he needed to stop the blood flow somehow, but his body refused to respond to even the simplest commands. The injury to his arm was bad; and it was getting worse by the second. He allowed his chin to rest on his chest. He just needed time to think....

The old man slapped himself in the face to stay awake. He'd imagined being enveloped in a warm white glow. *This must be the light that some people claim they see when they die*, he thought. In all the years that he'd fought against scavengers, gangs and slavers he never imagined that he'd be killed by a demonbroc. The creatures were extremely dangerous, but were easy to avoid as long as you stayed away from their nests or didn't anger them when you came across one. *What had brought this one into his son's home?*

"Easy, Dad. I've got you," Blake said.

"Huh?" Aiden muttered, allowing his eyes to focus. Blake crouched in front of him, tying a length of rope around his forearm. Skye stood further back, holding a large candle aloft, which cast a weak light across the kitchen.

"You killed a demonbroc, old man," Blake said as he continued with the tourniquet. "That's amazing."

Aiden's mind thought back to the battle and then he realized what his son was doing. "Hey!" he shouted. "Don't put a tourniquet on me; I want that arm."

Blake gestured for Skye to bring the candle closer. He examined the wound before saying, "I don't know if we can save it, Dad."

"Bullshit. Get Luke. He's the best doctor we have."

Blake's lips thinned. "Luke is dead."

Aiden nodded, he'd expected as much. "Alex?"

His son shook his head. "Dammit!" Aiden burst out. "What were they?"

"Slavers. They hit a few other houses. Most of the adults are dead on the western side and the children are missing."

His heart broke. Not the children. Slavers were the most despicable creatures imaginable. "Tanya?" he asked, his voice shaking.

Blake shook his head. "They didn't make it to Garrett's house. They're all safe."

"Why didn't anyone else respond to the alarm?" Aiden asked as his son placed wadded strips of clean cloth into the wound and then loosened the rope incrementally to see if the blood flow would stop.

"It looks like they came over the walls and killed all the sentries before they could alert anyone. They went to the houses on the west side of the compound and grabbed the kids. Nathan was able to ring the alarm a couple of times before he died; it wasn't loud enough for the families on the east to hear it."

"The west? Are Caleb and Varan safe?"

"No. They're missing."

"Humph," he grunted. "How'd that damn demonbroc get in here?"

Blake turned, picked up a device off the counter and held it up for Aiden to see. It was a long pole with a loop of metal cable on one side. "They must have brought it with them and released it inside the Homestead to cause confusion."

Aiden tried to stand and his vision threatened to go black. "Sit down, Father," Blake ordered. "I've already discussed it with the others. We're going after them at first light when our trackers can see. It doesn't do us any good to bumble around in the darkness outside of the walls."

"Good. That will give me time to make a cast for this arm," Aiden said, lifting his left arm.

"No. You're not going," Blake answered sternly. "Dad, you know that you'll slow us down. You're better suited to stay here and run the defense of the compound."

"I'm going after the children," he protested.

"Garrett and I have this, Dad," Blake said with a comforting hand on his thigh. "You have to trust us now."

Aiden knew the truth of his son's words, and the truth hurt. For as long as he could remember, he'd been the leader of the Traxx family. Over time, the mantle of leadership had slowly been transitioning to Luke. Now Luke was dead and Aiden wasn't certain which of his two remaining sons was strong enough to lead the family. The world seemed to be sinking even further into depravity—if that was possible.

He was rocked hard as a small pair of hands clasped around his neck. "Oh, Grandad! I'm so happy you're safe," Tanya squealed in his ear as she buried her face in his hair. "You can't leave us."

Aiden knew that he was stuck. His granddaughter had overheard him saying that he wanted to go on the search party. Now she'd requested that he stay. He reached across with his good hand and patted her head softly. "Of course, little one. Grandad will stay here and fight off any more of the bad men."

Tanya pointed across the kitchen at the bloody carcass. "Is that a demonbroc?"

"Yes, child," Aiden answered. "I told you and your cousins that they were very dangerous. Now do you believe me?"

She nodded her head, rubbing his scalp painfully as her forehead grated into the side of his head. "Are you okay, Grandad?"

"I'll be fine, little one. I just need some rest."

Tanya accepted his half-lie and asked, "Can you tell me the rest of the story about Aeric?"

"Yes, of course," he said. "I'm going to try and get some rest tonight. Tomorrow, I'll tell you about my childhood and the first time I saw a demonbroc."

"I'll tell Caleb and Varan that you're gonna continue the story!" she said, visibly excited.

The tears welled up in his eyes and threatened to spill onto his cheeks. He composed himself, he was a Traxx. He had to be strong for the others. "Caleb and Varan will have to hear the story later. Tomorrow will be just for you, little one."

Tanya nodded her head once again. She understood what his unspoken words truly meant; the family had seen it before. Her cousins had been taken by slavers. "Daddy and Uncle Blake will bring Caleb and Varan back home, Grandad."

ONE

Tanya fussed with the blankets that she'd piled high around her grandfather. She wanted him to be as comfortable as possible given the battered condition he was in after his fight with the demonbroc. "How's that, Grandad?"

"It's fine, child," the man told her with a weak smile. She'd overheard her father and uncle talking before they left to track down the slavers this morning. They were positive that an infection was going to set in and Grandad would lose his arm. The cuts were too deep and the muscle too torn to repair.

She made a face that her grandfather mistook for anger. "Varan and Caleb will be alright," he said. "They are both strong young men who know how to take care of themselves."

"Daddy said that you're gonna lose your arm," she replied. "Is that true? Is your arm going to come off, Grandad?"

The old man scoffed at her question. "No, child. Your father's a damn fool. I've had much worse injuries than this little scrape. Don't you worry, Tanya, I'll be around for a long, long time."

She smiled and gave him another hug. It must have been the hundredth one that morning. "Are you sure it's okay to tell me a story without the boys here? Won't they get mad?"

"It's alright. Besides, the boys don't want to know about Aeric's love life," he said with a wink.

"Oh, are you gonna tell me if our grandmother is Katie or Veronica?"

"Yes, child. Now, settle in on Grandad's lap—*Oof!* Watch the arm," he groaned as she adjusted herself into a comfortable position so she could hear the story.

Tanya watched his face intently as he stared off towards the fireplace. His eyes glazed over and then he began to speak.

*****

Aeric was settling into life in San Angelo. The people here were nice and he felt like he had a purpose in life instead of wasting time, waiting for the inevitable. He and Tyler had started out as members on the Gathering Squad six months ago. Over time and continual successful missions, Mayor Delgado promoted them and now they managed all of the squads.

As far as apocalyptic life ten months after a global nuclear war went, his was almost perfect. Everyone that he cared for was safe, he had a purpose in life and for now, there was enough food and water. Except for the raiders outside the walls, the only real issue he had was with the two beautiful women in his life.

His girlfriend, Kate, whom he'd dated since middle school, broke up with his senior year of high school and had begun dating again after he rescued her from a life of prostitution after the war, was pregnant with another man's baby. Then, there was Veronica. They'd only kissed that one time, before the war, but they spent time together almost every day and he felt more and more drawn towards her each time he said goodbye.

He'd developed a strong emotional bond with both of them and it was an interesting situation that he was in with the two women. When they first met, they'd been cold to one another. Over time, and with the limited space within the city, they'd come to realize that while they had different ethnic backgrounds, they were similar in almost every way.

Kate had been the prom queen in high school, Veronica was the homecoming queen at hers. Both had influential fathers,

Kate's had died years ago in a skiing accident, while Veronica's father was still alive and held the office of San Angelo's mayor. They had similar interests in clothing style, mannerisms and even their sense of humor. It was inevitable that they'd end up as either close friends or bitter enemies.

Luckily for Aeric, they'd chosen to become friends instead of enemies, both choosing to keep a wary eye on the other. Katie knew that she had Aeric's heart and allowed herself to open her own to Veronica. During the trip back from Missouri, she'd been jealous of Veronica before she'd even met the woman. Her jealousy seemed to have faded with the confidence that her impending motherhood had instilled in her.

She'd grown as a woman over the last year. When he'd returned to his hometown to find his father dead and his mother a prisoner in her own home, Katie had been a prostitute on the street, trading her body for scraps of food. Then, she'd been taken hostage by Justin, the former leader of the Vultures, and turned into a sex slave. It was Justin's baby that grew inside of her, not Aeric's. Kate had been able to use those horrible experiences to strengthen her character, allowing the pain and disgrace to fade away and not define her.

The scars that Justin had disfigured Aeric with, earning him the nickname "Traxx" were also fading. The youthful elasticity of his skin helped a lot, but so did the scar therapy cream that Veronica gave him from the old medical supply factory on the northeast side of town. He'd diligently used the cream on his face and most of the scars had paled. The ones on his jawline and neck were mostly hidden by the short beard that he wore, leaving only those around his eyes, nose and forehead visible.

His attempts to fade the scarring stopped at his face, though. He hadn't bothered to try and spend the effort on the ones that crisscrossed his body. They were simply too extensive and it was next to impossible to even know where to begin trying to treat them. Instead, he wore them as a badge of honor, proclaiming to everyone who saw them that he'd survived torture at the hands of the Vultures. They weren't the unbeatable force that everyone had thought that they were.

While the ash still fell from the skies almost daily, it wasn't the massive debris storms that had blanketed the earth with the remains of the old world like it had been in the early months after the war. The bulk of the ash stayed suspended in the clouds as Tyler had predicted it would and there'd even been a few times when the sun peeked through enough to bring the temperatures above the freezing mark.

Aeric rode his bike from his house to the warehouse where he worked. He and Kate lived three streets away from Veronica's with Tyler and Kate's little sister Julie, along with baby Kayla, who spent several nights a week with the guard Shellie when she wasn't on duty at one of the checkpoints. It was an imperfect system; one that they all knew would have to change as they readjusted to life inside a secure city, but having Tyler close to everyone made Aeric feel safer.

Every morning he and Tyler reported to the Stephens Arena, Angelo State University's old basketball arena, where they'd begun stockpiling every kind of supply imaginable from food and water to clothing and weaponry. It was a centrally-located, secure facility with wide-open fields of fire for the guards assigned there. The mayor renamed it the Provisions Warehouse and anything that couldn't be stored there was locked up in a few other smaller locations across the city. They'd even begun the construction of defenses around the arena to make it as secure as possible. The supplies were the city's lifeline.

When he could, Aeric made sure to leave a few minutes before Tyler so he could stop by and eat breakfast with Veronica. It was a habit that he'd developed soon after they arrived in San Angelo. It started out as a way to pass information that grew into one of the most anticipated parts of his day. She'd fill him in on the details of what happened in the city that she'd learned from her father and he'd pass along the Gathering Squads' targets for the day or go over any units on extended patrols. After the business was complete, they'd spend time together just talking as friends and laughing about her experiences at the soup kitchen that she ran for the city. He valued her friendship almost as much as the one that he had with Tyler.

Aeric turned his bike onto Veronica's driveway and braked in front of the garage door. Even though the mayor lived in the nicest part of the city, it was all relative in their post-apocalyptic world. He didn't want his bike stolen, so he wheeled it with him to the front door and knocked.

After a few seconds, Veronica opened the door. "Good morning, Aeric!" she smiled.

"Morning, Vee. Can I come in?"

"When are you gonna stop asking that?"

"Probably never," he replied as he pushed his bicycle through the door and placed it next to hers in the foyer.

"You're always welcome here, Aeric. Always," she whispered in his ear as she gave him a hug.

Veronica often made it plain to him what she thought about his relationship with Katie. Even though the two of them were strictly plutonic friends, she felt that Kate had used the situation in Missouri to get back with Aeric when he should have been with her. Sometimes he felt like one of those old kids' toys that got punched, fell over, and then popped right back into place to be hit from the opposite side.

He ignored her comment as he'd done for months and dug into his backpack. "I brought some cereal and powdered milk," he stated.

"Oh, yum," she answered with mock enthusiasm, quickly dropping the subject about him staying with her. It was one that they'd talked about often and they were at the point where she'd offer a friendly reminder and then move on. "So, where are you guys headed today?"

"We got a lead on a warehouse in a town near Midland-Odessa, so we'll be taking one of the military trucks to get as much as possible."

She smiled and said, "Good. I feel better about your missions when you guys take a truck."

"It's not the preferred method since we only have a finite amount of useable fuel, but since it's so far away we don't really have a choice," Aeric shrugged helplessly.

"How far away?" Her voice edged on alarm that she struggled to suppress.

"About seventy-five miles," he responded. "It'll be an overnight trip. If there's anything there, it'll be worth it."

"We don't know the status of Midland and Odessa. They were both a little bit bigger than San Angelo. It might be dangerous if they've taken the precautions that we have and set up long-range scavenging parties."

He handed the powdered milk to Veronica, who measured out two servings worth and used a whisk to mix in the water. While she mixed, he said, "Yeah, that's why we're taking two squads of Lorelei's Shooters with us. We're hoping that the two of them fractured enough along city lines that they're only concerned with each other and not what's further away."

"It's terrible that we're hoping for a war between other cities so we can swoop in and take stuff from under their noses," she stated. It was the way their new world was, kill or be killed, steal and survive or don't and die. "What's the name of the town?"

"It's a small town called Garden City. They're about forty miles or so from Midland, so I'm hoping that we'll be good."

"What about the people who live there?"

"We'll offer them the same deal that we offer everyone. They can come live here in the safety of San Angelo in exchange for all of their supplies or they could possibly become a trading partner. Or maybe we'll have to fight; we don't know yet. One of the advantages to this place is that it's isolated from everyone else, so those people may not want anything to do with us, which will suck since we're taking the truck up there."

"Can't be helped," she stated and poured the reconstituted milk over the two bowls of cereal that Aeric made while they talked.

They carried their bowls to the kitchen table and sat opposite each other, eating in silence for a few minutes. Then the sound of Aeric's spoon scraping against his empty bowl reminded them that he had to leave. He stood and put his dishes in the trash.

They'd had the good fortune to find a warehouse full of paper dishes and plastic utensils early on. Whenever possible, they tried to use the disposable dinnerware to avoid wasting their drinking water to clean dishes.

Veronica hugged him firmly from behind, resting her head on his back in a decidedly *not* friendly gesture of affection. "Take care of yourself and your men, Aeric. I don't know what I'd do without you."

He turned and wrapped his arms around her, hugging her back. "We'll be fine. Lorelei has trained her Shooters better than anything else out there. We can handle ourselves."

"Against a few people, yeah. But what if you run into a big group or if you guys come across some of those things that have been popping up?"

The *things* that Veronica asked about were mutated animals—and sometimes people. All the radiation had already begun to alter creatures on the genetic level. The ones that survived the winter passed along the mutations to their young in the spring. Some of the mutations were harmless, like extra limbs, while others had already begun showing frightening changes. There were wild dogs that had extra-long nails and larger teeth that could punch through heavy clothing, goats with wickedly-spiked horns, lizards with nearly impenetrable scales, and the list went on. Aeric wondered what those creatures would evolve into over the course of twenty or thirty years.

"We can handle them. The truck gives us all sorts of options to stay high out of their way."

"What about on the way back, when the truck is full and you're riding your bike?"

"We'll be fine. Don't worry."

"I *do* worry, Aeric," she insisted and squeezed his waist even harder, pressing herself into him. "You mean so much to me. You're my best friend and you know more about me than anyone left alive in San Angelo besides my father. You know that I'll worry about you nonstop until you get back tomorrow."

"I know. Just…don't, okay? Me and Ty got this."

Veronica leaned back away from him and looked into his eyes. "You take too many risks. You're the head of the Gathering Squads, you can stay in town and have other people carry out your orders."

"That's not me and you know it," he sighed. He'd gotten the exact same grief from Katie before he left. "I have a responsibility to this town. You've given me and my friends so much; we owe it to you to give back. Ty and me aren't desk people, we roll up our sleeves and get to work when things need doing."

She laughed and smacked him playfully on the chest. "You sound like some political candidate in a television ad."

He grinned along with her. "Yeah, I guess it was kind of corny, huh?"

"It was more than corny. More like clichéd and predictable." Her smile faded away and she continued, "You don't always have to be the hero, Aeric."

He snorted and tried to step away. Veronica stepped with him, still holding on. "I'm not a hero. I just think it's the right thing to do. I can't sit at a desk somewhere and ask my guys to put themselves in danger."

"I know," she said and buried her face in his chest. "That's why I love you."

Shit. Fuckity-shit, double shit! "Um... I... Veronica, you know how I feel about you. You mean the world to me."

"But not enough to be with me."

"I'm with Katie, your friend, remember? She's pregnant."

"Not with *your* baby, Aeric."

"Please, let's not have this discussion now," he answered uncomfortably. At times like this, he was painfully aware that he'd only really dated Kate; he didn't have any other previous experience with women to draw from. "I really need to get to the Provisions Warehouse so we can get going."

She held him tight, not granting him the escape that he desperately wanted right then. "I have one question for you, Aeric. I've never asked you before, and I won't ever bring it up again if you answer me truthfully."

"Um, okay."

"If Kate hadn't gotten pregnant, would you still be with her? I understand that you're trying to be honorable, but it's that gang leader's baby, not yours."

He got angry for a split second. Regardless of whose child it was, he would raise it as his own. The anger quickly subsided as he tried to see it from her point of view. She was looking for answers to help her deal with her own feelings. He wished that he knew what she needed to hear. If he said that he would have been with her, would that hurt the relationship that she'd developed with Kate? On the other hand, if he said that he would have stayed with Katie regardless, would that make Veronica feel inadequate?

God, he hated all the talking about this subject. He was so much better in the field, out where he could take matters into his own hands. No one ever second-guessed a decision that he made in the heat of the moment. It was so much simpler to define life by action and reaction than the various traps and snares that he had to dance around with the women in his life.

"Well, are you gonna answer?" she prodded.

He stared down into her deep, brown eyes. "I'm sorry, Veronica. I was thinking. You know that you mean the world to me—" he tried to say before she cut him off.

"No. I know that you care for me, Aeric. I just want to know: if Katie hadn't gotten pregnant, would you have been with me?"

"I can't answer that."

"It's really simple. Yes or no?"

He thought about it. The thought of finding Veronica safe back in San Angelo had kept him moving forward all along the trip from Austin to Springfield and even after he'd begun sleeping with Kate again, the thought of Veronica pressed close to him like she was now had driven him along.

Finally, he told her the truth. She wanted to know what he thought, and this was unlikely to do anything except complicate his life more than it already was. "Yes. If you'd have had me, as hideously deformed as I am, then I would have absolutely been with you."

She let out her breath in an audible sigh. *What does that mean?* he asked himself frantically. She answered him by pulling his head down to hers and kissing him.

TWO

What the hell had he done? He'd told the truth and now he regretted it more and more with every rotation of his bicycle pedals as he made his way to the Provisions Warehouse. Veronica had asked him that if Katie wasn't pregnant, would he have been with her instead. *Stupid.* He should have lied and told her that he was completely committed to Kate and had been since middle school.

He had a mission to focus on; he couldn't be sidetracked by his conversation about what could have been if things were different. And besides, what the hell had she meant when she said that she loved him and then followed that up with a kiss? *Dammit!*

His Gathering Squad was going on a potentially dangerous mission. No one had really been beyond a twenty mile radius from San Angelo in over three months. The last small group of refugees that they'd let in had been in April—they were the ones who'd told Aeric about the warehouse in Garden City.

He didn't know how much Veronica or Katie knew about the world outside the walls that they'd constructed. It had gotten much worse than when they were out there as the winter went unnaturally long and people began to starve to death. He suspected that Veronica knew a lot more than she let on, though. Her father was the mayor of the town and she ran the city's soup kitchen, so she interacted with everyone almost every day. She likely heard the darker tales that he tried to keep from her.

The perimeter guards were notorious for embellishing their stories, so there was the hope that Veronica discarded what they said, however, it was unlikely. The way that she'd refused to let him go proved that she knew something was not right out in the wastes. The mutations in the remaining wildlife had gotten worse, while the showdowns with scavengers and raiders had gotten downright deadly.

One of the ugly secrets that they didn't tell the good, hardworking citizens of San Angelo was the Gathering Squad's tactics. Besides the guy who managed the city's ammunition, Mayor Delgado and Colonel Henshaw, the Air Force base commander, were the only people outside of the squads who knew how often they got into firefights and scrapes out in the wastes. Aeric hadn't lied when he told Veronica that they tried to negotiate with people first. That rarely went well and they often got into fights rather quickly. Aeric's heavily-armed men and women were almost never received well and those initial meetings usually ended with the people dead. Luckily, the Gathering Squads had been better than those that they ran into so far.

He'd discussed the moral dilemma with Tyler and the Squad's lieutenants on multiple occasions. Were they any better than the psycho-scavengers roaming the land because they killed and stole things for the betterment of an entire city instead of themselves? Aeric wasn't sure. He knew how precarious the situation in the city was though. There were over thirty thousand people living in San Angelo—which was less than a third of the pre-war population. Even with the centralized food kitchen and supply point, the city's constables found people dead on a daily basis. The investigation almost always pointed to a fight over food. The simple truth of the matter was that until the temperatures warmed enough to grow crops, a population of thirty thousand wasn't sustainable. They needed to reduce the population down to a third of *that* number to be able to feed everyone without daily supply runs.

The Provisions Warehouse came into view around the corner. They'd spent a massive amount of time building concentric rings of fortifications around the warehouse so they could fall back to supplementary positions if there was a sustained attack on their supply storage site. Surveying the warehouse as he rode up, Aeric once again wished that they had working tractors. His long-term plan was to build earthworks behind each barricade so the defenders could shoot over the walls instead of using them simply as a barrier. It was a prudent plan to keep their supplies, literally their lifeline, secure. In time, when the squads weren't so busy, he'd make sure that his plan for the defenses were completed.

Two large military trucks called MTVs were parked out front of the Provisions Warehouse. The MTVs, or Medium Tactical Vehicles, were large trucks with a five-ton carrying capacity. Their cargo areas contained the Gathering Squad's bicycles for the trip to Garden City. The shooters and the actual men and women of the squad would ride back there as well. Then on the way back, the trucks would be full and the squads would ride their bikes beside the full trucks.

The MTVs were a major improvement over the contraptions that the Gathering Squads normally used during supply runs. They'd taken Aeric and Tyler's concept of a pull-behind trailer on their bicycles and increased the capacity. Since horses were in short supply, they'd fabricated a way to haul a lot of supplies at once. Aeric's rough design was developed by several engineering students and now they had several variations of long, flatbed trailers with lightweight metal side rails that were hitched to either four or six bicycles, similar to a team of horses.

Their carrying capacity was the next best thing to using the limited fuel in the military trucks. Unfortunately, the bike and trailer combinations' inability to maneuver also made them death traps for the riders if they were attacked. It was a lesson that only needed to be learned once. After that, they began sending heavily-armed single riders as well as the team and everyone in the Gathering Squads were trained in military tactics. The result was a militarized group of men and women who went out on the supply runs.

"Hey, Aeric, glad you could make it," Tyler called from between the trucks. "I thought for a second that you finally got yourself tangled up in bed with Veronica this morning." The musclebound Nebraska native was easily recognizable in a crowd of people. Even with the heavy coat and large hat he wore, at six foot seven, with a big black eye patch covering the puckered scar where Justin had plucked out his right eye and a shock of unruly blonde hair, no one would mistake him for anyone except Tyler Nordgren.

Aeric and Tyler had been roommates together at the University of Texas in Austin when the Vultures started the war that wiped out most of the big cities in America and, presumably, the rest of the world. The two of them had been through a lot together since then. Chief among their experiences was the trip to Missouri to find Aeric's parents and then their subsequent capture and torture at the hands of the Vultures' leader, Justin Rustwood.

"You just want the juicy details of something like that so you can spread the gossip," Aeric quipped as he grasped his friend's enormous hand. Aeric was larger than most of San Angelo's residents, but he was still dwarfed by his friend.

"You know it! *That* would be some good gossip that nobody could resist." Tyler held up his hands, imitating an old movie theater marquee and said, "The mayor's daughter and the Chief Gatherer entwined in a forbidden romance. That would sell, bro."

"Keep that shit up and Katie will kick you out of the house."

Tyler waved his hand dismissively. "Eh, I can handle her. She's a pushover."

Aeric snorted. "Maybe to you. She doesn't let me get away with anything." He smiled as his friend. Much like Kate and Veronica's relationship, Tyler had hated Kate when he first met her. He'd been convinced that she was using Aeric and would have ditched him at the first opportunity. When she'd killed Justin and rescued them, he became her biggest supporter. The woman could do no wrong in his eyes.

"She lets a lot of your puppy love with Veronica slide," Tyler replied slyly. He was one of the biggest gossipers in town and apparently, there wasn't a line that he wouldn't cross. To top it all off, he had a way of ingratiating himself with everyone and before long, people told him their entire life story, giving him more ammunition. Aeric hated walking around with him when they weren't busy because it took forever to get anywhere.

"Alright, can we keep my private life…private?"

"I'm just busting your chops, old buddy."

"So, are we ready to go?" Aeric asked, hoping to change the direction of the conversation.

"Yup. We've got enough food and water for three days in case we get out there and it's a bust, enough ammo to stop a herd of charging elephants and a total of twenty-six people. Fourteen from the Gathering Squad, two squads of Shooters with five people each, plus you and me."

"Alright, let's make sure everyone's ready to go, then we'll leave in ten minutes."

Tyler made an exaggerated effort to check his empty wrist and said, "Okay, I'm synchronizing my watch now."

Aeric pushed him playfully in the shoulder. "You know what I mean, asshole."

The big man flipped him the bird over his shoulder as he walked towards the group of people standing around. "Alright, folks," he shouted. "We're leaving in about ten minutes. You know where the outhouses are, make sure you do your business before we get in the trucks. Meet back here for the final brief from Traxx."

Aeric watched the group spread out as they went to use the restrooms scattered around the parking lot perimeter. They'd taken various porta johns from around the city and cut out the back side where the holding reservoir used to be. Then, they inserted metal buckets that could be taken away and dumped or burned. Almost every aspect of their lives had to be reimagined without electricity or running water.

When everyone had returned, Aeric cleared his throat and began, "Good morning, everyone. It's about seventy-five miles to

Garden City, assuming no major roadblocks or detours. The terrain should be open except for when we travel through Sterling City. The town clusters around the road so we need to be prepared to repel anyone who tries to get on the trucks. Other than that, we don't anticipate any problems until we get to Garden City itself."

"What's the read on GC?" Nicole, one of the members of his Gathering Squad, asked. She was one of Aeric's most trusted subordinates; if there were room for her as a lieutenant, he would have promoted her months ago, but those positions had already been filled by his predecessor. Since none of them were incompetent, he didn't feel right demoting them to make room for her. Nicole didn't seem to mind though; the job only came with more headaches, it wasn't like they were getting paid any more to put their lives on the line than the guys working over at the lake. Everybody got paid in rations, and no one got any more or less than their neighbor.

"We don't have any updates to our brief from yesterday," Aeric replied with a shrug to Nicole's question. "As of three months ago, there was an entire warehouse full of foodstuff without anyone guarding it."

"Why did the guys who found it come here instead of just staying there and keeping all that food for themselves?" someone yelled from the back of the crowd.

"I've talked to them on several occasions about that. Apparently, life in Midland-Odessa is violent and short-lived. They were afraid to take up residence so close to the city for fear that the people in Midland would find out about it and sweep in to kill everyone inside."

"How do we know that hasn't already happened?" Nicole asked.

Aeric sighed. It was a valid question; however, it should have been asked yesterday during the briefing, not today as they were getting ready to leave. "We don't know if all that food is still there. But the fact of the matter is that we need more food here. Until the weather stabilizes, trying to grow any crops is pointless. That means we're reliant on processed food that was made before the war. We've searched everywhere around San Angelo and have run into a few similar search parties to the east, likely from Austin. So far, we've had limited contact to the west, so we're hopeful that the Midland-Odessa survivors haven't found the supplies yet."

Tyler stepped in to help control the situation, "Alright, no more questions. You heard Traxx, this is our mission. If you don't like it, get the fuck out of San Angelo, I'm sure your collecting experience will be appreciated by the Vultures—that is, if they don't kill you first."

"Aw, come on, Tyler," Nicole said as she stepped closer and put a hand on the big man's arm. "We're trying to get as much info as possible before we go out and put our lives on the line. You know, it's like having sex one last time with your ex before they leave. You know what to expect, but you're still gonna try and knock their socks off."

Tyler's face turned red around the eye patch. "Uh, yeah. Let's get loaded up in the trucks."

Aeric laughed out loud at his friend's obviously uncomfortable response. Let him get a little of his own medicine. Nicole had been hitting on him since they arrived in San Angelo.

It didn't matter to her that he was homosexual and wasn't interested in her physically. She made sure to let him—and everyone else—know that if Tyler ever came over to the other side of the fence, she got first dibs.

"Alright, you heard him. We're leaving as soon as I get a head count," Aeric yelled while Tyler began counting men and women as they got in the trucks.

Within minutes, they were headed towards the Western Gate. The city's naming convention for the gates was a little confusing since the Western Gate shot off to the northwest, while the Southern Gate allowed access to the countryside southwest of the city. The only gate that was actually situated where its name suggested was the Eastern Gate, which fed out onto the old US Route 87. The Eastern Gate was the most heavily fortified and guarded gate into the city since Route 87 led directly to Austin.

The university's Engineering students had once again come to the city's aid in designing a wall for the city. Mayor Delgado and Colonel Henshaw had agreed right away that the city's old footprint was simply too big and not sustainable, so they'd cut off everything north of 19th Street. The students had wanted to exclude everything south of Highway 306. However, since that's where the mayor lived, along with most of the newer housing areas, they agreed to keep it.

A massive construction project began, initially with old cars turned on their side and then shored up with dirt and beams to keep them from tipping back over. They also tore down the homes outside of the new perimeter, using the parts for construction. The walls were five to six feet tall in most places, more than sufficient to hold off the small bands of marauders who'd begun showing up in the recent months. The plans were being drawn up to build a massive inner wall around the university area, including the Provisions Warehouse, that residents could flee to if the outer walls were overrun. The Air Force base would have to fend for itself.

The group drove past Old Fisher, the large lake where the city collected its drinking water. An elaborate system of PVC pipes had been installed, running at a slightly downhill angle from the lake to the city. Workers used bicycle-powered pumps to pull water from the lake into the pipes and residents collected the water inside the wall from a closely-monitored area containing multiple spigots. The water was then boiled at home to remove the contaminants that had built up during those terrible first months after the war. While gathering provisions was hard work, Aeric didn't envy those poor lake workers. In fact, the town's police officers used working at the lake and clearing the sewers as forms of punishment.

The lake disappeared behind them faster than Aeric imagined possible, having become accustomed to the speeds that he could achieve on his bicycle rather than the breakneck pace that the trucks moved at. He glanced over at the vehicle's speedometer; they were going about forty-five miles per hour, barely a crawl compared to the speeds that people used to drive on these roads.

He watched as the countryside *sped* by. The area wasn't particularly green before the war. The problem was compounded by the months of poor sunlight under the clouds of ash and the resulting chemical rains, turning the surrounding landscape into a bleak mockery of what it had been. They passed by a few abandoned homesteads that the Gathering Squad had already picked clean. Most of the population this far out had either died long ago or joined with the residents of San Angelo, choosing to move into the city.

The ruined land—the wastes as the city folk referred to it—passed by the door of the truck in a blur. Almost everything was a mix of muted, neutral colors since the vegetation had died, revealing patches of earth covered in a grayish residue. He assumed that the stuff was the result of the ash that had fallen to the ground and then the rains had turned it into a plant-killing slurry. Once the sun came out, it dried up and left behind the rest.

Every so often Aeric could see patches of green. Each time, he was hopeful that it was a living tree or even budding grasslands; unfortunately, it always ended up being the outline of a cactus. The cacti in this area had been particularly hardy, most of it staying green until two or three months ago. Most of them had finally succumbed to the devastation that had ruined the rest of the vegetation. He had faith that the vegetation would eventually return after enough clean rainstorms washed away the ash and sulfur.

What if it doesn't come back? he asked himself. San Angelo was holding on for now, but the fact that they were traveling more than seventy-five miles to raid a facility that *might* have food was indicative of the long term problem that the city faced. It was a simple fact that he returned to often. There were too many people living there.

It was a problem that didn't have an easy fix or workaround. Every one of the residents of the city deserved the opportunity to live. How would anyone ever make that sort of choice, anyways? They prided themselves on the fact that they were humane in their treatment of everyone, once they were inside the walls. He was glad that he wasn't the mayor; he wouldn't be the one forced to make the call when they were eventually forced to cull the population.

*****

The time—and miles—passed quickly. When they made it to the mile marker indicating that they were five miles from Sterling City, Aeric had his forces go to one hundred percent watch. His Gatherers and the Shooters all readied their weapons, pointing them out from the interior of the truck towards the wastes.

They entered the town minutes later. The road went right down the main drag of Sterling City, which, thankfully, wasn't that large. The road was wide and open, the few buildings set far enough off the street to allow them a clear view of the surrounding area. It looked abandoned. No roadblocks could be seen in front of them along the route and there didn't appear to be any junked cars sitting dead where they'd been when the EMP struck. Everyone relaxed slightly and breathed a collective sigh of relief. They'd been worried about the townspeople trying to stop the trucks, which didn't seem to be the case.

Then they took their first casualty.

They passed a red brick building with a sign on the side proclaiming that the squat, two story structure had been a hotel when the world exploded in gunfire. People had been waiting in the alley between the hotel and a rock-faced building. The rounds peppered the trucks, hitting several of the men and women in the back.

"Go! Go! Go!" Aeric screamed at the driver, who pressed the pedal all the way to the floor.

He looked in the side view mirror to make sure that Tyler, who was in the second truck, followed their lead as they sped through the engagement area. The noise of rifles and pistols firing in rapid succession made it impossible to determine if the San Angelians were returning fire or if they'd hunkered down to take whatever the ambush threw at them.

They were out of the kill zone in seconds. From his vantage point in the mirror, Aeric saw the barrels of several weapons appear around the corner of the stone building to fire blindly in their direction. That told him that the people in the alley were unwilling to follow them out into the street. He saw a few muzzle flashes from the back of Tyler's truck, so he knew his men were shooting back at the assholes who'd tried to ambush them.

They cleared the town with no further incidents. Aeric called a halt several miles outside of town to see if everyone was okay. Two of the Shooters in his truck had minor injuries. One of them was shot through the shoulder, the other had a broken wrist from when he dove to the floor of the truck. The second truck didn't fare as well. The townspeople had been able to fire into the cargo area as they drove away.

The most serious injury was to one of his Gatherers. The man had been sitting in the rearmost seat of Tyler's truck. He'd been shot through the side twice and once in the neck. By the time they stopped, Russ was dead. Several others had been hit as well. Thankfully, none of the other injuries were life-threatening.

Aeric was furious. They all knew that the town was likely going to be a dangerous place. It became real when they'd been shot at, not some imagined scenario during a rehearsal back at the Provisions Warehouse. Although about half of their missions to the various food storage points had resulted in a shootout of some kind, it had been months since anyone flat-out tried to ambush the group. He wanted revenge.

"Nicole, I want you to stay here with the injured and patch them up," Aeric ordered. "Darren and Sam, you stay here to guard the trucks and help Nicole. The rest of you, drop your gear, except ammo and water. We're gonna wipe that town off the map."

Tyler stepped over and whispered, "Are you sure? Our mission is to get the supplies from Garden City, not end up in a firefight in some piss-ant little town along the way."

Aeric thought about it for a moment, then answered, "Yeah, I'm sure, buddy. We can't leave these fuckers behind. They killed Russ with some lucky shots as we sped through town going forty-five. What's gonna happen when we're all riding our bikes through here on the way back? It's so quiet now that the sound of our trucks carries for miles. We caught them by surprise this time. You know we've got to put an end to them before they figure out another strategy for when we come back through."

Tyler nodded his head slowly. "You're right. You usually are in these situations. You make the hard, but necessary call. Alright, let's go."

The group rode their bicycles back down the highway until they were about a mile from town and then hid them off the side of the road. Since they didn't really know the layout of the town, except for what they'd seen when they drove through, Aeric sent half his remaining force, just nine men, to the south of the main strip with Tyler and the other half stayed with him on the north side, where the ambush had originated.

They moved into town rapidly, passing a sign announcing that the pre-apocalypse population had been eight hundred and fifty-three souls. Aeric wondered how many of those people were left alive. Probably not many since they'd been shot at by around twenty or so from the alley.

He led his group around the first building and stumbled into a man sitting in a lawn chair under the shade of an awning. He started to bring his rifle up and stayed his hand. He smiled and slowly raised his hand away from the weapon. One of Aeric's Gatherers slammed a spear through the watcher's throat. He didn't stand up and fire the gun like Aeric thought he would. Instead, he crumpled backwards into the chair and slid off, hitting the porch with a dull thud.

Everyone fanned out quickly, expecting an attack. When it didn't come, Aeric looked back to the man they'd killed. He wore multiple layers of clothing against the chill. Likely he was some kind of sentry on this end of town. He had some dirty brown water in a jug and a book sitting beside his post. The most interesting thing about his position was a rope that ran off towards the direction of the alley where they'd been ambushed.

Aeric pointed at it and asked, "What do you make of that?"

Charles, the man who'd speared the sentry, said, "I bet it leads to a bell or an alert system of some kind where the attackers are gathered."

Traxx nodded and grunted an affirmative. It made sense. They could post a sentry on either end of town, equip them with a means to communicate and warn the others of danger, then hide in the building. They likely didn't have enough people to build solid fortifications and any effort would have been a waste, so this was their answer to keeping the place as secure as they could.

"Hmm, wonder what that means?" Charles asked as he poked the body with the spear.

"Huh?" Aeric sidestepped towards Charles so he could see what the man was pointing at. He wore a tattered Texas flag bandana around his left biceps.

Aeric's mind was thrust six months into the past when he, Tyler and Katie had fled from Austin. They'd all been physically and emotionally battered, nearly starving and barely hanging on, when they came across the remnants of a massive firefight. Bodies littered the highway, about half of them wearing a Texas flag bandana on their arm. They'd gladly taken the weapons and bicycles from the dead, easing their journey to San Angelo.

Had the survivors who'd fought way out east of San Angelo somehow made it all the way to Sterling City? It was entirely possible that they'd bypassed San Angelo because of the large pseudo-military force that the town boasted and made their way here? If that were the case, what had happened to the original townspeople? They were questions that wouldn't be answered by staring at the corpse of a dead man, so Aeric had his team follow the rope towards the ambush site, watching carefully for any more sentries.

They made their way past several buildings until they came to a large, open parking lot where he called a halt. The stone building sat right in front of them and on the other side was the alley. Realistically, he knew that the people wouldn't still be there, it had been almost an hour since the ambush so they'd probably returned to their homes.

Everyone looked to him for guidance, what did he want to do now that they'd made it back into the town? He wished that he had a way to communicate with Tyler on the other side of the road. He thought about it for a moment. They had no way of knowing where the alley led on the back side. The anger that had fueled him immediately after discovering that Russ was dead had subsided now that he'd walked back into town. He thought about why they'd came back and what it would mean if they didn't clean out this nest of villains.

The idea that they'd have to face them again spurred Aeric into action. "Alright, let's go around to the back side of that building," he whispered. "We'll go two at a time for safety and when we get to the back, we'll see what's over there. Try not to use your guns if you run into anyone—unless you have to. Questions?"

There were none, so he sent the first two across the gravel parking lot. He cringed as the sound of their boots crunching on the rock echoed across the small space. Everyone scanned the area for activity in response to their noise. Nothing else happened until one of the men he'd sent across started gesturing wildly for him to come over to where he was.

He jogged across by himself, feeling foolish for crouching at a run. It was something that he'd seen in countless movies. *Guys always crouched when they ran in the movies, it makes sense, right?* he asked himself. When he arrived, he saw that it was Charles who'd waved him over.

"What'd you see?"

Charles held his fingers to his lips and replied, "Listen."

Aeric did as he was asked, straining to hear what Charles wanted him to hear. Then he heard it. The faint sound of music came from inside the building. It sounded like a couple of guitars and a set of drums. They were having a goddamned concert after murdering one of his people.

He peeked around the side of the building into the alley. It was empty. All of the rats must have gone back to their nest. His eyes fell on several vacant cars and he had an idea. "Block the back door with as much shit as you can," he told the Shooter that had been with Charles. "Quietly."

He waived a few men over from the remaining group and gave them a mission to go find Tyler's team and pass a message to them. Then he and Charles jogged back to where the old cars sat and saw that they'd conveniently already left all the supplies that he'd need sitting in the front seat of one of the vehicles.

*****

The residents of the town had been siphoning fuel from the vehicles around town, probably to start their fires each night, so he'd filled several jugs with the remaining gasoline and rifled through the trash to find five glass bottles. He kept one of the jugs for himself and sent a man up on the roof of the low building to pour the remaining ones across the rooftop.

The sounds continued to drift from inside the building. They were rocking to some old school punk rock. Whoever was playing the guitar hit every chord, but the drummer wasn't very good. Regardless, it sounded great to Aeric, who'd rarely heard any type of music since the war and reminded him of the people of Eureka Springs that he met on his journey back to Missouri. Not many of the band members from San Angelo State had survived the first few weeks when Mayor Delgado was on the road going after his daughter in Austin.

The ambushers must have relied solely on their outlooks on the edges of town because no one was guarding the building. Aeric took advantage of their overconfidence and emptied the container he'd kept all over the building's wooden front porch.

Once his man was off the roof, he lit the Molotov cocktails that he'd created in the glass bottles and hurled them high up onto the roof. The old tar paper on the roof caught quickly and he lit the gas he'd poured on the porch. Shouts of alarm spread from inside and Tyler's men, whom he'd placed across the street, shot several people as they burst through the front door. They fell dead onto the flames blocking the doorway.

Aeric threw the remaining Molotov through the open front door, spreading flames quickly across the inside as the old, dried wood caught fire. The heat from the roof combined with the blaze inside to create a raging inferno. Then the building blew up. Chunks of burning wood and superheated shards of glass flew in every direction. Whatever they'd stored inside with them had exploded once the ceiling collapsed.

Tyler's squad fired a few rounds towards the east as the sentry from that side of town came running up to see about the commotion. Aeric assumed that the threat was taken care of since they didn't continue after their initial volley and hoped that no one else would come out of the woodwork to shoot at them as they left town.

Aeric watched as the flames engulfed the building. He braved the heat to peer through the partially collapsed rock wall into the old store. Nothing moved inside, they were all dead. He wanted to feel remorse for what he'd done. He was only twenty years old, *I should feel terrible for their deaths*, he told himself, but he didn't feel anything except relief that his people were safe. The townsfolk had done this to themselves by choosing to attack his convoy. There would be no mourning from him. He'd grown exponentially during his experiences over the past year. Age wasn't a factor in the new world; you were either the hunter or the hunted. After his time with the Vultures, he would never allow himself to be hunted again.

He stepped back and continued to observe the fire while his team scanned the area for any threats. Finally, after ten minutes, Traxx was satisfied that no one would sneak up on them and whistled to bring everyone over to the parking lot next to the burning building. Once his team had gathered around, he took a breath to steady himself and said, "Okay, that isn't what we were expecting. I didn't want to kill everybody. I figured that we'd extract a little revenge for what they did to Russ and they'd never try to ambush innocent people again."

"You didn't know that they had explosives stored in there," Tyler answered for the group.

"I know," he mumbled, still wondering to himself why he didn't really care that every one of his enemies had died.

"What if there were women or kids in there, just enjoying a concert?" one of the Shooters asked.

"Stop," Tyler ordered. "We can't second-guess what happened. Traxx made the decision to attack and this is what happened. End of story. Beating ourselves up over what we could have done differently won't change a damn thing. They're all dead, end of story."

Aeric took heart from his friend's words. The big man could always be counted on to reinforce his decisions, regardless of how horrible their outcome was. He nodded his head, "You're right, buddy. Let's leave town and go back to the trucks before all this smoke attracts attention from out in the wastes."

They turned westward and began walking towards the edge of town where they'd stashed their bikes. When they reached the building where Charles killed the sentry, Aeric was shocked to see a blanket resting on top of the man with the edges tucked in like a shroud.

He immediately dispersed his team to check the surrounding buildings. They didn't find anything so they continued warily back to their bikes. Everyone had the feeling that they were being watched as they made their way out of town towards their bikes. No one said anything as they pedaled hard to put distance between themselves and the strange little town in the middle of the Texas wasteland.

THREE

Tyler watched his friend help the wounded back into the truck as they loaded up to continue on to Garden City. Traxx made the decision to keep Russ's body in the back of his truck instead of leaving it out in the middle of nowhere. It was the right thing to do and while the dead body in the cargo area may have made some of the Gatherers uneasy, they all knew that his family back in San Angelo would appreciate being able to bury him in the city's cemetery.

They were back on the road in under an hour. The rest of the trip to their destination was uneventful, except for a small pack of dogs that ran across the road in front of them. Tyler watched in amazement as some type of small furry animal chased the entire group. It took him a minute to work out that it was a badger chasing the dogs. He wondered what that was about. Badgers were known to be vicious, but weren't wild dogs supposed to be worse? Packs of the damn things had attacked their checkpoints before, how the hell was a single badger scaring the entire group?

He continued to stare after the strange procession while they drove past. Then they disappeared behind the trucks out into the wastes. A sign said that they were six miles from their destination so he put the odd animal behavior out of his mind and yelled to the men and women in the back of his truck to get ready to go.

They rolled down the highway until they passed a sign proclaiming Garden City's pre-war population was only three hundred and twelve. Almost immediately, Tyler saw a large, one story building on the left side of the road with a sign out front that said it was the Garden City Community Center, which is where they were told the food warehouse was hidden. It looked like a typical, abandoned building like they'd seen hundreds of times in their journey. They'd done an excellent job disguising the place.

Aeric's lead truck rolled past the building and they made a few turns down the narrow, dusty town streets to check out the town. It looked uninhabited. Their informants had told them that only a few people were left alive when they'd come through, maybe the residents had actually abandoned it. There wasn't much around in the way of infrastructure either. Even before the war, the residents had obviously been poor. The only highlight that he could see was the football stadium. The town was tiny, but they still had that famous Texas football culture and built a nice stadium. Maybe that weirdo Justin had been correct about the old society's priorities being misplaced. These people couldn't have afforded the stadium. Regardless, they still built it in the hopes that their team would do well enough to win an obscure six-man football championship.

As the trucks continued through the town, no one in Aeric's party saw anyone, so they returned to the community center. A few trips around the building didn't turn up any residents, or anything out of the ordinary, so Traxx decided to move in. They dropped a small squad of Gatherers behind the building to secure the back side and then parked the trucks across the street. He wanted to keep their primary means of escape out of the way of stray gunfire if it came to a firefight.

"Alright, buddy. You ready?" Aeric asked Tyler as the squads were getting off the trucks.

"Yeah. I know what to do," Tyler replied. He glanced around the Gathering Squad members until he saw Nicole. The fact that she wanted to get in his pants could be overlooked because the girl was one of the most tactically-proficient Gatherers on the squad. He usually chose her to accompany him on the more dangerous missions. "Nicole, you ready to go see if anyone's home?"

She broke away from the others, slinking over to him. "Are we just gonna walk up and knock?"

"You got a better idea?"

"We could try and sneak in a door on the back side or go through a window. Hell, we could even breach the side of the building and then storm in. Pretty much anything is better than knocking on the front door."

"That's not how Traxx wants to play this one. We're gonna try to recruit them instead of attack. If anyone's inside, he wants to point out that Midland-Odessa is only a little ways down the road and they're obviously all alone here. He's willing to offer a spot in San Angelo for whoever's here if the haul is good enough."

"I thought we had a population problem," she stated flatly.

"Yeah, well..." Tyler trailed off with one of his trademark shrugs.

"Fine. Come on, big boy," Nicole muttered and hooked a hand through his arm.

Tyler allowed her to lead him across the street while the remaining members of the Gathering Squad and the Shooters spread out around the sides of the building.

The moment that Tyler and Nicole stepped from the pavement onto the community center's concrete parking lot, a loud hissing noise came from the building and the clanging of metal grates falling into place over windows and doors filled the silence of the afternoon. He dove to the ground with his rifle pointed towards the building, willing someone to appear.

When they'd scouted the community center, it appeared totally abandoned. That obviously wasn't the case. "What the fuck was that?" Nicole asked. She stood above him, exactly as she'd been when the gates were released from their hiding places.

"No clue. Get down!" He pulled on her arm to bring her down to his level. *Dammit, combat training 101 was that when you get fired on, you either take cover or get down immediately,* he thought. *What is she doing standing up?*

"I'm fine. That wasn't gunfire," Nicole whispered in his ear.

He ignored her and continued watching the community center. Besides the metal grates that now covered every possible entrance into the building, it seemed just as abandoned as before the commotion. Tyler rolled slightly to his side and looked down the length of his body to where Aeric and the Shooters waited.

Aeric raised both hands up to shoulder height with his palms up in an exaggerated motion that could be seen from all the way across the road. Tyler took it to mean basically that he didn't have any fucking clue what to do.

"Okay, *somebody's* home. I guess we still try to go up and see if anyone wants to talk."

"Yeah, sure," Nicole snorted. "They've probably got the parking lot wired with explosives."

That made him pause for a moment. He didn't know if the EMP that wiped out all the non-hardened electronics in the US also knocked out things like detonators. He wondered if the old school box and plunger-type detonator from the Old West would still work. About the only thing he knew was that it created an electrical charge by pushing the plunger downward. Did the EMP destroy things that created an electrical current via kinetic means or what about items that were constructed after the EMP?

Then he remembered the old truck that he and Aeric had seen driving in Corsicana those first few days after the war. The driver had been able to get that old beast to crank, so the EMP hadn't knocked out everything. Tyler wished that he'd paid more attention in his high school shop class or that he'd signed up for an engineering class at the University of Texas before things went to shit. It was the simple things that he'd overlooked as a kid that could end up saving his life now that they were living in the apocalypse.

He thought for a moment longer and shook his head while he pushed himself to his feet. "There's nothing that we can do. We can't just sit here, and then go back to San Angelo, with Russ dead and nothing to show for it. I'm going to the door."

The big man stormed towards the metal grate covering the entrance and smiled to himself when he heard Nicole's boots scrape against the cement a step or two behind him. "Hold on, Tyler. I'm coming," she breathed heavily.

They reached the door and saw that the grate was comprised of two large pieces of metal that collapsed into place from either side of the door. The large, fake plants in the planters flanking the door had hidden them from sight while they were on the road. He glanced off to the right, the ones covering the windows had slid down from above. By hiding the security gates, anyone driving by wouldn't have noticed that there was anything different about the building. Hell, he'd had his own doubts about the community center as a place holding a lot of food. He would have thought to look in a school cafeteria, gas station, bank, or a grocery store, not the community center. The person who'd set this up knew how to deceive others.

It was also fascinating to see the ingenuity in the metal grates' construction. Whoever built them had drilled holes through the thick metal rods to allow bolts to pass through. They used large bolts with the ends bent over and wrapped the joints with heavy wire, finally securing everything with some type of soldering so the joints couldn't be easily broken. The molten metal would ensure that nothing short of a large hacksaw, and hours of hard work, would get past the grate.

They stared at the door for a long time until Nicole reached around him and pounded the flash suppressor on her rifle into the door. It echoed loudly outside, Tyler could only imagine what it sounded like inside the large cinder block building.

After a full minute without any indication that anyone was inside the building, Nicole banged on the door once more. This time, in response to her knock, a small metal plate set high in the door opened.

"What is it?" a man's voice drifted from the hole above their heads.

Tyler tapped Nicole's arm and said, "Hi, sir. Do you have a moment to talk about your lord and savior, Jesus Christ?"

"What the hell?" the voice asked. "No, I don't want to talk to you. I'm doing quite fine on my own. Please go away."

She slapped him hard across the bicep. "I'm sorry. My idiot friend thinks he's funny. We're from a city called San Angelo. Have you ever heard of it?"

"Of course I've heard of it. What do you want?"

"We'd like to talk to you about becoming a member of our community," Nicole continued.

"Why on earth would I ever do that? I'm perfectly safe here."

Tyler recovered from his amusement and interjected, "Did you know that the residents of Midland-Odessa are out, actively looking for supplies?"

The man inside the community center snorted, "They should be. We're all so stupid for living out here in the middle of nowhere without any resources or way to replenish what gets used."

"Do you have many people living with you?" Nicole questioned.

The voice didn't immediately reply, prompting Nicole to ask, "Sir, did you hear me? Are you alone?"

"I... Yes, I heard you. I've been alone since my wife was killed back in December. One of the pumpjacks collapsed on her."

Garden City was surrounded by the useless pumpjacks—the large, above-ground pumps that pulled oil from the ground and fed the crude into a storage container nearby. Tyler absentmindedly placed a hand on the metal grate blocking the doorway. The metal could have come from the oil pumps.

"I'm sorry, sir," Nicole answered quietly. "What was her name?"

Tyler nodded; she was trying to appeal to his emotional side. "Her name was Emily," the voice in the door responded.

"That's a very pretty name. What's your name?"

"Ted," he replied. "What do you want?"

"We'd like to talk to you, Ted," Tyler replied.

"Is that why you brought your army?" Ted asked bitterly.

"We didn't bring an army," Nicole stated. "We brought a few people to help protect us. The world is a dangerous place nowadays."

"It sure is. I've heard some stories from people passing through. That's why I chose to hole up in here."

"There was a group of people that came to us in April, led by John Pavlik and his wife. They met you and told us that you would be a good addition to our community."

"The Pavliks made it?" Ted asked, obviously relieved.

"Yes, sir," Nicole affirmed. "John said that you had a brilliant mind and could help us in San Angelo."

"They said that, huh?"

"Yeah, they said that you know your way around machinery."

Tyler nudged her and mouthed, *What are you doing?*

Nicole held up a finger and smiled when Ted replied, "Yes, ma'am. I'm a trained mechanical engineer, worked on the pumps in the oil fields for more than fifteen years."

"Ted, can we speak face to face instead of through the door?"

The man behind the door paused and Tyler began to feel uncomfortable. How much had he even interacted with the Pavliks? For all they knew, he could have turned them away like he was trying to do to the two of them. Nicole had taken a major leap to say that John Pavlik had recommended him to them.

The silence was almost palpable until finally, they heard a crank turning behind the door. The metal grate stayed in place while the door into the building opened inward, revealing a thin, wiry man who Tyler guessed to be in his mid-thirties. It was difficult to tell though because the skin on his face and arms had seen years' worth of damage under the harsh west Texas sun. His head was bald with a few spots indicative of skin cancer, and he wore a faded rock band t-shirt and jeans over standard work boots.

He opened their face-to-face conversation abruptly with, "My finger is on a button right now that will dump a hundred gallons of crude oil on your head and light it. It's highly flammable. The good news is that it will kill you in only a few seconds, so you won't suffer much."

"Thanks for the warning, Ted," Nicole replied. "I'm Nicole and this is my friend, Tyler."

"Nice to meet you," he replied. Tyler mumbled a likewise response that he didn't feel since he was potentially moments away from a horrible death.

"So, like we were saying, we want to offer you the safety of living in San Angelo."

Ted snorted once again, "Safety! You folks don't have any idea about safety. I can already tell your type. You think rolling around with overwhelming firepower is the way to go. Strongholds, that's what will see us through now."

"We agree," Nicole replied adamantly. "We have basic walls around the habitable parts of our city, but we need an expert to help us make them better." She pointed at the metal grates covering the doorway. "You're obviously the expert that we need, Ted. You did all of this by yourself and without any power tools."

He beamed under the pretty young woman's compliments. "Yeah, I guess you could say that I've had a lot of time on my hands." His laughter at his own joke seemed a little off to Tyler. Maybe the months of living alone in his fortress had slightly unhinged the man.

"There's something else, Mr.... I'm sorry, what's your last name?" Tyler asked.

"Winston. Ted Winston," he replied.

"You may have been safe before, Mr. Winston, but the cities are running out of food. Depending on how many people are left, they may already be starving. I guess you could say that San Angelo was lucky because we had our revolution early on, only days after the war. More than two-thirds of the population was killed, so we have a lot more food than other places. I traveled to Missouri right afterwards, and a little more than a month after the nuclear bombs fell, the people in Springfield were starving to death. They did some pretty awful things to each other."

Tyler tried to shut away the memory of baby Kayla's mother. He and Aeric had been outside on the street when they heard her screaming. They rushed in and interrupted her rape, but she was shot and killed during the fight with the two men who'd attacked her. They brought Kayla back to Aeric's childhood home and she'd been a part of their family ever since.

He focused his thoughts and heard the end of Nicole's comment, "And it will happen to you too."

Dammit! What had she said? he chided himself. "Yeah, she's right. You're in grave danger living here all alone."

"I don't know about that, Tyler," Ted answered. "I can pretty well take care of myself. You guys wouldn't have been able to get in."

"What if I strapped some C4 to the wall and blew a hole in the cinder block?"

The engineer seemed to consider it for a moment and sighed, "You're right. This place won't stand up to explosives. Holed up in this building, I don't have any sort of stand-off distance to keep marauders away. So far, I've relied mostly on staying hidden. If you folks knew where I was, then that probably means that others do as well."

"It's a good bet that they do, Mr. Winston," Tyler replied. "We can take you back to San Angelo, where you'll be safe, in return for your help with designing our defenses."

It certainly wasn't the mandate that they'd been given when they were told to go clean out the warehouse in Garden City, but Tyler thought that the engineer's addition would be a huge help to the city. He obviously knew how to design defensive systems and had done all of the work on the community center himself, imagine what he could do with a force of a couple thousand workers.

Ted Winston thought about it for a moment longer and made an exaggerated effort to remove his thumb from the button that would have coated them in oil. "Alright, I'm listening. What do you propose?"

*****

The rest of the day went by quickly as the Gathering Squad loaded the two trucks with food and supplies. Mr. Winston had amassed quite a bit of food from all over the town as the former residents left Garden City for the *safety* of Midland-Odessa, abandoning what they couldn't carry. They stacked water off to the side, if they had room for it, then they'd take it, otherwise it would be left behind and they'd have to continue to use water from the lake.

Once they'd cleared enough space on the floor, Traxx moved the trucks inside the community center's cargo doors and closed them so they could secure the location against the coming darkness. Their experience in Sterling City showed them that they didn't know much about this part of the country and all of them thought it was best to take as many precautions as possible. The crews worked long into the night to ensure that everything would be ready to go by morning.

Aeric had been prepared to offer Ted Winston a home in San Angelo, so he was fine with Tyler and Nicole's offer to the engineer. Ted seemed to be the real deal when it came to engineering—the type of person they desperately needed. The security upgrades to the building would have been impressive back in the old days, when there was electricity and scores of people to do the work. The fact that he'd dismantled oil pumps, dragged those parts here and turned them into near-impregnable gates on the doors and windows was amazing. And hiding the defenses so the building looked to be abandoned was a stroke of genius. If Ted could apply his expertise to the walls and checkpoints of San Angelo, it could improve the city's security a hundredfold. The possibilities were nearly limitless.

Aeric was sure that he could convince Mayor Delgado to allow Ted to stay, even with the current ban on new citizens. The city was overpopulated and the addition of another person wouldn't help. However, with the death of the Russ, it would technically be a zero sum gain in population for the city. Semantics.

Early the next morning, everyone was ready to go. Ted went through the building that had been his home for almost ten months one final time, ensuring that he hadn't left anything behind. He paid one final visit to his wife's gravesite where he'd buried her in the grassy area of the business next door. The town didn't even have a cemetery, but they had the damn football stadium. When Ted was satisfied, the group mounted their bicycles and began the long, slow journey back to San Angelo.

The trip was seventy-five miles, only about a two-hour trip in the vehicles. However, the men and women riding their bikes expected to be on the road for at least six or seven hours—if nothing out of the ordinary happened. Aeric considered trying to avoid Sterling City by traveling through the desert and ultimately decided against it. They'd been through the town after they burned the convenience store and other than the strange feeling of being watched, he felt the route that they'd already cleared would be the safest bet.

His estimate of the group's travel time was off. Including breaks and being overly cautious as they went through Sterling City, it was nearing nightfall by the time they made it to San

Angelo's Western Gate. Aeric was surprised to see Lieutenant Griffith on duty. It was odd since she almost always worked the day shift. He greeted her warmly as his bike coasted to a stop near the barricade.

"Hey, Lorelei! You're a sight for sore eyes." Aeric and the lieutenant had met each other only a few days after the war when he and Tyler were on the way to Missouri to find Aeric's family. He'd been the one to tell her and her Army platoon about San Angelo. Her soldiers were given the mission of guarding the interstate entrance in Richland, Texas before the war started. It turned out to be a stroke of luck for them since their base at Fort Hood was hit with a small nuclear missile that devastated everything in the valley where the base sat.

"Traxx! I'm glad that you're back. You've got to come with me."

"What's wrong?" he asked in alarm as Tyler's bike skidded to a stop beside his.

"Kate went into labor yesterday a few hours after you left."

Aeric did the math in his head, she was somewhere between seven and eight months pregnant. Not good. "Is she alright?"

"No," Lorelei stated. "She had the baby—a boy—and except for being small, he seems healthy. Kate isn't doing well, though. When I left this morning to come here and pick you up, she was barely holding on." Aeric appreciated that about her; she would tell it to him straight without trying to sugarcoat bad news. Information passed more efficiently that way.

Aeric glanced at Tyler. His friend's face showed concern for Kate. "I'm gonna go with Lorelei to the hospital."

"Don't worry," Tyler said. "I'll get the trucks to the Provisions Warehouse and make sure everything is unloaded. We'll send the trucks back to Goodfellow as soon as we're done so we don't burn that bridge if we need them again."

Traxx nodded and accepted his friend's hand, "Thanks, brother. Come to the medical center as soon as you can."

Aeric sat heavily on the passenger seat of Lorelei's tan Army Humvee. It was the same truck that she'd been in when he first met her over a year ago. They'd ripped out all the computers and the monitor that showed them where the other units were located. They were all alone now, there wasn't anyone left to see. They'd left the military radios installed so they could talk across the city for rapid dissemination of information.

The military equipment was designed with an EMP in mind, so it had been fine after the war. The lieutenant's platoon initially thought that their radios were damaged in the attack, but realized that their gear was good. It had been the repeater towers that were wiped out from the blasts. Once they made it to where Fort Hood had been, they'd understood why nobody answered them at the base.

Except for the low hum of static from the radio speakers, they rode in silence through the city towards the hospital. Aeric watched the houses fly by as Lorelei expertly maneuvered the big vehicle around obstacles in the streets, taking note of violators the entire time. Even though almost everyone was using bicycles and the occasional horse to move around town, the mayor still wanted the streets clear of debris so they could respond rapidly to emergency situations with the few working vehicles that they did have.

They reached the San Angelo Community Medical Center in less than ten minutes. Early on, it had been decided to consolidate the multiple clinics across the city to the one, centralized location. The much smaller population didn't need more than one facility and the medical center, while older than some of the others, it fit the bill perfectly. It had everything that a society living without electricity would need.

Aeric mumbled, "Thank you," to his friend and rushed inside. Stacey, one of the clinic's nurses, was in the hallway when he went inside. Gone were the days of a dedicated greeter sitting behind a desk performing administrative duties.

Stacey knew Aeric well from all the injuries to the Gathering Squad and the occasional death of one of his people. "I'm so sorry, Traxx. We tried everything we could do."

"Where is she?"

"Exam room three. Follow me."

She led him down the hallway to a small room. Inside, a standard hospital bed sat, forever positioned where it had been when the EMP struck. A body rested under a sheet. Aeric knew it was Kate.

"I'll go get Doc Huerta," Stacey said as an excuse to give him a moment of privacy.

He pulled the sheet aside. Kate's blonde hair fell over the edge of the bed. Her face was swollen in the effort of childbirth and her lips were blue with the loss of blood. He brushed the hair away and touched her cheek. Her skin wasn't cold like they used to show in the movies. Instead, it was the same temperature as the room her body had sat in for an untold number of hours.

Aeric reached down and touched her stomach. It gave and jiggled slightly, no longer holding Justin's baby that she'd carried since he raped her repeatedly. He wondered if the baby had survived the ordeal. Lorelei said that it was healthy, but her information was hours old. Kate had also been alive when she left for the Western Gate. There was no telling what had happened since then.

The doctor cleared his throat behind Aeric and he turned to see the older man standing in the doorway. "I'm sorry, Traxx. There was nothing that I could do for her. We couldn't stop bleeding after she gave birth to the baby."

"Is it… I mean, is the baby alright?" Aeric asked.

"Yes. The boy weighs four pounds thirteen ounces. He's small, but it looks like he's a fighter. He would have been put into the ICU before all this," the doctor gestured in a circle towards the ceiling. "Now the only thing we can do is to keep him warm, keep him fed with formula and make sure that he doesn't get dehydrated. That's about all we can do medically."

Aeric nodded dumbly. He hadn't expected to become a single father and was at a loss. The only baby he'd ever held had been Tyler's stepdaughter Kayla. He wasn't sure what he was supposed to do all by himself.

Sensing Aeric's apprehension, the doctor continued, "There is one thing that we could try, from the homeopathic standpoint. Now, keep in mind, it's not medical science, but there's plenty of observational evidence to back up the treatment."

"What is it, doc?" he asked. Aeric would try just about anything that the doctor told him. Katie had been the one with all the experience and who'd read the books, he'd always just planned on picking it up as it went, supporting her when she needed it.

Doc Huerta shrugged and said, "The best thing for the baby is to have skin-to-skin contact with a woman."

"Huh?"

"It helps a baby feel comforted, nurtured. That's extremely important for a newborn's development. Contact with the father is encouraged, but babies respond better to a woman for some reason. Kate was able to do it last night until she died. One of the nurses agreed to hold the baby for a little while this morning. Do you know anyone who'd be willing to help you for at least a few weeks, preferably a couple of months, until the baby has grown beyond the danger point?"

"I... Uh..." Aeric stammered. His world had changed once again. He'd adapted his life to the new reality of post-nuclear war America, but the rules had changed once again. His pregnant girlfriend had been dead for a few hours and the doctor was suggesting that he find another woman before she was even in the ground?

"I know it's difficult, Traxx. Your initial response is to mourn your loss. Your tears need to get cried out now, in this room, and then you've got to move on. That little boy needs his father to be there for him. You've got to learn how to compartmentalize your emotions and do what's best for the baby."

Aeric had learned to become a master at compartmentalizing his feelings while the Vultures held him in captivity. Every day they'd visit some new horror upon him, a favorite being the heated swing set chains that gave him the scars of his namesake. They resembled crisscrossing railroad tracks over almost every inch of his body. After a few weeks of the repetitive torture, he was able to suppress his body's desire to scream out in pain, vowing to deny his captors' the pleasure they sought. Yes, he certainly knew how to compartmentalize his feelings.

He thought about the doctor's words. There was only one person who came to mind when he thought about a woman who could help him with the baby. Veronica Delgado had been there for him from the beginning, even before he knew Kate was still alive. She'd certainly made it clear to him often enough that she would welcome a physical relationship with him, but did that offer extend to caring for an infant?

"I know someone, Doc. I'm not sure how she'll feel about a baby, though."

The doctor smiled, "Then convince her. Your son needs this."

Aeric nodded slowly. Would she agree to be a stand-in mother for the boy, just for a few weeks?

FOUR

"Oh, so *that's* who our great grandmother is," Tanya exclaimed.

Aiden took a drink of the ersatz tea that the family brewed from various plants in the region, including mint, which helped to hide the bitterness. "Yes, child. Aeric Traxx went to Veronica with his request to help him raise Kendrick—the baby. She accepted and they fell in love, eventually getting married and starting a family of their own. Five years after Aeric's trip to find Ted Winston, my father was born."

"Did he live?"

"My father? Of course!"

Tanya nudged his shoulder gently. "No, silly! Did Ken… Sorry, I forgot his name already. Did the baby live?"

The old man's brows furrowed deeply as he scowled. "Yes. Kendrick survived. He wasn't an imposing figure, like Aeric, but he was very strong like his real father had been and he was as smart as any prewar scientist. In fact, he apprenticed to Ted when he was only a teenager, learning the skills needed to become an engineer himself. The community accepted him, but he never quite fit in. He ran away when he was a teenager without telling anyone where he was going. Aeric searched the wastes for days without luck. They never found his body and assumed that he'd become the victim of some creature in the wasteland that drug him off to its lair.

"He returned to San Angelo almost twenty years later," Aiden continued solemnly. "Using his knowledge of the town's defenses, he sabotaged the walls and led an attack that destroyed our city."

"Was that when Aeric moved here?"

Aiden's eyes glazed over as he stared off into the room behind the girl. "No, Aeric didn't survive the battle for the city. It was... You know what? Let me tell you the entire story, it will make more sense for you that way. I was ten when San Angelo's wall fell and the Vultures burned it to the ground."

"You lived there?" she asked.

"Yes. It was a beautiful city. Most of the buildings were just the way they were before the war, not the ruins that the other places had become. Then, one day, the Vultures arrived and changed everything."

*****

"Ah, my back is at it again," Aeric protested as he stood up from the table pressing both hands into his lower back.

"You've spent your entire life working hard for our family. I'm surprised that you haven't already fallen apart," Veronica chided while she walked up behind him and slid her hand under his shirt. Her fingers curled playfully in the tangle of salt-and-pepper gray hair on his stomach. "You've got to take it easy, you're not a young man anymore,"

Aeric reached behind him and held her close while he turned gingerly to face her. "I'm still young," he mumbled. "Go to the bedroom and I'll show you!"

She giggled like a teenager and snuggled into his embrace. Then the front door opened and their oldest son, Mason, came in.

"Oh geez, are you two at it again? You have grandchildren for heaven's sake."

"Good morning, son," Aeric muttered forlornly as his wife separated from him, going over to embrace the man that their oldest child had become.

"Morning, Dad. I thought we had an appointment to go inspect the walls this morning."

"We do. Just because we're hugging each other doesn't mean anything."

"Do you need me to come back in thirty minutes?"

"Yes," Aeric said.

"No," his wife overruled. "You two go out and make sure no more of those nasty animals get inside the perimeter."

The animals that she referred to were known as *demonbrocs* to the San Angelians. The first known sighting of one of them had been by Tyler Nordgren on the mission when they found the engineer, Ted Winston. He'd seen a large badger-like animal chasing a pack of dogs. The creatures had continued to mutate and evolve in the thirty-five years since then.

Now, they more closely resembled some sick, twisted artist's version of a hellspawn than what a badger looked like before the war. The radiation had been the catalyst for the mutations and then evolution took over to help the creatures become some of the meanest sonsabitches in the wastes. Lately, there'd been several incursions through the walls by the animals, and they'd killed a score of the city's residents. No one knew how—or why—they were coming inside the walls. However, before they could go out into the wastes to investigate further, they needed to ensure that the walls were secure from any more incursions.

"Fine," Aeric said with a final peck on his wife's cheek. Then he asked Mason, "How's the ash today?"

"It's good. Sun's already made an appearance."

The environment had slowly been making a comeback in the last twenty years. They were able to grow crops to sustain the five thousand remaining people in San Angelo. A rash of diseases had halved the population about a year after Kendrick was born. Then, malnutrition and a few other epidemics had further reduced the population over the years until the sun finally began to peek through the clouds of ash, allowing them to plant crops for food. There weren't many people left anymore.

"Good, the lighting will help us see if there are any holes or if the damn things are climbing the walls somehow."

"I know, Dad," Mason replied. "You've taught me everything about wall maintenance." He leaned in to kiss his mother as well and then headed back towards the front of the house.

At thirty, Mason still acted like a teenager when he was around his father. Aeric snorted as he thought, *Too bad the apocalypse couldn't have taken away the snarky attitudes of young people.* Mason had his own children for Christ's sake; he should have been beyond the stage of not listening to his old man. Aeric had seen a lot of shit in his life and he needed to pass that information along to his family.

Thinking of his grandkids made him smile. "How are Alex and Aiden doing this morning?" he asked as he put on a light jacket and strapped his old respirator to his belt. The masks were no longer used every day, but most people still kept them at hand in case a sand storm blew in. A storm could stir up the radioactive dust particles and nobody wanted to breathe in any more of that if they could help it.

"They're doing well. I think Aiden's grown half a foot since you saw him the other day. Seriously, Dad, that kid is growing like a weed."

The older man slapped his hand on his son's back, "Good! That means he's getting enough nutrition. I hope we can all say that."

Mason turned and looked at Aeric, "How is Uncle Tyler doing? I haven't heard anything in about a week."

"I was over there last night. He doesn't have long, the damn cancer has consumed him. Nicole said that he hasn't eaten anything in a few days."

"How's she holding up?"

"She's devastated. That damn woman loves him—hell, maybe more than I do." Aeric had never truly understood Tyler and Nicole's relationship. Neither of them married and they'd lived together since Kendrick was born and Veronica moved into Aeric's home. Tyler still professed to be gay, and as far as he knew, they'd never been more than friends who'd developed a strong bond. Whatever it was, it worked for them and they'd always seemed truly happy in one another's company.

Aeric didn't know what Nicole was going to do now, though. She was fifty years old and had a lot of good years left if she stayed healthy, maybe she'd be able to find someone and possibly even start a family—which was something that the community sorely needed now that they were able to grow crops again. He just hoped that she didn't lose herself to despair like so many others had before her.

"I hope she's able to cope with it," Mason remarked. "Lord knows we don't need any more suicides."

"Yeah..." Aeric trailed off, surprised at Mason's insight. "Alright, Son, you ready to get out to the perimeter?"

"Sure. Let's get to it," he sighed as they walked out the front door to their waiting bicycles.

They rode slowly as the aging machines squeaked and rattled down the pitted asphalt roads. The city's infrastructure was completely failing at this point. They spent most of their available manpower guarding the walls, reinforcing the walls according to Ted Winston's designs or tending to the vegetables and livestock, leaving little time for maintenance. The roads had massive potholes that were filled with gravel from the early years of freezing and thawing. Aeric was thankful that they were in what used to be Texas instead of somewhere farther north where the ash cloud-induced climate change had surely hit hard.

Besides the roads, the buildings were falling apart as well. The dust storms and acid rain early on had wreaked havoc on the non-brick houses that didn't have siding, making those uninhabitable. The homes that remained were in need of repair beyond the paint that was available from the old hardware store. The ones that needed major structural repair were abandoned and marked for demolition, either to be used as additional material for the walls or chopped up and used in the cooking fires.

The trip to the southern edge of the city's wall took ten minutes at their leisurely pace. Over the years, the perimeter had decreased steadily; utilizing Ted's engineering expertise to build stable and defendable walls that had withstood countless attacks from scavengers and raiders in the wastes. Aeric's own stepson, Kendrick, had helped to build the current set before he was lost to the evils outside the walls. The boy's death had been hard on the Traxx family, threatening to tear them apart as Aeric repeatedly exposed himself to the dangers of the wasteland beyond the walls looking for him. It never sat well with him that he didn't find a trace of what happened to Kendrick. There should have been *something*.

"Alright, which way, west or east?"

Aeric focused on Mason and replied, "West. We'll leave our bikes here so we can look closely. All of the other inspections have been done by mounted patrols, so if there's something that they missed, we should see it. If we don't find anything, we'll be done by dinner."

His son dismounted and pulled the old chain lock from the basket behind his seat. He knelt and ran it through the tires and frame of both bicycles. Aeric was impressed, he'd half-expected him to complain about the walk. Maybe the last demonbroc kill only a few blocks from his home had changed his attitude about the duty.

They walked the perimeter of San Angelo—now only about seven miles around—in a few hours. Aeric remembered when the massive city walls stretched for miles and miles, encircling most of the old city. The huge decline in population meant that they could collapse their perimeter. They could still make it many times smaller if they wanted to move some of the infrastructure and force more people to move towards the old university buildings. It would mean that they'd need to rebuild the walls again, though; the population's appetite wasn't there to move them once more.

The walls were intact. They didn't find any holes or evidence of meddling on the inside. "Tomorrow, we'll have to check outside to see if there's a way they're getting in from that side," Aeric stated while Mason unlocked the bikes.

"Yeah, I was thinking the same thing. There's got to be a way that they're getting in. It must be over the top since we didn't find any holes."

"Maybe there's been some kind of damage to the walls and there are some jagged edges that they're able to use as handholds to climb up," Aeric suggested hopefully. They had to stop the damn things.

Their uneventful day ended with Mason promising to bring the boys over to Aeric and Veronica's house later that night. Aeric walked in to a house full of wonderful aromas. His wife sat in the kitchen reading a book. A large pot rested over a low fire.

"Mmm," Aeric said as he gave her a kiss. "That smells wonderful, what is it?"

"We got our meat ration today, so I made stew with vegetables from our garden along with some oats from the community fields."

"Sounds good. Is it ready?"

"Yes. I'll fix you a bowl after you wash your hands."

Aeric chuckled at his wife's statement. He'd been outside of their house, touching the fence, testing the wall that kept them safe, of course he'd wash his hands because of the radiation dust. But, raising three boys had instilled in her a lifelong need to ensure that everyone stayed clean—even Aeric.

When he returned, she had a steaming bowl of the stew sitting on the table and a glass of water. Aeric noticed a few things floating inside the glass. She saw his stare and said, "The filter is just about shot. We need a new one."

"I can clean it and get us a few more months out of it," he answered.

"Why not get a new one? Christy gets a new filter when hers goes bad."

He sighed. It was a debate that they'd had hundreds of times. "Veronica, we don't have an unlimited supply of water filters. I'll have to talk to Nicole about the rationing of non-replaceable items; Christy shouldn't be getting a new one all the time."

"Aeric, you bust your ass for this town and nobody else except for our family seems to suffer from the programs that you've put into place to keep us going. Don't you think that's bullshit?"

"I know, babe. The truth is, even without adhering strictly to the rationing program, by following even half of it, the community can sustain itself for a long time. Hopefully long enough for all the particulate matter to settle out of the water."

"Can't Ted design a filtering system?" she asked.

"He's a mechanical engineer. He's great with metal and steam powered things, not building water filters." It was true. They'd been able to design all sorts of steam powered equipment, converting the old rusting hulks of tractor equipment into useable, self-powered backhoes and bulldozers. It had helped them clear the parts of the old city tremendously and aided in the rapid construction of the walls each time they'd collapsed the perimeter.

"Well, there has to be something better than using blankets to filter out the filth. I just don't know what it is."

Aeric ate his stew in silence for a moment while he thought about the requirement. Then, he said, "What if we use old screens?"

"Huh?"

"All those houses that we've torn down had window screens. What if we overlay a bunch of them together to help filter out the crap from the water over at the spigots? We could use that as an initial filter and then continue using the blankets and sheets to further filter it. Then, the water filters here at the house wouldn't have to work as hard, so we could extend their life."

"That would help a little bit," she admitted. "Right now, the blankets don't last long before they're gummed up and all that crap from the lake needs to be scraped away."

"Good, I'll pass that on to the water folks. Maybe we can pick up some screens from the dumps when we go outside tomorrow."

"You're going *outside*?"

"Yeah. We didn't find any breaches on the inside of the fence, so there must be some areas outside where the demonbrocs are able to climb up and over the wall."

Veronica grabbed his hand and squeezed tightly. "Be careful, Aeric. I've had terrible dreams lately."

"What kind of dreams?" he asked apprehensively.

"About death and destruction...and fire."

"How long have you been having them?" It was an important question. Some of the younger people had begun to show signs of clairvoyance. Aeric was taken aback by his wife's admission, though, because it was always in those who'd been born after the heavy radioactive fallout of the war, not in people who'd been an adult when the old world ended. There was one little girl named Maria who had shown up alone at the Western gate several months ago. They'd accepted her into the walls; there was no doubt that she had the Gift. It was scary.

"About two weeks," Veronica replied to his question.

"Hmpf...that's how long the demonbrocs have been getting inside the perimeter. Do you think that maybe you're just worried about them—or is it something else?"

"You mean like predicting the future?"

"I don't know about that," Aeric replied in an attempt to ease his wife's fears. "We're facing extremely dangerous creatures that are getting inside our walls and have appeared all over the city. Maybe that's causing you to have these nightmares. I'd hate to think of what else it could mean."

She thought about it for a moment before answering, pondering the implications behind her dreams. "You're probably right about me having an overactive imagination," she admitted. After a moment, Veronica continued, "I'm scared, Aeric. Scared of what it means if I *do* have a touch of the Gift and that these things have a chance of coming true. The things that I've been dreaming about are absolutely terrible. Life-altering things. Attacks by humans *and* creatures from the wastes. Total destruction of the city. Our people—the ones who survive at least—are spread to the corners of the earth."

Aeric thought about his wife's statements, wondering what he could do. He didn't know Maria, the girl with the Gift, well enough to know much about the aspects of her clairvoyance. Was Veronica experiencing the same thing or was it simply an overactive imagination after having lived through some terrible times? He'd heard that the little girl went into trances in the middle of conversations, which was supposedly how she ended up out on her own. The group that she'd been born into had freaked out and banished her with no supplies. It was a miracle that they hadn't killed her outright.

"I... Honestly, I don't know what to say," Aeric stammered "We've dedicated our lives to this place. We made it past those violent early years when we lived almost like hunter-gatherers from Neolithic times, killing each other for resources. Then the fallout cleared from the skies and the sickness helped to balance out the population in the city. I thought we were past the worst days now that we can grow crops again and produce enough food to sustain ourselves."

"*We* can produce enough food," Veronica countered. "We have no idea what others can or can't do. I mean, when was the last excursion beyond the city's defensive perimeter?"

Aeric thought back. It had to have been more than five years since the Gathering Squad went outside of the ten-mile San Angelo defense zone that they'd established around the city. The need to go beyond that had ceased once they'd developed arable land inside the city perimeter and procured enough goats through trading to have a viable breeding program. Veronica was right. They had no clue what was happening outside their little microcosm environment that they'd carved out for themselves in the west Texas wastes.

He dragged his hand across his face and brought the spoon up to his mouth. The stew had gone cold, like the feeling of dread that had settled in his stomach. Finally, he answered his wife's question, which felt more like an accusation than anything else. "It's been years. The last big push we made outside of the area was to acquire the goats."

"God, it's been *that* long? I thought maybe a year. Can you imagine what others have done if they had a smart engineer like Ted or an aggressive war leader like Tyler? Hell, what if they had a smart, caring and shrewdly calculating civil administrator like you? There could be other functioning societies like ours out there. Considering your experiences outside the walls, it's not likely, but what if there are more like us? Or ones that have all those things, but are willing to do whatever it takes to keep it that way?"

Again, she was right. He'd allowed himself to become so self-absorbed and secure behind the massive perimeter walls that Ted had designed that they didn't know anything about the outside world anymore. It was a dangerous situation that they'd become complacent and he needed to change it. "I'll speak to Lorelei tomorrow about preparing an exploratory excursion beyond the defense zone."

"Good—"

Before she could say anything further, Aeric raced ahead and continued, "I need you to come with me tomorrow morning to speak to Maria. Maybe she's seen something and hasn't told anyone or they've ignored her because she's a child."

His wife blanched. "Why do you need me to go with you?"

"Because I need you to describe exactly what you've seen in your dreams. Maybe that will trigger her visions to start or something. I don't know how it works."

"She scares me, Aeric."

"She's a little girl, Veronica, how scary can she be?" His wife had interacted with Maria often at the soup kitchen, whereas he'd only seen her a few times during his incursions into the Barrio. In truth, he wasn't entirely sure that he could pick her out of a crowd of children.

Veronica Traxx sighed and placed her hands on the table, splaying her fingers wide. She examined them intently, replying without looking up, "You'll see. All of the kids with the Gift are a little off because of their visions, but she's…different. Sometimes the things that come out of her mouth are downright frightening. I don't want people to look at me like they do her. I don't want people to call me a freak and hide their children like they do with her."

*****

The city of San Angelo had fallen into disrepair, leaving the residents to fight a constant battle to keep their homes from collapsing. The parts of the city where few people lived were understandably worse off than other areas. The neighborhood that Veronica, Aeric and a young Shooter named Joseph found themselves entering the morning after Traxx decided to talk to the little girl with the Gift of future sight was known as the Barrio. The multiple contractions of the perimeter had inevitably left people homeless as the city shrunk inwards towards the larger concrete structures downtown. The homeless had successfully found homes in the first move after the big flu epidemic had killed off all those people, then when the walls were moved inward once more, less of them found homes, deciding to live in old commercial buildings. Finally, the third move had created the Barrio, a slum within the deteriorating city of San Angelo where the town's less than desirable population chose to live.

Veronica hadn't ever been to the Barrio before. She was scared. She dealt with everyone in the city on a daily basis in the relative safety of the soup kitchen, not in their own neighborhoods. Parts of San Angelo—like the Barrio—were unofficially off-limits to non-residents except for the police force and the specialized troops like Captain Lorelei Griffith's Shooters. Even Aeric confessed to her that he only went into the Barrio once every couple of months when he took the census to ensure that everyone had a job and worked towards the city's common good.

An old grocery store supposedly boasted a population of three hundred people, living in carefully portioned off pieces of real estate inside the building. Allegedly the large shelves helped to further subdivide the place. Murders and rapes were common in the Barrio. If it didn't happen to you or your family, though, nobody would talk to the police. It was a depressing way of life, brought on partially by the conditions after the war, but mostly because those types of people chose to live together in such a small area.

Veronica relied on her husband's limited knowledge of the neighborhood to find Maria. It had been a few days since she'd last seen her at the soup kitchen. The girl was probably nine or ten years old and skinny as a rail. Most people these days were thin anyways, but she was excessively so, almost like her body was eating itself.

The road they followed through the filth and wreckage was more of a path cleared of debris than an actual road. They traveled several blocks until it terminated at a large pile of rubble that might have been a house at one time. "This is the boundary for the Barrio," Aeric stated.

"Wait, I thought we were in the Barrio already," Veronica said, holding up her hand and gesturing to the detritus around them.

Aeric glanced at Joseph, who shook his head. "Not really. Joe spent the last few years of his childhood here before joining the Shooters. We were on the outskirts, the Barrio is a three-block square that's been claimed by the residents. The main structure is the grocery store and then there are lots of little cinder block structures that used to be gas stations, fast food restaurants and hair salons. Now that's where the people live."

Veronica stared at the young man who'd been with them from the start of their journey to find Maria. She hadn't known anything about him other than the fact that Aeric vouched for him. "What's it like growing up in there?" she asked.

He cleared his throat before answering. "You don't really know any different when you live there. We moved in about eight years ago when our old home fell outside the new city walls. It was either go to a place where you could have shelter from the elements inside the walls or take our chances out in the wastes. My dad chose to keep us inside. It's not all that bad, just like living in the barracks, except it's really dirty."

"Hmm," she muttered. "That's a good way of thinking about it. Why don't the residents clean it up?"

"The Barrio is different than any other part of the city. We have our own rules and ways of doing things. It suits most of the residents, so we're good."

Veronica wondered what he meant. With the help of the city council, Aeric—and her father before him—set the laws for the city. She thought those were established and followed by everyone, not that some community made its own rules. Her husband always acted strangely when the topic of the Barrio was brought up and had been pretty vague so far today about the neighborhood. She'd chalked it up to one of those things that you had to see to believe and had gone with the flow, so far. Now, her patience was nearing its end. "Why couldn't we have just told Maria to come meet with us somewhere else?"

"It's not that big of a place," Joseph answered. "But if someone doesn't want to be found, you'll never find them inside the Barrio."

"Huh?"

"What he means is that if Maria isn't interested in talking to us, then she'd disappear," Aeric answered. "If I'd led the life that she has, I wouldn't go with strangers either. You're our way of meeting with her. She knows you from the soup kitchen so hopefully she'll decide to talk to us."

Veronica accepted the explanation. Besides the few years that she spent in Austin where she met Aeric, she'd lived her entire life in San Angelo. Admittedly, the world was entirely different than when she was a child, but she didn't know that places like the Barrio could exist here. "Alright, fine. Let's get this over with."

In a rare display of deference, Aeric looked to Joseph for approval. The Shooter nodded and said, "It's morning, so most people are at their jobs. We'll have to watch out for the kids, though. There are a few street gangs that run the place while the adults aren't around. Most of the time, they're harmless and just want to be recognized as equals to anyone who enters. To get their attention, though, we may have to kill one of them."

Veronica looked at him in shock. "What?"

"If you kill one of 'em, that usually shuts them up and they scurry off to their holes," Joseph said with a shrug of his shoulders.

She turned to her husband, "Aeric, what's he talking about?"

He held up his hands at waist level and patted downwards. "We're not going to kill anyone."

After thirty years together, she knew her husband intimately and the daggers of warning that his stare sent towards Joseph meant that they'd talked about this beforehand. He knew about the killing of street children and kept it from her. It was unconscionable that he'd allow murders to happen inside the city walls without sending the police force in to put an end to it.

"The Barrio is...different," Aeric stated. "They are forced to do things that we don't like, and quite frankly, sometimes don't even understand."

"Then get some of Ted's equipment and bulldoze the walls!" she exclaimed while pointing angrily at the barricade. "Increase the police presence, provide incentive to the residents to follow the established rules of our society, educate the children about what's acceptable in a civilized city...."

"We've tried," Aeric replied. "They keep coming back. The best thing that we've found so far is to let them have their semi-autonomous neighborhood. They all contribute to the defense of the city and work in their jobs like everyone else. This is one of those things that we just have to let go. Trust me, Veronica."

She glanced back to Joseph, who nodded. "It works. It's what we—what *they*—want," he corrected himself. "There's enough opportunity to leave if someone chooses to leave. Nobody is forcing them to stay."

It went against everything she'd allowed herself to believe about her city. She thought that out of all the death and destruction, they stood separate and apart from it all, the proverbial shining beacon of society in a post-nuclear war world. Her perceptions had been false. Of all people, her husband had helped to perpetrate the myth. What was real and what was an intricate lie to keep the masses in check, she wondered.

FIVE

They left the path that they'd followed and trailed behind Joseph. He led the way around the perimeter of the Barrio until they came to an opening in the pile of garbage. Two kids, Veronica thought they were no older than thirteen, guarded the entrance with spears made out of old copper plumbing and kitchen knives. If their weapons hadn't looked so threatening, she'd have laughed at the absurdity of the children pretending to be soldiers.

"What you want, Joe?" the larger of the two asked. He ducked his head and acknowledged Aeric's presence. "Traxx."

"We're here to see Maria," the Shooter answered.

"She not here. You give ammo, you maybe see her," he said, holding out his grubby hand.

Veronica wondered about the pattern of the boy's speech. She hadn't ever picked up on the children at the soup kitchen talking like the boy at the entrance to the Barrio. Then again, she'd never seen either of these two before. She wondered if they didn't go to the daily communal meals that helped to cement the San Angelians together. At the very least, she should have seen them getting food to bring back here.

"I don't have any ammo to give you except for a bullet in the brain, Fish. Where is Maria?" Joe asked menacingly.

The boy sniffed and then rubbed the snot that dripped from his nose with his palm. "Don't gotta be fuckin' asshole, Joe. We tryin' to get more bullets for protection."

"We don't have time for it. Which rat hole is she staying in today?"

"No rats left. We ate them all," he answered matter-of-factly.

Veronica's mouth opened to protest that even in the darkest of days, she'd never served rat in the kitchen. She snapped it shut quickly when Aeric's hand gripped her wrist. He shook his head slightly, telling her to keep quiet.

"Yeah, I know," Joseph said. He sniffed and continued, "What are you cooking now, Fish?"

The boy grinned and wobbled his hand. "Little of this, little of that, Joe. You know how life in Barrio is."

"Where's the girl, Fish?"

"She in the old store. Little bitch bit Claw's dick off yesterday."

Joseph laughed out loud, startling Veronica. "She did? Good for her! That dirty, raping bastard deserves it."

The boy bristled at Joe's words. His partner placed a restraining hand on Fish's arm. He hadn't spoken until then, "She gotta go, man. If Claw lives, he gonna kill her. Make her pay first, though. Girl can't stay here no more, no matter what Mr. Edward say."

"We'll take her with us," Aeric stated.

The older boy turned to him threateningly. "Not talkin' to you, Traxx. You—" He was cut off by Aeric's fist smashing into his nose. Veronica yelped louder than the child that her husband punched.

"I'm not gonna take shit from some Barrio trash," Aeric scowled. "I'm done being nice. Either take us to Maria or I'm gonna let Joe start murdering you little fucks."

"Okay, okay, Traxx. You know we like you. You good guy," Fish replied in between glances at his partner's ruined face. "Don't know woman. Who she?"

"Veronica," Aeric answered. "Maria is going to live with her."

Veronica waved timidly and wondered at Aeric's choice of words. He purposefully left out that she was his wife, why was that?

Fish grabbed his crotch and rubbed it suggestively, "Wanna trade your woman for Maria? We take good care of her. *Real* good care."

She stepped back away from the degenerate in time to see the end of Joe's rifle slam into Fish's abdomen.

The boy bent over in pain and slapped at his bloody partner's leg. "Flame take you to Maria, man," Fish coughed.

Aeric smiled, "Don't try to double cross us once we're inside."

"You good, Traxx. No problem with Slashers."

Flame, the boy whom Aeric had punched in the face gestured for them to follow him inside the Barrio. Joseph led the way while Veronica fell into step beside her husband several paces behind the other two. "What was that back there?" she whispered.

"Violence is about the only thing that these kids understand," Aeric replied.

"Or maybe we could change that and try kindness."

He sighed and her temper spiked. If he dared to say something like she didn't truly understand the world that they lived in, then she would scream at him. It was an old argument between them. She'd never been out in the wastes besides the initial trip when her father brought her back to San Angelo from Austin. She'd heard plenty of stories from her famous husband and Tyler about the dangers outside the city walls. All three of her boys had followed in Aeric's footsteps and become members of the Gathering Squad as well, so she had enough knowledge about the outside world to inform her statement. These people were *inside* the city walls, it didn't have to be like this.

"You saw that...that urchin, Fish," Aeric continued in a hushed tone. "If given the opportunity, he'd rape you and then slash your throat or maybe vice versa. There's no saving those types of people. Times are tough all over—more so in the Barrio. That doesn't give the street gangs the right to be thugs and murderers, though. Like I said, violence is the only thing those kids understand. They respect people who are more powerful than them."

"Then why not go in and clear them out; empty the Barrio of the street gangs?"

"Now you want me to kill the kids? It would cause a massive uprising from their parents and leave the community in a state of fear over who's next to be wiped out." Aeric waved to a few dirty children playing with ancient toys beside an old ice cooler at a convenience store. He reached over behind her and placed his hand in the small of her back as they walked and continued, "The kids band together and do horrible things when they're trying to get through a tough period in their lives. You remember how awkward those years were back when we had everything in the world at our fingertips. Imagine how these kids are, their future is bleak at best. They grow out of it, for the most part. Joseph was a gang kid before joining the Shooters."

"What about the ones who don't grow out of it?" Veronica asked.

"We have a program for them."

She stopped and twisted away from his hand. "What program?"

"The ones who don't change their ways after they become adults work in the sewers under guard."

"You force people to clean up the filth of everyone in the city?"

"All that piss and shit has to go somewhere," he answered and began walking again. "It's not a job that anyone is going to volunteer for, so we take the degenerates down there and they spend ten hours a day scooping refuse into buckets and hauling it through the sewers out to the south side of town. So far we've only had one person who hasn't reformed and seen the error of his ways after a couple of weeks."

"What happened to him?"

"He's in charge of the Barrio."

"What?"

Aeric shrugged, "He still works down there, hauling shit every day. Has been for more than twenty years. But the residents of the Barrio love him and have elected him as their spokesperson."

She blanched at the idea of someone being in that filth without the convenience of showers. "You've had people down there for twenty years?"

Aeric shrugged, "Edward Huerta is a degenerate who hasn't done enough to be banished into the wastes. It seems like every time we allow him to come up, he does something else and gets thrown back down there. Petty theft, vandalism, drug production and sales, that sort of stuff."

"If he runs the Barrio and these street kids do whatever he says, why does he keep getting in trouble, not one of them?"

She could tell that her husband had never thought of it that way before. "I don't know."

"Have you been down in the tunnels to see what's going on down there?"

"Sure. I mean, not all of them. There are miles of crisscrossing sewers, but I've been along the main routes."

"Maybe there's something else going on and that's why he keeps going down in there," she proposed. *How in the hell has he not wondered what's going on in the tunnels that keeps this guy down there?*

"You're probably right, babe. I'll send some of the police force or maybe borrow a few more of Lorelei's Shooters to go down there."

"I don't know, it seems like—"

He cut her off, "We can talk about it later. We're coming up on the old grocery store where Maria lives."

She nodded and walked slowly beside her husband. It was probably best to discontinue the conversation anyways. There seemed to be a feeling of being watched inside the Barrio, so there was no telling who was listening to her tell Aeric that Huerta's actions seemed shady and needed to be investigated.

They passed by a rough-looking group of young men lounging around a fire pit in an open area near the trail through the garbage. These boys were also about the same age as the kids at the entrance, but a few were older, fifteen or so—maybe. Veronica swore that they might have been the vilest group that she'd ever seen. They wore ragged clothing of various styles with a square of bright green cloth sewn onto their shirts above the left breast.

Veronica had seen the cloth sewn on clothing before at the community soup kitchen, never really thinking anything of it. Now that she saw it displayed on ten boys all at the same time, she knew that it was their gang symbol. The boy at the gate didn't have the green cloth sewn on his clothes, but he was clearly in a gang according to Aeric and Joseph. *They must be rivals*, she concluded.

Some type of animal, about the size of a medium dog sat on a spit over the fire. The cooking meat smelled wonderful, making her wonder what type of ration they'd been given. One of the boys stood up and closed the distance between them.

"What you doin', Flame?" the boy asked the rival gang member, ignoring the adults that he led.

"Traxx needs to talk at Maria," Flame stated.

The boy with the green cloth sewn on his shirt looked over at Traxx. "That true? Why you want my girl?"

Aeric sighed. "Seriously, kid. I know she's not your girl. And I'll talk to whomever the hell I want."

"Oh yeah?"

"I've about had enough of you little shitheads!" Veronica screamed, causing everyone—including Aeric—to flinch involuntarily. "We need to have an important discussion with her and all of you think that you're bigshots in this little shithole. You're not; you're just a bunch of wannabe gang banger thugs. Now, where the hell is Maria?"

The boy puffed up his chest and pointed to himself with a thumb. "I'm leader here, not Traxx. He don't give orders."

"Stand down, Bull," Joe said as he leveled his rifle at the gang leader's midsection. "You know I ain't got no problem shooting you."

The boy stepped back with his hands up. "This ain't over, Traxx. You allowed in the Barrio one time a month, ten days after meat ration. You early."

"Don't make me confiscate your illegal meat, kid," Aeric threatened.

"That our meat. Touch it, you die."

Aeric brought his own weapon around. The ancient lever-action 30-30 had been with him from that night in Austin when Veronica first met him and Tyler. "Threaten me again and *you're* the one that will be buried, little man."

Bull seemed to consider his words carefully before replying, "Fine, take bitch. We sick of fucking her anyway." He made an exaggerated circle with his hands. "She all stretched out after we done with her." Then he turned and went back to the fire.

Aeric gripped Veronica's elbow lightly and steered her towards the large structure looming in front of them. "Let's go," he muttered quietly. "They scare off easily enough. Unfortunately, their own inexperience allows them to get over their fear quickly. Better to be inside when they figure out that they outnumber us three-to-one."

The relative closeness of the Barrio seemed like wide open grasslands compared to the dark and damp that greeted her inside the grocery store. The walls bore the signs of thirty years' worth of habitation. Dirt, graffiti...blood, it was all there. The lack of the original overhead lighting made it nearly impossible to see since the discolored skylights above were caked with smoke film. Filthy children of all ages sat alone or played in small groups among hundreds of individual family campsites. It was the most depressing thing that Veronica had ever seen.

Obviously, she'd become accustomed to things being generally more run down and dirty since the days of her youth. However, the conditions in the supermarket took everything to an entirely different level. It seemed to her that the residents were content to merely survive and not improve their situation at all. She immediately identified several quick fixes that would have been easy to do and likely increase morale, primarily cleaning, increasing the lighting and opening the skylights above to allow the smoke to escape.

"Maria lives on row one three," Flame stated. "Leaving now." The boy didn't wait for Aeric to answer before turning to leave quickly.

"What the hell was that about?" Veronica asked as she hugged herself tight in an effort to shrink away from the grime in the building.

"They don't like her," Joseph replied. "She scares them."

"That hasn't stopped them from raping her," Veronica scoffed.

"Eh, I doubt they've actually done it. Lots of talk from little boys who want to be big men," Joe countered. "The girl has the

Gift, so she knows when they're going to try something. Besides, you heard what Fish said about her biting Claw's uh...er...."

"His *dick*," Veronica offered. "I had three boys, Joseph. I've heard it all."

He nodded and continued, "Yeah, she did that to him. So she knows how to defend herself."

"Good point." She stared over at the smeared sign above the aisles indicating that row thirteen used to contain charcoal and paper products. The little girl had survived on her own in the wasteland before coming to San Angelo. *Maybe she really can predict the future and she's learned to avoid trouble*, Veronica thought.

"Okay, we came all this way," Aeric interrupted her thoughts. "Let's go over and talk to her. If what Joseph says is right, she already knows that we're coming anyways."

They walked slowly, exaggerating their efforts to not inadvertently step on someone sleeping in the piled up blankets and heaps of discarded clothing. At the end of row thirteen, it became immediately apparent to Veronica where Maria lived. Each aisle they'd passed had been filled from one end to the other with the personal belongings of the row's residents. Aisle thirteen had a noticeable vacancy between the end of one family's area to a small "camp" in the middle of the aisle and then another empty space on the other side between the camp and another family. A small bundle sat hunched over in the center of the blankets. Obviously, the residents had chosen to shun her instead of help her.

"That's gotta be her," Aeric mumbled as they followed Joseph down the row. Veronica watched where he put his feet and carefully placed her foot where the Shooter's had previously been. It certainly wouldn't do for her to step on someone or to break one of the few possessions that these people owned.

"Hello, sister," a frail child's voice drifted from the blanket when the group neared her.

"Uh… Hello?" Veronica answered. "Are you Maria?"

"Yes. I am. I've been waiting for you and the masked man to come."

Veronica was already beginning to get freaked out. She'd scared herself with the dreams that she'd been having. What really made her skin crawl was that the girl hadn't looked up from underneath the blanket and she knew that Aeric Traxx was there. Surely, the "masked man" was her husband. The scars that disfigured his face could certainly resemble a mask to a child who'd never seen him before.

"Uh… Hello, Maria. My name is Veronica."

"Oh, I know who you are," the girl replied, still hidden in the blankets. "You run the food kitchen for the city. I've seen you surrounded by death, it's not pretty."

"Jesus!" Aeric exclaimed as he stepped over to the blanket. He snatched it off of the girl's head and admonished, "I know you like to be mysterious and creepy, but you don't open a conversation with how someone is going to die."

The girl blinked up at him. Her dirty face was framed by stringy, black hair that likely hadn't seen soap in months, if ever. Up close, Veronica could see that she was probably closer to eleven than the nine that she'd originally thought. The girl was just skin and bones, although it was hard to tell with the way she was huddled up. She seemed entirely ordinary except for her eyes. They were the strangest shade of blue, almost like she wore purple contact lenses like the girls at the university used to wear before the end of the old world.

"I didn't say that she was going to die," Maria corrected him. "Death follows closely beside her."

"Maria, we came to talk to you about—"

The girl's face snapped back towards Veronica. "You've been having them too, haven't you?"

"What are you—"

"The visions. Death. Destruction. Torture," she intoned. "The city is going to fall and everyone living here will die."

Aeric looked to his wife and mouthed, *What the fuck?* Veronica squinted and made the face that her children knew well. She was silently telling Aeric to get control of the situation and do it quickly.

"Maria," Aeric tried to get the girl's attention.

"You're all dead! You've stayed too long." Maria began to thrash about in the blankets. She was going to hurt herself.

"Maria, stop!" Aeric's voice boomed across the grocery store. Several tiny heads peeked around the corner at the edge of Veronica's peripheral vision. They had to get this under control before the other children started to panic.

"They're going to eat us and use our skin as coats. You!" she pointed at Aeric. "You're the masked man that caused all of this. It's your fault! Everyone will die because of you. The walls will fall and the city will burn. Everyone who survives the fire will become the playthings of the giant birds!"

Veronica had heard enough. *That didn't take long,* she thought. They'd come to discuss her dreams, but that wasn't going to happen. Maria was clearly disturbed and incoherent. She could pity the girl, but they weren't going to get anything useful out of that little head.

"Aeric, this has to stop," Veronica ordered. "She's scaring the other children and their parents are all at work. We should just go."

He nodded and stepped in close to stop her crazy rant. Maria avoided him by standing up quickly and backing against the vacant shelving unit. She twisted her head back and forth and then lunged towards Aeric, grabbing both of his wrists.

"But wait!" Maria yelled. "The colossus can save one of the tribes if he chooses to abandon you!"

"One of the tribes?" Aeric asked.

"The Birds!" Maria screamed, changing her grip to grasp his forearm. "*The Birds are coming!*"

As she finished yelling, she collapsed against Aeric. He caught her to keep her from falling. "What the hell was that?" he muttered as he held the limp figure in his hands.

"She's gotta go, Traxx," Joseph stated. "I doubt that she's been screaming like that around the others. If she did, you can bet that they'd beat her to death for it. The Barrio is no longer safe for her."

Aeric's eyes searched his wife's face for a clue as to what they should do. She certainly didn't want the responsibility of caring for this crazy person. She was probably going to have night terrors and interrupt their way of life. Then, Veronica's heart softened. Maria was just a little girl and she needed help; help that they could give her.

"I guess we can take her to our house and figure out what to do with her," Veronica finally conceded with a sigh.

Aeric agreed, so they gathered the few belongings that were in the immediate area and Joseph carried Maria from the refuse.

SIX

Once they arrived safely at the Traxx home, Joseph took his leave of them to return to the Shooter's barracks over near the old Air Force base, which had been annexed to the city after Colonel Henshaw's death. It didn't make any sense to anyone to maintain two perimeters, so they cut off the worthless old airfield and tore down the student hangar for construction material, which also gave them excellent fields of view to the east.

Maria had woken up after they left the Barrio, choosing not to say much of anything besides mumbled words of acknowledgement when they tried to talk to her. Although she seemed more coherent than she had been inside the grocery store, Veronica wouldn't let him ask her about the visions until she'd been cleaned and fed. While his wife took the girl upstairs to take a lukewarm bath and outfitted with a new wardrobe of their grandchildren's clothing, Aeric busied himself with rekindling the fire to heat the stew that his wife had made the day before.

He didn't know what to think of the girl's outburst in the grocery store. There was definitely something off in her head, unfortunately, they no longer had the medical staff that they once had—the last round of the flu had ensured that. There were several other children in San Angelo that he'd heard of who had a touch of the Gift, as they called it, although no one else was as vocal or open about their talents as Maria.

Her warnings about the birds scared him. He obviously had no clue how her visions came to her, whether they were voices or only images, but a vulture could easily be mistaken for another type of bird. The Vultures were the bastards who'd tortured him and Tyler, while their leader, Justin, turned Kate into a sex slave. Justin's final parting gift to Aeric before his death had been to get her pregnant, which had ultimately killed her during childbirth.

The Vultures were a vicious, dangerous gang of murderers who'd taken power in the former capital city of Austin. The last he'd heard, they were heavily involved in a civil war between Sanders, the former Army officer whom Justin had bribed to come work for him, and some upstart looking to unsettle the balance of power.

That had been more than ten or twelve years ago. He hadn't learned the outcome of the fight for the gang's leadership. Not knowing about the Vultures, along with Veronica's questions from the previous day about what lay beyond the San Angelo defense zone, haunted him. He honestly had no clue what was out there beyond those ten miles anymore. With the smaller population, they had plenty of supplies and simply didn't need to continually expose themselves to the dangers of the wastes far away from human habitation.

Maybe they needed to begin patrolling again. Hell, maybe a scouting mission all the way to Austin was needed as well.

The sounds of feet scraping on the stairs brought him back to the present as the girl appeared in the kitchen doorway. Veronica stood behind, leaning against the doorjamb with her arms crossed over her chest.

Aeric was shocked at Maria's transformation. The bath had done wonders for her. Underneath the layers of dirt had been a pretty, olive-skinned little girl. Veronica had given her a haircut, likely because the hair had been too matted to wash. Now her hair was the length of her chin all the way around, giving her a softer appearance than before. Except for her eyes, which were still a strange purple color, she looked like a child and not a psychopath.

"Hello, Maria," he said softly.

"Hi, Mr. Traxx," she replied dutifully. Her eyes darted towards the metal pot suspended above the fire.

"If you're hungry, we have some stew for you."

Maria smiled and Aeric noticed that she even had a dimple on her cheek. "Oh, please!" she exclaimed. "I'm so hungry. I hardly ever got to eat all of my food before someone else took it from me."

He busied himself with preparing her a bowl of the stew from the pot. It hadn't gotten as hot as he liked his soup to be, but figured that the lower temperature would be good for the girl. She waited eagerly at the head of the table, holding her spoon expectantly like she planned to fight off others for the opportunity to take a few bites.

When he set the bowl down, she plunged the spoon and began to shovel the food into her mouth. He chuckled and held up his hands to catch her attention. "Maria, you can slow down. Nobody here is going to take the food from you. Take the time to taste the food; we won't get another meat ration for a few weeks."

She made a visible effort to slow down and take her time. Aeric used the ladle to scoop out two more bowls of stew and then sat them down on the table across from each other. Veronica padded over softly in her old house shoes and took the seat nearer to the fire. Everyone ate in silence until Maria finished her stew and burped, causing them to laugh.

"There, wasn't it better when you slowed down?" he asked.

"Yes, sir. It was delicious. Thank you."

He pointed across the table at Veronica with his spoon, "Don't thank me. Veronica made it yesterday while I was out inspecting the fence line trying to figure out where the demonbrocs were getting in."

"They're not getting in, they're getting *out*," Maria replied nonchalantly as she looked around the small eat-in kitchen area.

"Excuse me?"

"The demonbrocs," Maria answered. "You said they were getting *in*. A few of them have escaped the pens recently, so you're probably finding those."

He set the spoon down on the table. What the hell was she talking about? "What pens?"

"In the Barrio. They eat demonbrocs and some of them got out."

Her words hit her like a brick to the forehead. Those idiots in the Barrio were keeping demonbrocs for food? He remembered the meat that the gang members outside the grocery store were eating and thought it was dog or maybe a goat. Aeric would never have thought that anyone would be stupid enough to keep a demonbroc inside the city walls. Except for today, his inspections of the Barrio were always announced ahead of time to avoid any problems with the residents. They must have hidden the evidence each time. No wonder that kid, Bull, had been against him being there.

"How long have they been keeping demonbrocs for food?"

She shrugged, "I don't know. They've been there the whole time I've lived here."

"That's been more than a year, Aeric," Veronica stated.

"Yeah, I know. What are those idiots thinking?"

"They want the meat, so they're willing to risk it," Maria replied with a simplicity that only a child could assign to such a major issue.

"It's not just them," Aeric countered, speaking more to himself than to Maria. "They're putting the lives of everyone in the city at risk." He turned back to the child and asked, "Do you know who's keeping them?"

"Oh, sure. It's Mr. Edward. He keeps them down in the tunnels. I think he has too many though and that's why they're getting out."

"Too many? Wait, I thought you were talking about a couple of them. How many does he have?" *Well, that answers Veronica's question about why he keeps going back down there*, he thought.

Maria stared intently at her empty bowl. "I wasn't supposed to go down there. It was an accident that I saw them, I promise. I don't want any bad things to happen to Mr. Edward; he's nice and has kept all the boys away from me, except Claw. He tried to do things to me, so I beat him up."

Aeric wondered how she made the connection between emasculating the would-be rapist and "beating him up." It might have something to do with her mind protecting her from the reality of what could have happened if she hadn't fought back.

Veronica cleared her throat and asked, "So, Edward Huerta is breeding demonbrocs in the tunnels under the city for meat?"

Maria nodded her head. "Oh sure. They make them fight too, that's how a couple of them escaped. They were betting on which ones would win and they got out. I was hiding up in the rafters and saw the fight."

Shit, Aeric thought. If they were betting—he assumed either food rations or ammunition, both were used as currency these days—it was likely that other citizens were involved, not just the residents of the Barrio. You can only trade so much amongst yourselves before it became stagnant. The residents worked all across the city, they could easily have been bringing select individuals to the fights. How had the police who patrolled the Barrio missed it?

"Maria, do the police officers who work inside the Barrio know about the demonbrocs?"

"Oh, the police don't come into the Barrio," she uttered. "Mr. Edward pays them in meat to stay away and we take care of things ourselves."

Once again, her revelations about what was currently happening rocked Aeric. They'd get to the girl's future predictions soon enough. First, he had to take care of the here and now. He thought back to the police reports from the Barrio. It seemed like he got one every few days and the officers who "patrolled" that neighborhood constantly dragged Huerta in front of the magistrate. Was it all an elaborate ruse to keep him in the sewers so he could further his business? Aeric wondered how he could have been so stupid.

"Do you know who else goes to the fights or gets meat?" he asked.

"No, I only saw the fights that one time. I know that the boys deliver meat all over the city, though."

"Son of a bitch," Aeric muttered. That meant it was a systematic problem, not an isolated event or two—and confirmed his fear that it was spread across the city, not just to the residents of the Barrio. The demonbrocs multiplied much faster than the goats that he'd brought in for the same purposes, so it made sense that people would try to breed them for meat. It was just colossally stupid.

He let his simmering anger subside. There was nothing that Maria could do about Edward Huerta and his collection of crooks. He would definitely have a talk with the police officers and the Barrio's chief degenerate to put a stop to it immediately.

For now, he wanted to talk to Maria about Veronica's nightmares, the girl's visions, and what she called 'The Birds.' If there were any truth behind the idea that the Vultures were still out there, he sure as hell wanted to know about it.

"Okay, I'll talk to Huerta—Mr. Edward," he amended. "We'll get to the bottom of things and find out what's going on. Thank you for bringing this to my attention, Maria. I would have been walking the walls looking for holes or ways over for weeks without any luck."

She stared blankly at him with her strange eyes. "Ahem, well… Veronica, has been having some dreams," Aeric began.

Veronica adjusted her chair and the loud scrape of its wooden legs across the tile ran up his spine like a cold winter blast that caused him to shiver. "Let's talk about your Gift, Maria."

SEVEN

Captain Griffith looked up to see Shooter Joseph come through the door to her office. She cinched the strap on her bag down tight and then used the side of her desk to surreptitiously help herself up. Her features remained controlled and blank while she looked at the newcomer. There was no way that she'd let one of the young guys see that her old body was stiff just from packing her backpack with supplies.

She laughed to herself. Before the collapse of the old world, she wouldn't have batted an eye at facing life at fifty. Now, with a serious lack of diversity in their diets and all the multivitamins long gone, her body felt like she'd been beaten repeatedly. Standing for too long hurt her, then again, too much sitting was painful as well.

Thirty-five years ago, she was a young, married lieutenant in the US Army, intent on getting out as soon as her five year commitment was up. Then the Vultures initiated World War Three and destroyed the future of mankind. Her husband was killed, along with everyone else she knew, when Fort Hood was obliterated by a small-yield nuke.

She made her way to San Angelo with her platoon and joined up with the Air Force commander at Goodfellow Air Force Base. Her team made do for a little while under the Air Force as guards on the gates, then eventually separated to form the nucleus of the Shooters, an organization that worked directly for the city's mayor. The Shooters were a hybrid of police SWAT and an army infantry platoon, tasked with keeping the wastelands surrounding San Angelo safe. Over time, the commander of the base died and the military base was annexed into San Angelo. The Shooters took over one of the buildings near the walls that cut off the runway and expanded operations to be in charge of both the ground defense area and manning the gates.

Lorelei Griffith promoted herself from lieutenant to captain as the commander of the Shooters and established several platoons with lieutenants in charge of each. She'd become more of an administrator than an operator after that, only going out on operations sparingly. She was in the final preparation stage of an operation now.

Aeric stopped by in the morning to discuss operations beyond the San Angelo defense area and to borrow a Shooter to escort him into the Barrio. She'd been as surprised as he'd been when they started looking through the patrol reports. While it hadn't been five years like he thought, it *had* been more than two years since they'd conducted a patrol outside of the immediate area around the city. *That was way too long,* she told herself.

Events outside the walls had settled drastically over the years and she'd allowed the Shooters to get lazy. It was inexcusable and Lorelei promised Aeric that she would personally lead a patrol before the end of the day. The group was ready to go, the only thing that she'd been waiting on was Joseph's return from the Barrio.

"How'd it go? Did you find the girl that Traxx was looking for?" she asked the young Shooter standing a respectful four feet from her desk.

"Yes, ma'am. We found Maria and brought her out of the Barrio to Traxx's house." His eyes darted towards the ground, indicating to Lorelei that he wanted to say more.

"What is it, Joe?"

"Well, it's just… The girl is strange." He took a moment to organize his thoughts. The captain had known Joseph a long time, from when he was a little gang banger in the Barrio, through the Shooter selection and training. Then he'd spent two years at the garrison up in Tennyson where they'd set up a secure location to retreat to in the event that San Angelo ever became compromised and, more recently, another year with him in the city. He'd grown exponentially over the years, but his formative youth in the slums without a proper attempt at education sometimes held him back from speaking fluidly without pausing to ensure the old accent didn't emerge and to put things in the correct order in his mind. She could be patient.

"Maria has what they call the Gift."

"The Gift? You mean the children who supposedly can predict the future?"

"Yeah. Ma'am, I know it seems like a bunch of lies," Joseph stated. "I've seen some of the things that she's said come true. I don't know about the other people who say that their kid has it. They could be lying. Maria is different."

"Okay, so convince me. What have you seen?"

He thought for a moment before answering. "The crop boost last fall. She said something about there would be so much food that we wouldn't know what to do with it. That came true."

"There was a lot of clean rain last spring and even in the summer we got some," Lorelei countered. "Even a little girl could have seen that coming."

"She also said that it would be a mild winter. We only had a few deaths last winter because of the cold."

"So the 'Gift' is good for predicting the weather?"

"No, ma'am... Um, well, I guess so. She predicted that attacks by the bandits and mutants from the wastes would stop. We haven't had a raid attempt in more than a year."

"When did she *predict* that?" she asked with mild interest.

"A few days after she arrived here. We took her in and there were only a few more attacks on the perimeter before they stopped."

"Interesting. So, what is she saying now that's caused Traxx to want to seek her out?"

"She said that San Angelo is going to burn. That the birds were coming to destroy the city."

That caught her attention. "What else did she say about the birds?"

He thought for a moment, "That they'd eat us and use our skin for clothing. She also said that the walls would fall."

"How old is this girl?" Lorelei asked in alarm.

"Ten or eleven."

That's some gruesome shit for such a young person to be going around telling people, Lorelei thought. She wondered if it was better to remove her from the public eye before she caused a panic in the population. She'd have to ask Traxx if they should segregate her somehow.

Joseph chilled her blood when he continued, "She also said everything that will happen to San Angelo is Traxx's fault. That he brought the curse on us."

"The Vultures," she muttered. She knew without a doubt what Maria had seen. It made her upcoming patrol all the more important. How could she have been so stupid and lackadaisical in the performance of her duties? "The girl is talking about the Vultures."

"The Vultures, ma'am?"

She glanced up at the young man. He'd been a part of the Shooters for several years now, but was still too young to know anything about the early days of the city after the war. "Have you ever wondered about the scars that cover Traxx's face and arms?"

He shrugged, "No, ma'am. They're burn marks, that's plain to see. I figured that it was some kind of fire or maybe an injury from the war."

"The Vultures are a real gang—not like those kids in the Barrio pretending to be meaner and bigger than they are. They started out as computer hackers." She stopped. She'd lost him. "A computer is a machine from the old world. They helped to control our daily lives and a hacker was a person who would invade someone else's computer from far away and take it over, then cause the computer to do whatever they told it to do. The hackers took over a computer that started the war and destroyed everything."

"If it was so easy to take over the computer, why would people in the old world have the…" He searched for the word before remembering it, "Why were the *bombs* controlled by the computer? Why didn't they carry them around with them or keep them locked up? Why did they have bombs that could destroy the world?"

"Good questions," she conceded. "They made the more powerful bombs to keep up with our enemies, each of them making bigger and stronger bombs to intimidate the other. As to why were they controlled by a computer? That's just how it was. Everything was run by computers. People even had a tiny personal computer in their pocket for communication called a cell phone. Hell, computers were everywhere, now the ones that you still see are ancient pieces of junk.

"Anyways, the Vultures started the war and made sure that Austin, the city where they lived, wasn't destroyed. They were led by a crazy man named Justin who took over the city during the war. They tortured people, murdered, destroyed and stole everything in the surrounding area. Aeric Traxx and Tyler—the commander of the Gathering Squad—were taken prisoner by the Vultures and tortured. They're the ones who burned him and put out Tyler's eye. They escaped and killed Justin, then came here. The last we heard, the Vultures had crumbled from the inside as they fought amongst themselves to see who would be the new leader after Justin's death."

She took a deep breath. It had been years since she related the story to anyone and it took more of a mental toll on her than she thought it would. "The Shooters were established specifically to fight the Vultures if they came here. Of course, we had thirty or forty thousand residents back then and made a much more lucrative target. We've fought raiders and mutants, and turned back people seeking shelter, but we never ended up going head-to-head with the Vultures. If what that little girl is saying is true, then we're in trouble."

"We're ready to fight, ma'am. I remember how bad it was as a child without much food. We have a stable way of life now. We'll defend our home if it comes to that."

"I know we will." She smirked and said something that she'd been taught as a brand new officer in school, "The best defense is a good offense. We have a patrol that's going outside of the ground defense area. We're leaving in a few minutes if you want to go."

This time, the Shooter didn't deliberate or take time to arrange his thoughts before answering. "Absolutely, ma'am. Let's go see what's out there."

*****

The heavy trucks chugged along at eleven miles per hour, belching smoke and steam into the early afternoon. The engineer, Ted Winston, had long ago converted several of the old gasoline-powered trucks into massive steam engines because he foresaw that the quality of fossil fuels would degrade over time and be unusable to power the vehicles. He was right, of course.

It had been more than thirty-five years since the last tanker of fuel left a refinery along the gulf coast. Gasoline that remained unused was now worthless for transportation and barely even able to be used to start fires. The first thing that Ted converted was the earth-moving equipment—bulldozers and backhoes, primarily—to keep the ever-changing walls repaired. Next were a few flatbed trucks that the Gathering Squad could use to continue their operations as they had to range farther and farther during the lean years of acid rain, and finally, he retrofitted three of the big military transport trucks for the Shooters.

Lorelei hated riding in the damn things, though. The trucks reminded her too much of what they'd lost over the years. The city was riddled with remnants of the old world, from defunct street lamps to the old basketball arena. Everywhere you looked, one could see what had been lost when the Vultures started the war.

The rough coughing of men and women from the cargo area made her turn and peer through the missing window into the back. Ten of her Shooters sat along a row of benches in the middle of her truck, facing out. Their mixture of old Air Force uniforms pilfered from the base stores, combined with bandanas and ragged strips of cloth covering their faces to keep the smoke and grit from the engines and the surrounding wastes out of their mouths. Everyone also wore goggles of some type, most were the military-issued ones, but a few of her men had old swimmer's goggles and one even had a full gas mask, anything they could use to keep the debris from their eyes.

Nearer to the cab, two men steadily fed a mixture of coal and other flammable material into a chute that led to a fire bin underneath the boiler that Ted had designed for the overly-simplified steam engine. Water in the boiler was converted to steam, which then forced a piston to move through a cylinder, allowing for vehicle movement. The excess steam was then trapped and piped back into the boiler as it cooled. The whole design was much less complicated—and more efficient—than the old locomotive engines that used to run all over the country.

"You doing okay back there?" she shouted over the roar of the engine. Several of the Shooters gave her a thumbs up without answering verbally, so she turned back around and stared out of the windshield, which was spider-webbed on her side from a long-forgotten battle with marauders.

The desolate landscape stretched on for miles in all directions. She'd sent two trucks out the Northern Gate, one going north and the other going west to see what was beyond their normal patrol routes. She'd purposefully chosen to take her truck out of the Eastern Gate. Back when they used to get in fights with scavengers and bands of raiders out in the wastes, it was almost always on the eastern side of the city where people had fled from the larger cities of Austin and possibly San Antonio. Even though she knew that they were all dead and gone, she still contributed all of the fights on the east to the Vultures.

They passed by the remnants of Wall, a small town that the Gathering Squad had dismantled, taking everything usable into San Angelo. The old concrete foundations of the buildings were as far as anyone from the city had been in several years. She remembered the weeks upon weeks of boring protection duty as her Shooters guarded the Gatherers when they tore apart houses and the few businesses. Those times were interspersed with several firefights; she lost two Shooters on the mission. Of course, there were always more volunteers willing to become a Shooter in exchange for steady meals back in those days so it hadn't been an issue.

Lorelei couldn't help that she held her breath as the truck bounced down the jutted highway beyond the town. They used to go on patrols far into the wastes and she knew these areas were more dangerous. They'd stopped going so far once they stopped coming in contact with survivors of any kind. The dwindling population of San Angelo needed more and more protecting at home as they fortified their position and began sustainably growing their own crops and producing small herds of goats instead of eating them right away.

She glanced through the rear window once again and saw the whitened knuckles on several of her troops as they gripped their weapons, which were a mixture of military and civilian rifles, it came down to whatever ammunition they could find. Most of the Shooters had been with the team for a long time, so they remembered the troubles that could be experienced beyond the ground defense area. Demonbrocs bred and grew to maturity quickly while the insect population had grown in size exponentially. It wasn't uncommon to see centipedes and scorpions that were three or four feet long once their genetic makeup had been altered by the radiation all around them.

The last of the concrete foundations faded behind them in the truck's rearview mirror, causing her to feel like they were truly on their own in the wasteland. Everything familiar to them was now gone.

The long, dusty road snaked off into the distance. It was so covered by the drifting dirt that if the skeletal remains of trees and the occasional rusted sign hadn't been present, then she wouldn't have been able to say definitively where it was. The landscape had changed so much since her platoon had first arrived here. Back then, there was grass and the occasional tree as well as green cacti dotting the roadway.

The cactus plants were still a staple in the sands, but they'd changed as much as the wildlife. What people used to think of as thorns were laughable little stickers compared to what they'd become. The need to develop larger and more dangerous spikes to keep away the birds and other creatures had caused a rapid evolution in the plant life as the shorter-thorned varieties were quickly consumed for the moisture contained inside of them. A man could be impaled on the forest of spikes jutting in every direction on the remaining varieties of cacti.

It wasn't long before the flat, barren landscape lulled Lorelei into a daze. The occasional dilapidated home with the remains of a few trees were the only thing to break up the monotony of the open wasteland. Occasionally, a demonbroc would appear near the road; usually not long enough to get a shot off at the creature, though. It was a tedious task and she couldn't help but allow herself to believe that there was nothing out here.

They were almost thirty miles from San Angelo and the captain was having a hard time keeping her eyes open. The other crews must be in the same state out to the north and east of the city. The years of cold weather and acid rain followed by heat and near-drought conditions had done their job in west Texas. No one remained alive outside of the larger concentrations of people and those who did survive certainly weren't going to leave the safety of their walls.

She decided that it was time to turn around. There wasn't any point in being out here anymore. It turned out that Aeric's fears about raiders had been unfounded. Still, she planned to continue sending Shooters on regular patrols further into the wastes. It was an oversight that could have been dangerous if there were some type of large, well-provisioned force remaining in Austin.

She studied the tattered map in her lap for a moment and saw that they were almost to the town of Eden. She'd done a few sweeps through there in the early years when there was still a lot of fuel and enough manpower to dismantle an entire town for its supplies. The town had already been brutalized by gangs by the time they got there so they didn't have to compete with residents for supplies, it was a ghost town.

Her worst memory from those days was the old prison on the east side of town. The guards had abandoned their post and went to their homes, leaving the prisoners to fend for themselves. Unfortunately for them, the magnetic locks had stayed engaged when the EMP knocked out the electricity, only an electrical pulse could have unlocked the failsafe measure built into the doors in the event of a power outage. The prisoners had starved in their cells, dying by the hundreds. The Gathering Squad didn't even bother trying to salvage any building material from there. Once they'd cleared out the kitchens and supply buildings, they abandoned everything else. Presumably, the skeletons of those men would be locked away forever.

Lorelei tapped the driver on the arm. "Hey, Ollie, we're gonna head back. In about half a mile, we'll come to the old town of Eden. Take a left on the main road. We'll go north on that for a few miles, then when we come to a big four-way intersection, we'll go left and head back west towards San Angelo."

Ollie nodded his head and shouted over the roaring steam engine, "There's nothing out here, ma'am. It's all just desert."

"That's why I'm calling it. There's no sense in going any further out this way. There's only more sand and dirt."

The truck chugged into Eden and Ollie followed her directions. It had been a successful and uneventful mission with nothing significant to report. Just the way the captain liked it.

EIGHT

He watched the truck turn north up Main Street through his binoculars and breathed a sigh of relief. The watcher thought that he'd finally been compromised. Oh, he knew that he could hide in the prison, the ones who used the dirty, foul-smelling machines of the past never entered his home. His friends scared them.

The black smoke pouring from the truck had been easy to see for miles—or was it leagues? Maybe even furlongs? The man scratched at the bald spot on the side of his head where he'd long ago rubbed away the hair that grew wildly everywhere else. He didn't know what an appropriate measure of distance was now that everything was measured in how much water someone could carry. His fingernail slipped under the scab where his fingers scratched and he lifted it away, placing the course disc of skin and blood on his tongue.

He sucked at the scab while he watched the truck disappear in the distance. Satisfied that they weren't stopping or coming nearer to his home, he chewed on the softened treat and then wiped away the smear of blood that had welled up at the scab's former site. He licked the salty red smear from his fingers and waddled over to the guard tower ladder.

Several painful minutes later, he limped towards Cellblock B, which was his primary home. His right knee bent outwards at an angle, a lifelong gift from his master. He remembered the man who'd maimed him, for all intents and purposes trapping him in the Eden Detention Center. His master had been a young man, so angry and full of hate, even back then.

Seventeen years prior—or was it one hundred? Maybe forty-one? He could never keep such a trivial thing like time straight in his head either. Anyways *a long time ago*, Judd Carlisle had been a survivor, living in and around the town of Eden. The soldiers in the trucks searched the town, but they didn't find him, no they hadn't! He'd hidden cleverly in the refuse and watched them taking the supplies that he'd stockpiled for himself.

He didn't have any weapons besides a knife, so he knew that going up against them would be suicide. Judd may not have had much to live for—even back then when he was healthy—but he was alive and planned to stay that way. He hid and observed in silent rage at the loss of his food and resources. They stayed for days, loading up their giant trucks with basically everything that was moveable.

After three days, the hunger in Judd's belly had grown beyond his ability to control any longer. His friends whispered to him in the darkness that he would be safe if he snuck up to one of the trucks and took back some of the food that they'd taken from him. He'd argued that he would be caught. His friends wouldn't listen to the logic he presented to them. They were convinced that he'd be okay if he waited until the middle of the night—*and they'd never apologized for being wrong*, he thought angrily as he walked towards his room.

He'd finally relented to their murmurings of safety and crept up to the side of a truck where he'd seen them place the canned goods they'd stolen from his home. His friends had promised to watch his back for any type of trouble; he'd been foolish enough to believe them. They typically weren't very reliable and abandoned him when he needed them the most. They'd missed the approach of the youth sneaking up on him in the darkness.

He was caught off guard by the cool muzzle of the youth's rifle pressed against his jaw as he reached underneath the tarp. Judd knew instantly that all the years of sneaking and hiding since the big booms had come to an end. He remembered television—oh God, did he miss *that!*—and the damage that a gun could do. He'd watched a show one time where a group of bikers ambushed a policeman and spread his blood like paint on the side of his car. He definitely did not want his blood painting the truck, so he held up his hands in surrender.

Judd couldn't help but giggle at the idea that he was afraid of his blood *painting* a truck. *Was that my inspiration?* he wondered as he tapped the nub of his index finger on the side of his head. Out loud, he said, "I never realized that's where it came from. Wow, funny."

He stopped thinking about painting and remembered the master. Judd had turned to the youth who held the gun against his face and tried to smile. Unfortunately, the jagged, rotten stumps where his teeth had broken on cans before he figured out how to use a can opener scared the boy. He lashed out with the wooden part of his gun and knocked poor old Judd to his knees.

Judd cried out in pain and the youth wrapped a gloved hand over his mouth, dragging him away into the darkness away from the trucks. He was beaten savagely with the rifle and begged for mercy. None came. The youth was relentless in his anger at Judd for trying to steal the things that were rightfully his.

He'd passed in and out of consciousness until finally, the beating stopped and he awakened in the prison yard. The youth told him that what he'd experienced was merely a sampling of the pain that he would visit upon the watcher if he didn't do what he asked. Of course, Judd promised that he would do whatever the man wanted him to. He would have been crazy not to—and that was one thing that Judd was not, no sir, he was not crazy. Those kinds of people, the *crazies*, lived in the isolation ward. The nurses used to let him walk around outside the ward, even gave him important jobs to do like keeping the windows on the guard shacks clean so they could keep the crazies locked away.

The youth didn't believe him that he wouldn't run away, so he broke Judd's knee and then left him in the warden's office. The next night, the youth returned with food and several large bottles of water. He gave Judd a bottle of pills with careful instructions about how many to take and when, he said that they'd keep the infection away and that his leg would heal.

The trucks left and Judd thought he'd never see them again. The food that the youth had given him ran out so he crawled through the prison to the cafeteria and found enough scraps to last him a long time. He made new friends with the men behind the bars in their old cells, although they never wanted to come outside, so he always had to go to them to talk, which got annoying sometimes. Why did he *always* have to be the one who sought out their company? Wasn't he a good enough friend that they'd want to come see him? *Kinda rude when you think about it, yes sir*.

Even though his knee flared out at a painful and awkward angle, his leg did eventually heal enough for him to walk unaided. The injury made running or traveling for long distances impossible, though. One day, he was minding his own business, rolling down the cellblock hallway in the warden's chair when the youth materialized in front of him. He'd aged into a man by that time and asked what Judd had seen since their last encounter.

Judd tried to avoid the question and asked his friends behind the doors for help. Again, they abandoned him, choosing to look the other way and not offer any assistance. The man beat him with a heavy stick, screaming at him that he had to be the eyes and ears outside of Salmon-Jello. He was the watcher.

Judd had been confused. Why was the man so angry about fish-flavored gelatin? The pretty nurses used to give him Jello and it was one of the only things—besides television!—that he missed about life before the big booms. Of course, fish Jello sounded nasty, but it wasn't reason to beat up poor Judd. Finally, he realized that Salmon-Jello was the name of a place. He begged for forgiveness once again and the man relented as Judd told him all about his friends in their cells and the food supply that he'd found. Telling the man about his life in the prison before the big booms seemed to calm the man slightly. He introduced himself as Kendrick Rustwood.

Kendrick told Judd that he worked for him now and his job was one of the most important out of all the people that Kendrick had working for him. He was to be the watcher. If any soldiers in the trucks came back from Salmon-Jello, Judd had to find a way to contact his new master.

Judd wasn't a fool. He promised to work hard at being a watcher and Kendrick seemed satisfied with his vow. Then the man turned and left the cellblock, telling him that he'd be back with an army soon.

From the window, Judd saw him get on a bicycle and pedal off in the direction that the sun came up in the mornings, which seemed silly to him. It was so hot, why anyone would want to go closer to the sun was beyond his understanding. He watched until Kendrick disappeared and began planning how he could watch for the soldiers as he'd promised he would.

A long time later, it could have been months or maybe years, Judd didn't really have a good way of keeping track of time, Kendrick returned with trucks of his own. These were smaller than the ones that the soldiers had used and had paintings of giant birds all over them. Judd liked the birds and planned to draw them on the walls. He thought that would please Kendrick.

About twenty men came with Kendrick, all of them mean and vulgar. Judd's friends didn't like the men, so they kept quiet, which only made them the butt of the men's jokes. They laughed and used the ends of brooms to reposition his friends, who couldn't get out of the way. It infuriated Judd that they'd pick on his friends, but knew better than to mess with their kind. They were just like the nasties over in Cellblock A; he didn't like going to Cellblock A because of all the mean and rude things the prisoners over there said to him.

The images of what Kendrick's men had done to his friends made Judd stop as he limped through Cellblock B. He peered into Jake's cell and asked, "You doin' okay, buddy ol' pal?"

I don't like when you think about what they did to me, Jake replied.

"I'm sorry, Jake. I know you don't. I couldn't help it. The soldiers came back! I have to tell the master that the soldiers were here. I couldn't help myself from thinking about it. I was just remembering about when I met him."

It's humiliating. My eyesight is still blurry, Jake muttered accusingly.

Judd squeezed his eyes shut in an effort to not remember. Every time he tried not to remember something, it only reminded him of what he was trying to not remember, which made him remember what he was trying to forget. *Why is the human mind so difficult?* he asked himself and then cut off his thoughts. *It certainly wouldn't do to be answering your own question; that's what the crazies in the East Ward did*, he giggled out loud again.

The images of that night flooded back into him and even though he felt bad for the hurt that it would cause Jake, he couldn't stop the memory. One of the men had reached through the bars and pulled Jake's head towards him. Part of Judd's mind realized that the skull had come completely off of the skeleton's body, but *that* part of his mind wasn't usually allowed to speak. All it did was make day-to-day life harder for Judd when that part voiced its opinions.

The thug had pulled Jake's head over to the bars and shouted, "Hey, you know how we always say things like 'I'm gonna skull fuck you?' Well, watch this!" He unzipped his trousers and poked his dick back and forth into poor Jake's eye sockets. His friend screamed in pain as the men howled in laughter. Several of them tried to position a couple of his other friends with their rear ends towards the cell doors so they could rape them. Thankfully, Judd's friends had collapsed and refused to cooperate. Charlie hadn't talked to him since that night, though.

Come on, Judd! I told you not to think about that! Jake admonished.

He ducked his head low between his shoulders. "Sorry, Jake. I didn't mean to. I..." He remembered why he was in the cellblock. He didn't have time for small talk, he had a mission to perform. "I gotta go tell Kendrick about the soldiers!"

Judd hurried away from Jake's accusatory, if blurred, stare and made his way up the staircase to the warden's office where he kept the machine. He wished that he could have kept it in his room so he could be encouraged by his friends, but the office was the only place where the antenna would reach the roof and have a clear line of signal to his master.

He limped past the squiggly, rust-colored birds that he painted in the stairwell in his own blood a few months prior. In hindsight, that had been a bad idea. He got lightheaded halfway through the project and birds four and five looked a little off to him. He wanted to fix them, but couldn't bring himself to cut off another finger.

That night, long ago when the Vultures visited and did those awful things to his friends, Kendrick had given him a gift. Several gifts, really. First off, he didn't allow the men to harm poor old Judd and then he gave him more food and several barrels to collect rainwater so he could stay healthy. The best gift that he'd given the watcher was a way to contact him.

Somehow, Kendrick had found a radio—a radio!—that worked. It was green and had black keys with white numbers and green letters on the front. It was a very fancy piece of equipment that only specialized operators like Judd knew how to use. The master had showed him how to operate it and said that he must always leave the batteries out of it and could only use the radio if the soldiers returned.

His hands shook in anticipation. He'd waited oh so very long to talk to Kendrick again. Sure, they'd gotten off to a rocky start with the beatings, but old Judd had deserved it for not knowing what the master wanted. Besides, he'd been beaten his whole life by the people in the prison, so he could handle little things like a few bruises and broken bones. The master was only trying to teach him the correct way of doing things. He'd even broken Judd's leg so he could stay safe with his friends behind the safety of the prison fences. That way, he didn't get hurt out in the wild lands around the town. It was for his own good, after all.

In the warden's office, he worked the latch to open the compartment where the battery went and folded the hinged lid over. Inside the drawer was a battery that had never been opened, it was sealed in a metallic foil bag of some sort. Judd made quick work of the packaging with his knife, wrinkling his nose at the strange odor that came from inside.

Once the battery was free of the foil, he examined it until he found the indention where the plug down inside the battery box would fit and aligned the two before pushing the battery home. He tapped it gently several times to ensure that it was seated properly and then closed the lid, latching it to ensure a good connection between the post and the battery.

He connected the wire that ran to the antenna on the roof to the upper left of the radio like he'd been shown and then fiddled with the knob on the left until he rotated it all the way over to the letters "**FCTN TST**" and waited. Judd didn't know what the letters meant, but Kendrick had told him that it was important to do that first to get it going.

The little screen lit up with a pretty greenish-yellow light and the word "**GOOD**" appeared in black letters. That meant the radio worked, so he twisted the knob back up to the "**ON**" position. He pulled a notebook out of the desk drawer that had a secret code written on it.

Judd couldn't help but mumble the words out loud as he pushed the buttons. Sometimes talking out loud helped him to concentrate and not screw it up. "One. Two. Three." He tore his eyes away from the screen and verified the next number in the code before continuing. "Four… Five!"

He waited. Nothing happened so he checked the notebook again. That's right, he was supposed to hit the "**STO**" button. He depressed it and again, nothing happened. Judd picked up the radio and looked at it. *Why wasn't it working*? Kendrick had made it work to show him. *Had all that time caused the radio to go bad, like all the rest of the electronic stuff, like the television*?

Then he remembered about the black handset with the twisty cord. "Oh, man. How could I have been so stupid?" he yelled, startling himself with the noise. He plugged in the handset and examined it. There was a button on the side of it that he had to push to talk.

He pushed the button in with his middle finger and what remained of his pointer. "Uh, hello. This is Judd. Master?"

He listened to the receiver and still nothing happened. *Maybe I should have practiced this a few times*, he told himself. He thought back to that night when Kendrick had shown him how to operate the radio and remembered that he had to let go of the button for them to answer.

His fingers flew open to allow the radio to work and he almost dropped the handset in the process. He listened for a few seconds and then pressed the push-to-talk button again, "Hello. This is Judd."

He released the button immediately this time and a woman answered, "Hello, Judd. My name is Starr. The Vultures have been waiting for your call."

Judd was ecstatic that the radio worked, but he was disappointed also. He'd wanted to talk to the master, not some girl. The only girls that he'd ever talked to were the nurses and his momma, but they'd abandoned him to the prison with only his friends for company. "Uh…hello?" he asked into the handset. "Is Kendrick there?"

"Rustwood is presently engaged. Do you have a message for us?"

He thought about what "presently engaged" meant. He knew that before people got married, they were engaged. Did this Starr-woman mean that Kendrick was getting married and that's why he couldn't come to the radio? That must be it! He was happy for his master, getting married was a big deal.

"Tell him that old Judd says congratulations!" he stated emphatically. "That's exciting."

"Okay… I'll let him know that you said so." She sounded angry to him, had he said something wrong? "Do you have news from your location?"

"No ma'am, the television in the cellblock doesn't work anymore, so there's no news."

"What the hell are you talking about you crazy bastard? Kendrick said you were a fucking looney, but Jesus!"

Her insults slid past him and didn't affect him. Before he came to stay at the detention center people used to say things like that to him all the time. The only time it had ever really bothered him was that one time when the O'Connor boy said that mean stuff and then hit him. Judd didn't really know what happened after that. The next thing he knew, there were police officers everywhere. They were really nice and gave him a free ride to his new home. The part of his mind that didn't get to talk much told him that he bashed the boy's head in with a baseball bat. Of course, that wasn't true, that part of his mind just liked to make him feel bad. That's why it wasn't allowed to talk much.

"No, ma'am, I'm not a looney. The crazy people live in the East Ward and the baddies stay in Cellblock A. I live in Cellblock B and make paintings and talk to my friends. Sometimes we play cards."

"Stop. What the hell are you talking about?" the woman asked. "Do you have information about San Angelo or are you just wasting the battery on the radio?"

"Oh!" She reminded him about why he'd called. "Yes, the Jello soldiers came through in their trucks today."

"Jello? What the fuck? Oh, you mean *Angelo*. The soldiers from San Angelo came in to Eden today. Is that what you're saying?"

That's what he'd just told her. *She* was the crazy one. He'd already told her about the soldiers three or four times. Talk about not listening. He thought that maybe she was slow in the head, so Judd spoke slowly and made sure to enunciate each syllable. "The soldiers from Salmon-Jello came through town today. Kendrick told me to call when they came back."

"Alright. Got it," she answered. "I'll tell Rustwood about your message. Keep the radio connected, he'll contact you soon."

Judd leaned back away from the radio and smiled. The master would come back to him soon. He had to tell all of his friends! They would be so excited—well, everyone except Jake. He didn't like the Vultures and told Judd that constantly. Everyone else would be happy to see their old friends though, especially the guys over in Cellblock A, they really liked the Vultures a lot.

NINE

"I've always been able to know what would happen in the future," Maria mumbled, choosing to stare at the empty bowl of stew instead of either adult seated at the table. "I didn't start having the visions until a few years ago—that's when my family got mad at me and made me leave."

"Where are you from?" Aeric asked.

The girl shrugged. "I don't know the name of the place. I was too little to learn it; San Angelo is a lot bigger. There were ten or eleven houses behind a big wall."

"That could be just about anywhere, then," Veronica interjected. "Does it really even matter where she's from?"

Traxx glanced at his wife, "Of course it does. If there's a powerful settlement nearby, then we need to know about it."

"They obviously weren't that powerful if they were scared of Maria's visions."

"Oh, they're probably all dead by now," the girl said without a hint of remorse. "Nobody liked me because of my dreams. I told them about the birds coming there too and they wouldn't listen. That's when they made me leave and go out into the wastelands."

"These 'birds' that will attack San Angelo, can you describe them?"

Maria seemed to sink into herself and she picked at one of her fingernails. "I don't like to talk about my visions. They're scary."

"You certainly didn't seem to mind talking about it when we were in the Barrio," Aeric said.

She frowned. "I'm sorry, Mr. Traxx. When a vision happens, I can't stop myself from saying whatever I see. I don't mean to be bad."

He smiled at her use of the words and reminded himself that even though she certainly seemed older, the girl was way too young to be carrying all the baggage that she had. "It's alright, you're not bad. Were the birds black, maybe with a hooked beak?"

She nodded, obviously intent on not speaking about the vision. "Do you know what a vulture is?" Aeric asked gently.

"No, sir."

"Hmm. Okay, I think I know what you're vision meant about the birds. There's a gang in Austin called the Vultures. They're a really nasty bunch—or at least they used to be. We'd thought that they all died out or killed each other off. Now I'm not so sure that we were right."

He paused to organize his thoughts into a manner that would be understandable for her and then continued, "They took me hostage right after the war. My girlfriend killed their leader when we escaped and came here."

Maria's eyes widened and she looked over at Veronica. "He *killed* someone?"

"No, honey," Veronica interjected with a pointed stare at Aeric. "Mr. Traxx had a girlfriend who was in a very bad situation and she killed the Vulture leader. Aeric didn't do it." Aeric agreed with his wife's tactic; it was probably best to not upset the girl any more than she already was.

"What happened to her?"

Veronica chose to avoid the obvious question about what her bad situation had been. Maria didn't need to know the details of what happened to them in Austin. "Kate—that was her name—died in childbirth."

"Oh. I'm sorry to hear that," she answered with a sad smile. Then, her eyes glazed over and she stared intently at Aeric for a moment before saying, "Your son is going to kill you."

"What?" Aeric's voice boomed across the little dining area.

Maria jumped and scooted her chair backwards, causing the same noise that had grated his spine earlier. "I said I'm sorry that your girlfriend died," she whimpered.

"No, the other thing," he demanded.

"I... I don't know what you mean."

Veronica's eyes flashed an angry warning at him. He took the hint and sat back in the chair with his arms folded across his chest. She reached over and grasped the little girl's hands. "Sweetie, you said that Aeric's son was going to kill him."

She looked back and forth between them. "I did? I'm sorry. I didn't mean to say that."

Veronica waited a moment and then asked, "Is that normal for you to say strange things in the middle of a conversation? Do the wrong words sometimes come out, or is that part of your Gift?"

"I, uh... I don't know. Most of the time I know what I'm saying. It's like I'm standing beside myself and I watch my mouth move and words come out, but can't stop it from happening."

"So maybe it was a slip of the tongue then," Veronica offered hopefully.

Aeric knew what the girl said, even if she didn't realize that she did. *Telling someone that their child was going to kill them wasn't something that you accidentally say*, he told himself, fuming in silence while his wife tried to defuse the situation.

He thought about his boys, Mason, Anthony and John. Could one of them actually kill him? How was that even possible? Of course, it could always be some type of mercy killing, like if he was disemboweled by one of those damn demonbrocs that Huerta was raising in the Barrio. Whatever the reason, it didn't sit well with him that Maria had so casually stated that one of his sons would kill him, without realizing the impact that her words had on him.

He tried to relax and cleared his throat, "Ah, I guess... I guess we should get back on topic. You said the Vultures were going to attack—"

"I said the *birds* were going to attack. I don't know what it means. Maybe there are giant birds out there that you don't know about."

He nodded his chin for show, but he wasn't naïve. He knew exactly what the reference about birds meant. "Okay, good point. *Something* is going to attack San Angelo and it's my fault. You said the walls would come down and everyone would die. That about sums it up, right?"

She thought about it and then replied, "Yes. I think that's all that I saw."

"Do you know when?"

"No. I'm sorry. You looked roughly the same, not gray-haired or anything."

"Hmm…" Aeric rubbed his chin as he thought about a way to figure out a timeframe for the attack. "Was it harvest time or were there vegetables on the crops?"

"I didn't see that," she said. "Everything was on fire. I saw you and several men run towards the birds and then they…"

She stopped talking once again. "It's okay, Maria. I've lived a full life and can handle what you're going to say. What about me?"

"They're going to put your head on a pole by one of the gates. Maybe the Northern Gate. I'm not sure."

Veronica let out a sob and pushed away from the table. Aeric watched her rush off towards the bathroom. He considered going after her and discarded the idea. It would be better to let her be alone for a moment and give her time to calm down. He glanced back at Maria, who was staring at the empty bowl once again. "Do your visions always come true?"

"Mostly," she replied.

"Are you sure that you don't have any idea of when this is going to happen?"

"No. Sorry, Mr. Traxx."

"It's okay. Looks like we need to start preparing our defenses better though, huh?"

She shrugged, "Couldn't hurt."

He smiled and pushed himself up from the table. "Okay, kiddo. Thank you for telling me everything that you know. I'm gonna go talk to Miss Veronica. Make yourself at home. There's more stew in the pot if you're still hungry."

Aeric didn't wait to see if she acknowledged him before walking into the next room. That girl gave him the creeps. He knocked gently on the bathroom door and heard Veronica pour water into the toilet's tank behind the seat, then flush away whatever had been in it.

"It's open," she said.

He turned the handle gently and slipped inside. The air smelled of partially digested stew. "We don't get much meat, can't be wasting it like that," he teased.

"Shut up. I couldn't help myself." She wiped her eyes with a rough hand towel that had seen better days. "I thought that we've set up a nice, safe home here and... And I'd hoped that all of that stuff with the Vultures would be in the past."

She wiped away more tears and jabbed her finger towards the door, "That girl is talking about them cutting your head off. Babe, I can't..."

Veronica trailed off, not wanting to finish her statement. Aeric reached out and pulled her to him. He wrapped his arms around her, resting his cheek on the top of her head as she cried into his chest. "We've lived far longer than most people have in this screwed up world, love," he mumbled into her hair. "I don't want to die either."

"Then let's leave," she said unexpectedly, leaning back and wrapping her fingers around his jaw. "We can go. If the Vultures want you, then we can leave and they won't even have any reason to attack the city. We can choose our own future, regardless of what that little girl says."

He shook his head gently. "I can't do that. I am the mayor of this city. I can't run away and leave them to whatever the Vultures have in store for them."

"If we leave and that will save the city, then isn't that better for everyone?" she pleaded.

"I wish it was that easy. You've heard the stories about them, the Vultures won't stop until they've finished the job they started when they initiated the war. The fact that I'm here is just a bonus to them."

"So we're going to wait here to die?"

"No, we're not," he answered. An idea had been kicking around in his head from the moment he heard Maria say that the birds were going to burn San Angelo to the ground. "I'm going to Austin to stop them. They'll never expect an attack."

*****

"How are you holding up, Ty?" Aeric asked his best friend.

"I'm good, bro. You?"

Traxx nodded his head noncommittally. "Is there anything I can get for you, maybe some aspirin for the pain?"

"Nah, save that shit for someone who has a chance. I can take it," Tyler replied. "It's been a couple of days since you were over, what's going on?"

"Nothing. Everything is good. We're doing alright," he answered woodenly.

"Yeah, you can tell me what you did with Aeric, you pod person... Body snatcher!" Tyler reached over playfully from the couch towards his friend.

"Tyler, be careful," Nicole admonished. "You don't want to start coughing again."

Aeric eyed the bloody towel on Tyler's lap, evidence that something was majorly wrong with the big man. He'd seen him go into a coughing fit a few weeks ago from exertion while walking to the Provisions Warehouse where he worked.

Tyler stuck his tongue out at Nicole, who snorted. "Oh, that's really dignified for such an old man," she scoffed.

"Old? I'm only fifty-five! I've got thirty good years ahead of me."

His comment hung in the air, silencing the banter between the three friends. Tyler was sick, most likely cancer, and Aeric doubted if he'd survive the upcoming winter. Even with their masks, the two of them had spent months upon months on the open road immediately after the war on Aeric's quest to find his family, planting the seed of guilt firmly in Traxx's mind that his friend's illness was his fault. Added to that were the decades that Tyler spent as the leader of the Gathering Squad as the city struggled to procure every usable resource in the surrounding area, breathing in the shit in the air and eating food that was probably tainted with radiation.

Aeric plastered a fake smile across his face and said, "I didn't know they let the nursing home patients talk that way to their caretakers."

Nicole folded her arms under her breasts and cocked her hip out to the side. "Aeric, this old fool wouldn't know what to do with a nurse as hot as me. Nah, I'm just here to make sure he doesn't crap his pants."

Tyler grinned and mumbled, "Thankfully, *that* hasn't happened to me yet."

"Can I get you anything to drink?" Nicole asked Aeric.

"No, thank you, I'm fine. Have a seat; I've got some news that is going to affect everyone."

She started to sit on a side chair, then thought better of it and sat on the couch beside Tyler and gripped his hand in hers. "What is it this time, Aeric?" Tyler asked. "Are Martians invading and we're Earth's last hope? Do we need to go fight some dinosaurs that hatched from million year old eggs?"

"Oh man, I wish it were that easy," Aeric replied. "Do you guys know Maria Salazar?"

Both of them shook their head so Aeric tried another approach, "Have you heard of the children with the Gift? It's what people in the community are calling the kids who can predict the future."

"And this girl, Maria, can predict the future?" Tyler surmised.

"Yeah—well, not really predict, she has visions of what will happen. The other kids seem to be able to determine a few things here and there, but they're not reliable and she has a much better track record with her visions. Like a hundred percent success rate."

"Pretty good odds," Nicole smirked. "Can I take her to Vegas?"

Aeric laughed at her attempt at lightening the mood in their home. "She says that the Vultures are coming."

Tyler sighed and asked, "To San Angelo?"

He nodded. "Granted, she didn't say the *Vultures* were coming, her visions aren't that specific. She saw giant birds attacking and burning the city. So unless there's some type of crazy mutation in the bird population that we don't know about, I'm pretty sure that she means the Vultures."

"Yeah, I think you're right about that, not much else it could be," Tyler admitted. "What else did she say?"

Aeric spent a few minutes relating the details of Maria's vision until he got to the final part about his own death and that the colossus would save a tribe. Tyler interrupted him at that point, "What does that even mean?"

He shrugged, "I don't know. Hell, she doesn't even know what the word means; it just came out when she started talking."

"The Colossus of Rhodes was one of the Seven Wonders of the Ancient World," Nicole stated. "What? I liked history in high school. The Colossus was a giant statue that stood over the harbor in the Greek city of Rhodes. It only stood for a few decades before an earthquake knocked it down."

"So, a giant statue is supposed to save a tribe? Of what, Indians?" Traxx muttered.

"Maybe she meant a group of people or a family," Nicole offered. "A tribe can be both."

"So, what, we build a large Trojan horse, put a family inside it and hope the Vultures don't look inside?" Tyler snickered. "Thanks, for telling us what the word meant, Nicole, but it doesn't really help."

"I don't care if you are sick, Mr. Nordgren. I will kick that big ass of yours if you don't play nice."

"You see what I have to deal with?" Tyler pleaded. Aeric chose to remain silent, ignoring the peculiarities of their relationship. They'd lived together as platonic friends for over thirty years and often got into minor squabbles, which helped to keep their friendship strong.

"I can't help you, buddy," he replied.

A knock on the door made them all turn towards it. "Expecting company?"

Tyler looked thoughtful for a moment and then shook his head. Aeric pulled a large knife out of the sheath on his hip and held it against his forearm as he trailed behind Nicole. He felt foolish. Maria's words had him spooked; they were safe behind the walls.

"What are you doing?" Nicole hissed.

"Taking precautions. The mayor and the two leaders of the Gathering Squad in one location makes for a pretty lucrative target."

He positioned himself near the door. "Just don't stab anyone," Nicole muttered before she opened the door. When she turned the knob, pulling the door inwards, the smile on her face made him relax.

"Hi, Kayla! How are you?" Nicole asked as she leaned forward hug Tyler's step-daughter. "Oh, good, you brought the baby! She always makes Tyler so happy."

Aeric slid the knife home, feeling even more foolish when Kayla stepped through the doorway and saw him standing in the shadows. "Hi, Uncle Aeric. What are you doing behind the door?"

"I, uh… I was just stretching my legs. Your dad and I have been talking for a long time."

She accepted his answer and gave him a brief hug before walking to the living room where Tyler waited. Nicole shook her head at him and he walked slowly back to the room where everyone waited.

"And then, at the warehouse, Greg got into a scuffle with some boy from the Barrio. The police broke it up and took him back home. Can you believe that?"

Kayla, baby Ketchup, was all grown up now. She sat beside Tyler on the couch holding her own daughter, Anna. She gently passed her over to him and he played with her hands while Kayla continued to talk.

"It's been crazy. People are scared of those demonbrocs that keep getting in. Dad, have you heard about that?"

"Hmm?" Tyler asked with the goofy grin of a proud grandfather plastered across his face. "Demonbrocs? Yeah, Aeric told me about them a week ago. Did you ever figure out where they're getting in?"

"We, ah, we have a pretty good idea."

"And?"

Aeric glanced at the three adults in the room, all of them were extremely close to him and he'd give his life for them. However, if the information about the demonbroc breeding for meat got out, then there'd probably be a riot. People would storm the Barrio and demand that the dangerous creatures be put down, which would likely result in their cages—or whatever Huerta had them in—getting opened. He trusted everyone present, but Kayla would tell her husband Greg and there was no telling who he'd pass the information off to. *No*, he thought, *it's better to keep it to myself.*

"We think they may be coming in from the sewer, so we're going to explore that further," he said, which was true. He just hadn't had the time to deal with Huerta and his illegal operation.

"Hmpf. Makes sense," Tyler answered while he made a funny face at the baby. "Those sewers deposit out in the wastes, all sorts of things could follow them back up and inside. We should make sure the grates are still in place."

Aeric smiled at his friend. "Don't worry, buddy. We've got it; you just stay here and rest."

His friend looked up to him and said, "I hate this crap, Aeric. I feel like such a drain on the community."

"You've given your entire life over to this city, Ty," Aeric countered. "You can take a few weeks off until you get better."

"What if I don't?"

"Dad, don't say that!" Kayla exclaimed. "You're gonna pull through whatever is making you sick. Anna needs her grandpa in her life."

Tyler's grim expression softened. "Oh, I'll be here. Don't worry, sweetie."

Anna started to cry and he handed her back to her mother who slipped the baby under her shirt to feed. Aeric stood aside and watched the small family's interaction with one another. He'd been the one to slight the Vultures, causing them to seek him out. If it wasn't for him, they probably wouldn't even know that San Angelo still existed. He needed to do whatever he could to keep his friends and family safe. It was his duty to protect them and put a stop to this whole mess.

He'd made up his mind about what he was going to do, regardless of Veronica's protests. He'd vowed to himself long ago that he would never allow himself to be hunted down again. Aeric was a hunter; he didn't cower in the corner, waiting for someone to attack him. He went out and met them on his *own* terms.

His friends and family were the most important things in his life, a close second was the city of San Angelo, and he'd do whatever he could to end this before it even began. He planned to leave for Austin first thing in the morning.

TEN

"The little girl, Anna, that's *Grandma*, right?" Tanya asked with wide eyes.

Aiden adjusted the pillow under his arm and used his good hand to pull it in closer to his side. "Yes, child. Kayla, was the little girl that Aeric and Tyler rescued when they went to Missouri to find Aeric's family. She grew up and had Anna, whom I married years later, after the fall of the city."

"Are you making all of this up, Grandad?"

He chuckled and accidentally swallowed a little bit of saliva, causing him to choke. Tanya backed away, frightened that he was going to be sick. He raised his hand to let her know that he was fine. "I'm okay. I'm okay, just swallowed some spit."

He gestured weakly and said, "Come back over here. I promise that I'm not making this up. It really happened."

"What about Kate's sister, uh…"

"Julie."

"Yeah. What about Julie, is she in this story too?"

"No, I'm sorry, child. Julie died of the flu or dysentery or one of the other godawful diseases that hit the city after her sister died. So many people died between when Aeric first came to the city and when I was born. It's a miracle that most of our family survived."

Tanya's eyes fell to her lap. Aiden had to strain to hear her tiny voice, "Grandad, why does everyone die?"

"It's a part of life, sweetheart. Everyone—and everything—dies at some point. There's nothing we can do about it. The real measure of a life is how you choose to live it."

"Like you and Aeric?"

"Yes, like all of our ancestors. I'll die one day—no, not *today*," he smiled at her expression. "When I do, I want you and your cousins and all of the family to say that I lived an honorable life. That you are proud to be related to me."

"Of course I am, Grandad," she said and hugged his neck a little too roughly.

"Then I can die a happy man, and know that I did my duty for our family."

*****

Aeric waved at the trucks as they headed back towards San Angelo on the old road. He'd gone to Lorelei and asked for a lift to the edge of the renewed patrolling area. He hadn't wanted to risk going any closer to Austin in the Shooters' loud, steam-powered trucks, so he figured the town of Eden would be fine. That way, the city's defenders could make a loop through the outer defensive perimeter and it would save him about thirty miles of riding.

Of course, Lorelei had insisted on coming with him, which he'd refused. Her place was leading the defense of the city and ensuring that all of the residents there were safe. She eventually relented. It didn't stop her from trying to load him down with more weapons than he could feasibly handle. He'd taken a 30.06 rifle with a high-powered scope and silencer, instead of the 30-30 that he'd had forever, because he needed the stopping power at a distance that the larger caliber would give him. He also had a military style M-4 rifle for close targets, ammo for both weapons, and his fighting knife. Everything else was too unwieldy to balance on a bike for the two hundred and fifty mile round trip.

He watched the twin rooster-tails of dust recede in the distance and then lifted his leg up over the frame of his bicycle. He had about a hundred miles to ride; if he pushed it, he could be on the outskirts of the old Austin city limits within a few days.

"Mind if I tag along?" a familiar voice called out from behind the wreckage of an old car beside the highway.

He turned slowly back to where Joseph emerged pushing a bicycle of his own. He must have been in the second truck and hidden until they were too far away for Aeric to call them back. "What the hell are you doing here, Joe?"

"You need help. You can't do this on your own."

"I *don't* need your help. I'm not planning on staying long; just gonna snoop around, see what they're up to and then get out."

"Don't lie to me, Traxx. If that were the case, you probably wouldn't have taken a sniper rifle as well as an assault rifle. I think you want to take out the leader of the gang and you hope it will be enough to end this."

Aeric set his jaw. That was exactly what he planned to do. The only person he'd told that to was Veronica, though. How had Joseph learned of it? "Who told you that ridiculous story?"

"Call it a hunch," Joe replied. "Look, you can't make it there in one day, so you'll need someone to share guard shifts with at night and I can be a spotter for you when you're using that big rifle."

Dammit! He had a good point about sharing responsibility during the night. Travelers who fell asleep unguarded tended to end up dead—or worse. He absently rubbed at the chain scars across his hand; there were much worse things than death to contend with in this world.

"Fine, you can come with me." Aeric held up a finger in warning, "If you get in my way, we're done. If I see a target, man or woman, that I think is a threat to San Angelo, then I'm taking the shot. Understand?"

Joseph smiled, "Of course, sir. I wouldn't have it any other way. Let's go see what these Vultures are made of."

Aeric ducked his chin in approval and hopped on the bike. He had to readjust the big sniper rifle across his back and then adjusted the Velcro straps on the handlebar so he could secure the M-4 rifle. Once all of that was done, they began the first leg of their journey towards Austin.

They made it less than a mile out of the remaining one hundred and fifty before Joseph saw movement in the old prison that caused them to veer sharply off the road. A man with a horribly disfigured leg that angled outwards limped rapidly across the yard.

Aeric pulled the strap holding his rifle to the bike and pulled the weapon up against his shoulder in a practiced motion. He fired one shot along the man's line of escape, kicking dirt up into the air. The man stopped and raised both hands over his head.

"Grab him!" Aeric ordered, causing the old man to begin running again.

Joseph weaseled his way through a cut in the chain link fence while Aeric kept his rifle sites in the small of the man's back. The chase was over before it began; the disfigurement to his leg made him an easy target for the physically fit Shooter. He picked up the older man like he weighed nothing and carried him back towards the road. After a little maneuvering, the Shooter was able to get him out of the prison's fence and into the street where Aeric stood waiting.

Besides the wretched leg, the old man was as thin as a pole and absolutely filthy. His clothing must have been an orange prison jumpsuit at one time, now it was a dull, muted brown with splatters of what must have been either paint or blood. Aeric looked him up and down, noting the rags on both of his hands, one of them clearly missing at least two fingers.

"What are you doing out here?" Aeric asked.

"Old Judd lives here! This is my home!" the man replied.

"Shut up, don't tell them *anything*!" he said in a different voice.

"It's better to tell them the truth. Maybe they'll let you live."

Aeric held up his hands and shouted, "Stop! What the hell is going on?"

The man, whom Aeric realized was probably insane, got a sly grin on his face and in a completely different voice, he said, "Don't tell them about the Vultures. Let the fools stumble into the master's trap."

"Darn it, you fool! Stop thinking about it, they can hear your thoughts." The old man collapsed to the ground and held his hands against his ears as he writhed on his side.

Aeric's eyes met Joseph's. "What the hell is wrong with this guy?" the Shooter asked.

"He's crazy. Normally, I'd say we should just bypass him except that he mentioned us getting trapped by the Vultures," Aeric replied. "So that means he knows something... We've just gotta figure out how to get it out of him."

He looked back down to the pathetic creature on the ground trying to "hide" his thoughts from the newcomers. "Alright, you...uh, Judd? Hey, stop that. We can't read your thoughts."

"Even if we could, why would we?" Joe snorted. "He keeps telling us what he's thinking."

The watcher stopped and looked up at Joseph. "What did you say?"

He crouched and got at eye level with Judd. "I said that you keep talking out loud and telling us what you're thinking."

"Dammit, Jake!" he shouted, causing Joseph to jump back involuntarily. "I told you to stay inside your room!"

He glanced over at Aeric and adopted an apologetic countenance. "I'm sorry, sir. My friends sometimes shout things from their cells." Then he put his hand up beside his mouth, hiding what he said from the prison, whispering, "They're kinda crazy sometimes. They're locked in their room, but boy, they like to shout like a bunch of monkeys at the zoo!"

Aeric didn't know what to make of Judd. Clearly, he was insane; his eyes spoke volumes in that regard. What he didn't know was whether the old man was truly alone or if there were more people inside. And he sure as hell hadn't expected to get sidetracked before he even left the drop-off point.

"So, your *friends* are locked inside? Do you have any who come outside with you?"

"Of course he does! I'm here," Judd muttered. "I'm always being dragged places I don't want to go."

"Lawrence, I thought you liked the fresh air. Don't be like this," Judd accused himself.

"No, *I* like the fresh air," he countered. Aeric sensed that whoever was talking now was at least the third personality inside the old man's mind.

"Look, this isn't getting us anywhere," Traxx stated. "How many people do you feed?"

"Hmm?" Judd asked, clearly confused. "Feed? Like who eats in the prison?"

"Yeah. How many people eat your food supply?"

"I, uh…" His face screwed up in thought for a moment and then he replied, "I guess just me. Nobody else ever asks for any food. But I don't have enough for you to take any! We'll die if you take our food."

"Okay, that's what I thought." Aeric motioned to Judd and told Joseph, "It's just him. We can probably relax a little bit."

He nodded in agreement and then picked Judd back up, pulling him into the shade of the watch tower that he'd observed them from originally. "Okay, old man," Joe said as he slid his hands out from underneath Judd and then wiped them on his pant legs. "What did you mean about a trap set by the Vultures?"

Judd recoiled as if he'd been slapped. "I… I didn't say anything about a trap."

"Don't tell them anything!" he said immediately after the word "trap" was out of his mouth.

"Alright, I've had just about enough of this crap. I want to talk to Judd," Aeric demanded.

"I'm right here talking to you. No need to shout at me," Judd moaned.

"What trap are the Vultures setting?"

"I don't know! I promise. They gave me a radio—a real-live, working radio!—and told me to call them when the soldiers from Salmon-Jello came back. So I called them."

"Shut up you fool," Judd's second—or third—personality said.

Aeric ignored Number Two and asked, "Did they tell you what they were going to do?"

"No! The master wouldn't trust poor old Judd with that. Think about it, dummy. I'm here, all alone...since *my friends are hiding!*" he shouted. "If they told me what they were going to do, people like you would find out."

Aeric clenched and unclenched his jaw. The old man had a radio to contact Austin? Maybe he could call them and find out what their plan was. "Okay, get up," he ordered. "Where's this radio of yours at?"

"It's upstairs, in the warden's office."

"Let's go, then," Aeric said. "I want to see your radio."

Judd looked back and forth between Aeric's stern, fatherly appearance and Joseph's overtly hostile demeanor and apparently decided to do what the men ordered. He pushed himself up painfully, "The master will be very mad at us."

"Shut up. You've already told them about the radio. There's nothing I could do to keep your mouth shut."

"Okay, stop it!" Aeric thundered. "I only want Judd to talk. The next *person* to say anything, whether it's Lawrence, Fred or goddamned Michael Jackson, I will beat the shit out of you guys. Understand?"

The old man nodded his head forlornly. "Sorry, sir. They can't help themselves sometimes. We do love Michael Jackson though. Do you have any of his music?"

Judd started bobbing his head to some imagined tune and Aeric sighed, "No, Judd. Nothing electric works anymore."

"Ha! You're wrong!" he said, hopping on his good leg while he held his bandaged hand in the air. "I have a working radio. It doesn't play music, though. A woman talks to me on it."

"Well, then let's go see this radio of yours."

He stopped dancing and pulled his hands in close to his body while he hunched himself up. "You're not going to try to take my radio are you?"

"You can't take our radio! The pretty lady —"

The other personality was cut off by a quick punch to the side of the head from Joseph. "Traxx said only Judd could talk."

"You're right, you're right," Judd said rubbing his head and then pulling away a scab there. "The master will be very mad at you for hitting me. Only he's allowed to hit me."

The old man popped the scab into his mouth and Aeric cringed. "Take us to your radio. Now," he ordered.

Judd looked hurt emotionally, not physically. "You two are mean-spirited. If the nurses were still here, they'd put you in solitary for being so rude."

"Talk and walk, Judd," Aeric sighed again. Judd was wearing on his nerves.

"Huh? Oh yeah, you want to see my radio. This way!" He turned sideways and slid through the chain link fence and limped off into the compound.

They followed him across the courtyard and into a building marked **CELLBLOCK B**, then through a dark, smelly hallway. Cells lined both sides, their occupants long dead. Some of the cells had bones scattered around like they'd been torn apart by animals who couldn't fit the bones through the bars, while others had complete skeletons, resting peacefully on their beds. Aeric had seen these same prisoners decades ago when they were here and guessed that the locks wouldn't open after the power went out and everyone in the cellblock starved to death. What a shitty way to die.

Just before the stairs to the second floor, they came across something truly disturbing. Giant birds, presumably vultures, were painted on the cinder block walls. The paint was mostly a dull, light brown color, sometimes dark brown where the fluids had pooled heavily. Aeric stepped closer and saw bloody rags along the base of the wall and a knife.

"Judd, did you cut yourself to create these?"

He unwrapped his hand and held it up. A partially-healed scab covered the injury where his index finger had been chopped away at the closest joint to his palm and a fresh wound indicated a more recent removal of his middle finger at the first joint. "Paint! We needed paint! We learned after the first time," he grinned as he pointed at the nub where his index finger used to be. "Oh yes, we learned. This one was too far, too much gone! Now, when we need more paint... Just the tip! Easy peasy, lemon squeezy!"

"You sound—"

"Shut up! He'll hit you again."

"Both of you, shut up," Aeric told Judd. "So, you painted these giant birds, why?"

"*Vultures!* They are vultures! The master will be pleased when he sees them."

"Your master, when was the last time you saw him?"

Judd's face fell. The joy and elation at showing off his masterpiece drained away from him. "It's been forever. What's it been?"

"At least ten years."

"More like fifteen, you idiot."

Aeric held up his hands to quiet them down. "Okay, it's been a long time. It's a dangerous world out there, are you sure that your master is even alive anymore?"

Without warning, Judd sprang at Aeric. He landed on his chest, knocking him backwards. As they fell, Judd beat weakly at Aeric's face screaming, "The master loves me! He said he'd reward me for telling him when the Jello soldiers returned. They know! The Vultures are going to kill the Jello people."

Aeric hit the ground hard, then rolled to the side. Judd scrambled after him and Aeric kicked out with his boot, catching the insane watcher squarely on the chin. He dropped, out cold.

"Where the hell were you?" Aeric asked Joseph.

"I was in shock that the... Holy shit, you should've... You should've..." Joseph started laughing uncontrollably. "That little old crippled man just attacked you. Oh god, that was funny."

"He could have had a knife and that 'little old crippled man' could have killed me as quick as a demonbroc, Joe."

The Shooter sobered and wiped his eyes, "Yeah, you're right. I'm sorry, Traxx. I didn't think about it like that."

Aeric grinned at him "Okay, you've got me. It *was* a little funny. We need to be careful out here, though. We're not in the San Angelo defensive area anymore. We have to assume that everyone we meet out here is a killer. They'd have to be to survive this long."

"So what do we do with him?" Joe asked, pointing towards Judd with his chin.

"Let's tie him up. Here, cover him, while I grab a bedsheet."

Judd sat up groggily and stared into the barrel of Joseph's rifle while Aeric went to the nearest cell and reached inside. "What are you doing?" Judd screamed.

"Relax, he's only going to get a sheet. You need to have your hands tied."

Aeric pulled hard on the sheet he'd grasped, sending the skeleton clattering to the floor. Behind him, Judd let out a godawful high-pitched keening sound. "Jake! You've killed Jake! Oh my god. Oh my god. *Jake!*"

"Who the hell is Jake?" Aeric asked, walking up carrying the bed sheet.

Judd sobbed on the floor. "You bastards! Jake didn't do anything to you. He was my only real friend in here. And you killed him."

He looked at the sheet in his hands and then thought about the skeleton that had lain atop it for thirty-four years. Had the old man been a prisoner here who'd somehow been outside of his jail cell when the power went out? "I... Uh, I'm sorry, Judd. I saw an old skeleton lying on the bed. I didn't think anything of it."

"What? What are you talking about? Jake was just there this morning!" Judd started crawling towards the cell. Aeric and Joseph stood by, watching him.

He made it to the cell and used the bars to pull himself up. Judd stared inside the small room for several long seconds before whirling away to look up and down the hallway. "Jake! Jake you old sneak! How'd you get out this time? Where are you, buddy?"

Joseph leaned over and whispered, "Traxx, this guy is absolutely insane. We gotta watch out for him."

"That's what I tried to tell you a minute ago when you were laughing at him for jumping on me," Aeric retorted. He looked back at Judd and called, "Hey, Judd! Hey, I think I saw Jake run upstairs to the radio room."

Aeric could almost see the light turn on above Judd's head. "Oh, you're probably right. He likes girls and that Starr sure sounds like a good-looking woman."

The old man limped quickly past them. Aeric reached out to stop him. "Hold on, Judd. We need to tie you up. I don't want you attacking us again."

Judd stopped and stared at his hands before holding them out. "You're right, sir. I'm sorry that I acted like that."

The constant flip-flopping of personalities was exhausting to Aeric. The old man was as inconsistent as the weather back in Missouri when he was a kid. The weather would turn from hot and sunny to chilly and rainy, then back again, all within a few hours in the spring and fall. Preparing for a day outside was mentally draining, just like speaking with Judd.

He tied Judd's hands in front of him and they followed the man up the stairs. He couldn't put all of his bodyweight on the leg with the destroyed joint, so he negotiated the stairs by sitting backwards and hopping up each one. Aeric briefly wondered about the ladder to the watch tower; with enough arm strength, anything was possible.

At the top of the stairs, Judd pulled himself up with the help of the railing and hobbled down the hallway towards an open doorway. They allowed him to enter as he called out for Jake, choosing to stay back out of the room in case there really was someone in there. Satisfied that they were alone, they went into the room.

Sitting on the desk was a military style radio, like what Lorelei's Army Humvees used to have before the damn things finally crapped out. Aeric remembered that it was called a SINCGARs radio; hell if he knew what the acronym stood for, though. This one looked like it was brand new. There weren't any chips in the green paint and all the numbers on the keypad could clearly be read.

"How long have you had this radio, Judd?"

"Hmm? Oh, I don't know... Kendrick gave it to me when he was here last time."

The floor dropped out from underneath Aeric and he had to put a hand on the desk to steady himself. "What is it, Traxx?" Joseph asked in alarm.

His heart beat loudly and the edges of Aeric's vision started to close in on him. Kendrick? Had the crazy old fool said that *Kendrick* gave him the radio? Was it the same person? Was his son still alive? Did he come here before going on to Austin? If he went to Austin, that meant he was a Vulture, which meant....

"You said Kendrick," he gasped, fighting off the nausea that threatened to make his breakfast of oatmeal rise out of his stomach. "What do you mean?"

"Kendrick. He's the master!" Judd exclaimed, clapping his hands wildly.

"These people don't listen to a word you say, Judd. Let's go find Jake."

"Dammit, Lawrence, you're supposed to keep silent!"

"Shut up! All of you!" Aeric roared and stood straight to his full height. "Do you know the master's last name?"

"Last name? Hmm, the last time I saw him, he had the same name," Judd said in confusion.

"No, like his family name. I'm Aeric Traxx, he's Joseph Purvell. Traxx and Purvell are our last names."

"Oh! The *second* name, you mean," Judd giggled. "Of course I know it. Don't you think it would be silly for me to work for the master if I didn't know his second name?"

Aeric pounded his hand on the desk. "Okay, what is Kendrick's *second* name, you crazy fucker?" His head was pounding as loudly as his fist had sounded against the wood.

Judd looked properly admonished and mumbled, "It's Rustwood. Kendrick Rustwood, the master of the Vultures. Duh."

Aeric sat heavily in the seat across from the desk and put his face in his hands. *How had this happened?*

"Who is this Kendrick Rustwood, Traxx?" Joseph asked.

The missing pieces of the puzzle that Maria had presented him with fell into place. Kendrick had helped Ted design the walls, so theoretically, he could know of a way to breach them.

Maria said that they'd "fall down," to a child a hole in a wall could look like they fell down. Kendrick planned to bring the Vultures to San Angelo and use his knowledge of the city's defenses to destroy their only real protection.

The girl had also said that the destruction of the city and the murder of its inhabitants would be Aeric's fault. When Maria told him that his son was going to kill him, he'd thought she meant one of the boys that he and Veronica had together. Until this moment, he'd thought that Kendrick had died when he disappeared almost fifteen years ago. Kendrick planned to attack San Angelo in retaliation for his real father's death at the hands of Kate, who'd killed him trying to help Aeric escape.

"Traxx, who's Kendrick?" Joseph repeated, more forcefully this time. He wouldn't have heard of the Rustwood boy before; Joseph had been too young when he ran away.

"He's the *master* of the Vultures, haven't you people been listening?" Judd said.

Aeric looked up at the young Shooter with red-rimmed eyes, "Kendrick Rustwood is my son."

ELEVEN

The sound of his boots echoed across the old, yet clean, marble floor. When he'd arrived here all those years ago, Kendrick found his father's palace in Austin in poor repair. After he'd killed that idiot, Captain Sanders, and took his rightful place as the leader of the Vultures, he made it his mission to clean up the inhabited parts of the city. Call it a lesson that he'd learned while he lived in San Angelo. If you let the garbage and filth build up, then disease was surely not far behind. It was a small point of pride for him that there hadn't been a major outbreak of disease since he'd taken charge of the Vultures.

Not that he particularly cared for the residents of Austin. It was simple really, he needed an army to defeat Traxx and sick people couldn't fight. The city of San Angelo was a fortress in every sense of the word. That bitch, Griffith, had taken her experiences in the Middle East and been involved in every step of the fortification process with old Ted. They'd collapsed the perimeter to a much smaller and defendable area that encircled the city, systematically removing the structures outside of the walls to give them greater stand-off distance. It had been years since he'd personally seen their progress; his observers had told him that everything was gone now.

Luckily, he'd been able to add a few special touches to a sizable portion of the southern section of the new wall. Once the Vultures were in sight of the walls, the alarm raised by the defenders would signal his man on the inside to start the fires. The heat would ignite the fuses on the dynamite and blow the wall apart. It wasn't a fool-proof plan, but it was a pretty good one.

He'd waited his entire life for revenge. He'd pretended to be one of the San Angelians as a child for as long as he could stomach. Then he'd left without a trace and returned to Austin, declaring himself the rightful leader of the Vultures. Sure, he'd had to fight that fat, bloated bastard that had stepped in after his father died, but the man had been easy to defeat in hand-to-hand combat.

Two decades of subjugation under the oppressive Sanders had quickly brought the population over to his side. He introduced farming to the Austinites to offset their total reliance on the Vultures for food in exchange for their promise that at least one member from every family would join the fight when he called upon them. The people really had no choice except to agree to his terms once he stopped providing food for them. It was a win for him on two counts. He got to save the precious little pre-war food remaining and he was able to guarantee himself a full army while only employing a relatively small group of people full time.

Kendrick sighed as he stepped lightly up the stairs to his bedchamber on the third floor of the palace. His father had set up the suite in the north wing and then Sanders had ruined it so he had to have it repaired. He finally felt at home in Austin, more so than he could ever have felt living among the enemy. The time was drawing near, though, that he would have to leave the city and go into the field with his troops.

The watcher at the prison in Eden had finally called to let him know that Traxx and his people were once again patrolling the surrounding area. It meant that they felt themselves secure enough in San Angelo to leave the safety of their walls to conduct routine patrols. That false sense of security would be their undoing. He'd crush them; make them regret the day that they'd taken his father away from him.

"Mmm, lover. What's wrong? You seem so tense."

Kendrick looked up to see Starr standing at the top of the stairs. He'd been so engrossed in plotting the death of Traxx and his people that he hadn't realized he'd stopped on the landing before the final flight of stairs to the third floor. His breath caught in his throat at the sight of the beautiful, yet ruthless woman.

Starr Munoz was, quite simply, a young man's dream. She was tall, for a woman—maybe five-ten—which complimented Kendrick's six foot frame perfectly. She had an athletic build with dark, black hair that framed her face. Her chin was slightly pointed, without being severe or giving her the appearance of an elf, while her cheekbones where high and strong. The shape of her dark brown eyes hinted at her Japanese ancestry several generations before and the olive skin gave away the Hispanic heritage of her recent relations. Like her height, everything about Starr paired well with Kendrick, whose own creamy skin darkened considerably in the sun underneath his sandy blonde hair.

Her intoxicating visual appearance was renowned throughout the city. So was her sadistic nature. No one who'd ever crossed her had survived. She was well-known for having rivals skinned alive or slowly tortured by her servants, something that Rustwood found stimulating. Starr would go to any lengths to please him—and to make sure that she was the only woman who crossed his mind.

"I'm fine," he answered. "I'm just irritated that the preparations for the army aren't going as well as they should be."

Starr nodded her head in understanding. He was the only person that she lowered her voice for, the only one to whom she'd offer deference e towards and the only one who she would ever attempt to comfort. She grasped his forearm and tugged gently while saying, "Come to the bedchamber, let me help you relax."

His feet carried him behind her as he inhaled deeply of her fragrance. She always had a supply of scented soaps and shampoos, even after all these decades when no one was producing anything new. He wondered idly how she continued to procure the goods. *Some questions were better left unasked*, he thought.

Kendrick saluted the guards awkwardly, being dragged the way that he was. He thought he saw a twitch at the corner of one of the men's mouth, causing him to stop short and jerk his arm away from Starr. "Do you think something is funny?" he screamed, spittle flying across the short distance between them.

"No, sir! No, I—"

His attempt at an explanation was cut short by a hand clamped across his mouth. "I'll take him out back and discipline him, sir," the captain of the palace guard stated. The man had materialized out of the shadows, which was highly disconcerting.

The heat and rage that threatened to burst out of Kendrick receded gradually. He took a deep breath and nodded to the captain, "Thank you, Quellan. I want him to remember that I am the master of this city. The Vultures answer to me and any who mock me will suffer the consequences of my wrath!"

"He will be properly disciplined, my lord."

Kendrick's eyes blazed for a moment longer and then he turned to follow his woman through the doors into the bedchamber. He ruled the city with an iron fist and everyone knew not to cross him. The fact that one of his Vultures had smirked at him when he was about to make love to Starr made him want to cut the man's eyes out and then piss into the empty holes. He smiled at the thought. Maybe he *should* do that to the guard, and let him wander the halls of the palace as a beggar, to remind the others that he was the master here.

Starr's hand splayed open on his shoulder and spun him around to face her. She held a knife low, ready to stab into his stomach. Kendrick's heart raced at the anticipation of what she would do as she shoved him roughly back onto the bed. She walked over to him and glared down at him as he unbuckled his pistol belt and then unsnapped the buttons that held his military-style cargo pants closed.

She kneeled before him and took him in her mouth while she slid the knife softly along the top of his thigh, leaving a trail of crimson behind. The blade crossed over multiple dried lines of the same kind, causing him to wince in pain and writhe in pleasure at her tongue on his penis. The combination of the two sensations made him finish quickly into her mouth and she slid along his body to kiss him roughly.

"Better, my lord?" she purred.

"Yeah. You know exactly what I need."

Her fingers trailed down his stomach to fondle his drained testicles. "What has you so worked up?"

He jabbed a finger towards the windows. "Those damn peasants. They love me when I give them seeds to grow crops, provide them with goats for milk and chickens for eggs. But when I tell them that it's time to repay my generosity, that the army is being stood up and they must fulfill their part of the bargain, they cry out and make every excuse in the book.

"I would murder them all if I could. I would rip open their chests and eat their hearts while they watched me do it. As soon as we're rid of Traxx and that meddler, Tyler, then we'll come back here and cleanse the city."

Starr squeezed her hand tightly, causing his breath to catch in his throat and an uncomfortable pain to spread across his stomach. "Your father initiated the first cleanse. It's only fitting that you carry on his work. This is your city; the people live and die by your command. If they've outlived their usefulness, then get rid of them."

A smile spread across his face. "Yes! We need a purge to clean out all the malcontents and worthless freeloaders. We'll do it after I burn San Angelo and bring Traxx back here in a cage. Then we'll have an old-fashioned pig roast here in Austin."

The look of confusion on her face made him realize once again that she was much younger than him. While he hadn't seen them himself, he'd heard plenty of stories about pigs and how to cook them growing up. "It was an animal that lived before the

Reset," he said, using the term that his father had coined to describe the war that he'd initiated.

"Oh. Did they all die out?"

"Probably. Filthy animals I'm told. Anyways, they ran a stick from their asshole through their mouth and then cooked them over a fire." He hated the need to stop his rant to explain things to her. "*That's* what we're going to do to the people who piss me off after we destroy San Angelo."

"You're the smartest man alive, Rustwood" she demurred. "Wanna fuck now?"

He pushed upwards, throwing her roughly across to the other side of the bed and descended upon her giggling form. Of course he wanted to fuck; it was the only thing that sated his thirst for revenge against Traxx.

Unbeknownst to Kendrick, it was a trait that he shared with his father.

*****

After breaking Judd's radio and antenna, Aeric and Joseph traveled down the old highway towards Austin. It took them a few more days than they'd planned due to the encroachment of Mother Nature upon the pavement as well as increased activity as they got closer to the city. Mechanical monstrosities that were US Army tanks at one time or another tore up the ground and blocked the main roads, causing them to divert towards the lakes and travel down back roads. The Vultures were preparing to move.

They approached Austin from the west. The last several miles had been brutal on their thighs and hamstrings as they traversed the ups and downs of the hills on that side of the city. Once they topped the final rise and were barely able to see the downtown area, they made their way to the Vandegrift High School which sat on the top of a hill overlooking the city. The sign out front still had the phrase, "Go Vipers!" plastered across it, making the place appear both abandoned and pathetic.

The odds were that the place was empty. They didn't take any chances, though, and they approached cautiously. As they neared the school, nothing seemed out of the ordinary, so they went through the front doors, long since broken and shattered. Their boots crunched across the broken glass as they searched for a way onto the roof. A thick layer of dust, probably heavy with radioactive fallout, covered everything, which they took as a good sign that no one had been in the building in a long time.

They found a stairway leading to the roof. They had to jimmy open the door with a small crowbar from Joseph's pack, praying that the noise didn't attract any unwanted attention. Once they got up on top of the school, they had good three hundred and sixty degree views for security. More importantly, they could see the downtown area about five or six miles away.

Aeric was shocked. It had been a long time since he'd seen the city—the day he finally escaped with Katie and Tyler was the last time he saw it—but the skyline had changed drastically. He slid the 30.06 off of his shoulder and used the powerful scope to get a better view.

When he first returned to Austin and was captured by the Vultures, he'd been utterly surprised at the transformation; they'd apparently continued their wrecking spree in the intervening years. There were less than a handful of high-rises now, and those had clearly fallen into disrepair beyond the normal wear and tear of neglect. Even from this far away, he could see holes in the sides of the remaining buildings. He cursed under his breath, for him to be able to see those holes from this distance, they must have been large, probably hits from the tank ammunition that the Vultures had.

It made no sense to him for the high-rises to get knocked down. What was the point? If anything, hundreds, if not thousands of people could have lived in those buildings...all up against one another in the cramped space, without proper cleaning or ventilation. *Actually, maybe it was a good thing that they knocked them down*, he thought. They probably didn't want people getting sick and then spreading the disease to the rest of the population.

He shifted the focus of the scope and could see what looked like green fields all over the place in between buildings and the truth hit him. They wanted the people to live in houses so they could farm the yards. People who lived in a high-rise building didn't have a lawn and would likely have relied on others to provide their food. This way, people were now responsible for their own food supply. It was a smart move on their part and the spark of a plan began to form in the back of his mind.

Aeric passed the rifle over to the Shooter and walked him in on the high-rises. "See those there? I bet there are a few of them left that have line of site to the old Texas State Capitol where the Vultures used to have their headquarters. I'd be willing to bet that they still occupy the place; there's no reason to have moved."

"The Vultures' headquarters is that pink building?" Joseph asked.

He smirked; the granite *did* look pink in the morning light. "It's the type of rock that they used for construction. It's more brown than pink."

"Eh, I don't think so, looks pink."

"I want to get up in the top of one of those buildings and see if we can take out Kendrick. End this thing before it even starts."

Joe pulled the binoculars away from his eyes and squinted at him. "I knew it. Are you sure you can do that, Traxx? I mean, Kendrick is your kid."

Aeric dropped his eyes and then looked away, back towards the city. "I used to think that, once. Not anymore. I've had a lot of time to think about it since that crazy old man told us that he was the leader of the Vultures. I think Veronica and I made a huge mistake by telling him the truth about his father. We should have never let him know that he wasn't my child and the differences in appearance could have been explained away that he took after his mother, who died in childbirth. When he learned the truth about his heritage, he made himself an outsider.

"I loved that boy like my own and didn't treat him any different than my other children. I guess it wasn't enough for him. "He took a ragged breath, surprised that he felt so emotional about this, he was usually fairly stoic. "I have to kill him, Joe. If I can kill him before they attack, maybe they'll start fighting among themselves again and leave us alone. I can't let my feelings for him cloud my judgement about what's best for more than five thousand people."

Joseph seemed to consider his words for a moment and then stated, "When the time comes, I'll take the shot."

Traxx smiled, "Nah, Joe. I appreciate it, but I've got to do it."

"I'm a much better shot than you. I've trained extensively with that rifle."

Aeric patted the 30.06 that Joseph had leaned against the side of an old air conditioning unit when they began talking. "I don't know…you've never seen me shoot. Besides, you wouldn't know who Kendrick is—hell, it's been fifteen years, *I* might have a hard time figuring it out."

"Then point him out to me."

"See, here's the part where we start talking about a plan. I don't intend for this to be a suicide mission. If we both went to one spot and fired, they'd probably home in on us pretty quickly. If both of us are shooting—and moving—from different locations, then they won't be able to mass on us, we'll keep 'em guessing where the shots are coming from."

Joseph nodded slowly in understanding. "So we're splitting up, in a hostile city? Wasn't the whole point of me coming with you to watch your back?"

"It was. This strategy gives us a greater chance of survivability, though. We'll disguise ourselves to infiltrate the city and get a feel for the place, then split up to go to our shooting positions. In two days, we'll meet back here."

"Two days from now or two days after we spilt up?"

"Good point," Aeric acknowledged. "Two days after we split up. That'll give us probably one day of shooting and one day of evading."

"What if we don't see any targets? Do we still come back here?"

"This would have been so much easier with a radio," the older man muttered as he rubbed the scars across the bridge of his nose. "Okay, we'll meet here in the evening of the second day after one of us shoots our weapon. It could be a week before we see anyone, though."

"Got it. That makes more sense."

They spent the remainder of the day hiding their bikes in the skeletal forest surrounding the campus and finding a defensible place to sleep. They settled on an outbuilding near the back side of the school grounds, which would allow them an easier escape than the roof of the high school if it came to that. Aeric took first watch while Joseph slept. He figured that he had a lot of thinking to do before he could go to sleep anyways.

After all, he'd signed up to murder his son.

*****

"Oh, sorry. I didn't mean to... I didn't see you," Aeric protested as the guard turned menacingly to see who'd bumped into him.

"Do you know who I am?" the man, dressed in army-style camouflage pants and a grimy t-shirt with a green square sewn on the left side, asked.

"Yes, sir. You're one of them Vultures."

"What the hell happened to you?" The gang member pointed at Aeric's face, "Looks like you got caught making love to a stove!" He laughed while his buddies congratulated him on what they thought was a witty comment.

All of them wore the green square of cloth and it reminded Aeric of something that he'd seen before, but couldn't quite remember where. As his mind clutched at the significance of the fabric, he had to abandon that line of thought and deal with the immediate situation in front of him. There'd be time to ponder the Vulture's fashion choice later. "I was on the outskirts of San Antonio when it got bombed. Got trapped in a burning apartment," he lied. "That's why I can't see so well, sir."

"Well get the fuck out of here, old man. I don't have any food to give you." He raised both his hands and "shooed" Traxx away like he was trying to scare away birds from a table. "Go on, before I change my mind."

Aeric dragged his leg behind him like he'd been doing for the last two blocks as he hurried away along the palace's fence line. His hip hurt like hell from limping as a part of his disguise, but it was necessary. He'd been able to verify that the old state capitol was still the Vulture's headquarters and now he had a place to focus his attention. Now all he needed to do was to link back up with Joseph and find a building that would allow him to fire down into the palace grounds when he saw Kendrick.

He turned down a street that he remembered from his college days. Back then, it had been named San Jacinto Street or Boulevard, he couldn't quite recall. Now, a sign hung from an old lamp post that said it was Murder Lane. "Cute," he muttered, dragging his leg until a building blocked the palace guards from view. Then he walked normally back towards where he'd left Joseph in an alley with most of their weapons.

Since coming into the city, he'd been surprised at how clean everything seemed to be compared to San Angelo. If he pretended that the war hadn't happened, he could almost think that it was the Austin of old. There weren't the large piles of trash that had littered the city the last time he was here and, thankfully, the bodies had been hauled away as well. He wondered if they'd gone through their own round of illnesses, like had happened at San Angelo, that forced them to change their ways.

They'd taken the cleanliness to the extreme, which was a strange combination when you mixed it with the totalitarian rule of the Vultures. From the renamed streets to the furtive glances of residents as they passed by, it was clear that the people were repressed by the gang.

The Vulture's oppressive rule worked in Aeric and Joseph's favor. Even though they were easily recognized as outsiders and carried their weapons openly, no alarms had been raised against them. If anything, the people seemed surprised by the two men, traveling through the city, not marked as Vultures, without a cart or wheelbarrow of some kind. The residents were curious about the two of them, but they continued their work and didn't ask any questions of them.

The children seemed to be the exception. Here, like in San Angelo, if a child was too young to work, they had the run of the streets. There were three of them in the alley with Joseph when Aeric returned.

"Okay, you guys need to get out of here," Joseph told the kids.

"You gon' try to steal our food?" one of them asked.

The first child was quickly followed up by another, "You get caught stealin' an they chop off you hands. Both of 'em."

"Yeah, den dey beat ya to deaf for not workin' on ya farm."

"We're not going to steal anything," Aeric muttered. "We got tired of living alone in the wasteland so we're moving into the city."

"Sho, sho. How you get over da fence if you wasn't sneakin'?"

Aeric grinned, hoping that his disfigurement didn't scare the children. "We want to set up our own place, without the Vulture's help, so we climbed over."

The third child finally spoke, "You just don't wanna get called up for the army. You must be a wimp if you don't wanna fight."

He kept the grin plastered across his face as he said, "We've been fighting in the wasteland our whole lives. Maybe we *will* join the army. What are they putting an army together for?"

"The boss man, he says it's time to pay back for all the seeds and animals," the third boy continued. "There's some bad guys outside that want to come take our crops and murder everyone, so we gonna go stop them."

Aeric nodded his head solemnly, "Yeah, there are lots of bad guys outside the walls. When is the army going to go get those dirty murderers?"

The boy shrugged, "Don't know. My dad and both brothers are going to keep me and momma safe. I'd go if they let me."

"Believe me, kid, you'll end up seeing war sooner than you expect. You shouldn't wish for those sorts of things. Hey, do you guys know of an empty house where we could stay?"

"What 'bout one of dem on five-one ess tee? They's a buncha empty ones over there."

"Five-one ess tee? Oh, do you mean Fifty-First Street?" Aeric asked.

"Sure, whatever. You can stay there."

"We'll go see about it then." Aeric pretended to have a thought pop into his head, "Oh, hey! What about one of these big tall buildings? Are there any rooms in there where we could stay?"

The talkative boy of the bunch shook his head emphatically. "The boss man don't let *nobody* live in those no more. Didn't like people not havin' a farm. Now they're empty. Don't try to live there, you'll get arrested—or worse."

The grin reappeared on Aeric's scarred face; that was exactly what he wanted to hear. "Thank you for the advice. I guess we'll be going up to Fifty-First Street to see what's available up there."

He motioned for Joseph to follow him as he turned towards the north and headed in the general direction that they'd been told housing was available. They continued their ruse for three blocks, making a few turns here and there to ensure that they weren't being followed, before ducking down an alley and jogging back towards the shadows near one of the high-rises that overlooked the grounds of the Vultures' headquarters.

They hid until nightfall and then split up to go into the separate buildings like they'd planned when they were at the high school. Aeric watched Joseph walk casually into the night and then he used the wall to push himself up.

"Ugh," he grunted. "Geez, I'm getting too old to do this."

He thought about running towards the boarded-up entryway that they'd passed on the way into the alley and decided against it. It would be better to find the emergency exit door to see if he could get in that way. It was a long shot that he'd find an open way into the building except through the front.

His hands trailed across the dry, dust-covered brick as he groped blindly for the opening. The few remaining high-rise buildings conspired to block out the moonlight from above, casting the entire alley into a deep, black shadow. He could barely see anything in the closeness of the alley.

His fingers finally ran into a set of hinges. Aeric turned and faced the door so he could keep one hand on the hinge and search for the handle with the other. He cursed as his fingers rubbed against a jagged piece of metal sticking out where the handle should have been. He felt blood dripping from the ends of his fingers, but it was too dark to see how badly he'd been cut.

More cautiously this time, he probed the area where the handle should have been. He felt the circular opening where the knob had been knocked off at some point in the past. The shard of metal that had stabbed him protruded from the door along the lower side of the opening, probably where the knob had ripped it away as it fell.

Aeric slid his fingers into the top of the hole and tugged gently on the door. It didn't budge. He cursed silently once more; there was no getting into the building from the alley. They'd purposefully made it so someone couldn't sneak in that way. While he hadn't expected it to be so easy, he'd allowed himself to become hopeful. *Gotta stop doing that*, he told himself. There was no reason to be hopeful about anything in Austin; he was probably going to die there.

He crept down the alley, still trailing his hand along the wall, more to keep in contact with it and go in one direction than in hopes of finding another door. Ahead, the gray of the sidewalk pavement nearly glowed in the dark compared to the alleyway.

When he neared the opening back to the main streets, he paused to listen. Nothing seemed out of place, so he peered cautiously around the corner of the building, first one way and then the other. Nothing moved along "Murder Lane" so he walked around the corner as casually as he could manage. There was no sense in drawing suspicion to himself by acting like he was trying to hide his movements.

About halfway down the building, he came to the doors that led inside. They had a chain through the handles to keep people out, but the glass had long ago been smashed in, granting access to the lobby. Aeric checked his surroundings once again before he drew the large fighting knife from the sheath on his belt as he stepped through the door into the building.

Darkness once again enveloped him like a shroud. He held the knife before him, letting the blade lead the way into the void. If he was attacked in the lobby, there would be almost nothing that he could do. He couldn't see a thing. A moment of panic hit him; what if there was a demonbroc in the building? What if there was an entire nest of them? Not that it mattered. Even one of those fuckers was enough to kill an armed man in broad daylight. His chance of surviving something like that in the pitch black that surrounded him was exactly zero.

He stumbled on something in the darkness and fell to the floor with a yelp. *So much for being quiet*, he thought. Thankfully, he'd kept his hold on the knife and had the presence of mind to throw his hands wide when he fell so he didn't stab himself. Traxx felt around his ankles and discovered an old blanket wrapped around them. He'd gotten tripped up by a stupid blanket; he was definitely not going to be nominated for a hero of the year award, he told himself bitterly.

Despite his fear of the darkness, the thought of some kind of superhero award made him grin. He was an old man who'd done a lot of ass-kicking in his life—even if he'd survived mostly by luck and by having good people around him. The only formalized training that he'd gone through was the hand-to-hand fighting classes and some marksmanship instruction with the Shooters. Most of his success had come from trial and error, figuring out what worked in their new world and what motivated people to perform the duties that he asked of them.

And he'd asked himself to end this war before it started, so sitting around remembering the good old days wasn't going to get the job done. He pushed himself up off of the floor and staggered blindly through the darkness. There was no way of telling where the stairs were. Some buildings had them tucked off in corners where they were out of the way for all the ritzy guests who used to stay there, while others were designed with simple functionality above anything else.

The building that he'd chosen to be his sniper perch didn't have any windows on the ground floor. He'd have to check every door that he came to in the darkness. It was convenient for his safety, but the gloom was a horrible choice for trying to get around. Without any type of ambient lighting, his eyes hadn't adjusted to the pitch black and he was just as blind now as when he initially entered the lobby. He wished that he had a flashlight or a torch....

Aeric slapped himself on the forehead in his mind. Of course! He had several lighters in his pack. He'd used them to start their cooking fires at night. There had always been an abundance of the damn things around. Even thirty-five years after the end of the world, they were everywhere. He shrugged out of his backpack and unzipped the top flap. The sound of something hard scraping against the floor in the darkness made him pause and stare blindly towards where he thought it had come from.

He waited several seconds. When he didn't hear anything else, he dismissed it as his mind playing tricks on him and jammed his hand into the pocket where his lighters were. He pulled one out and zipped the bag closed before slinging it up onto his shoulders once again.

Light blossomed from the precious little tube of plastic, bathing the area around him in a soft orange glow. He stood, more or less, in the middle of a large hotel lobby. The furniture had long since been hauled away, whether for use as it was intended or for firewood, he'd never know. What he thought was a blanket was the fabric from a couch or chair, though, so he leaned towards the firewood explanation. Not much else remained in the small circle of light around him.

Far across the open space, he saw three sets of eyes glittering brightly back towards him. The glow from the lighter's flame reflected green in the darkness. He breathed a sigh of relief; green usually meant a dog or cat, both things that he could handle. If the eyes were red, he would have been worried. Rodents' eyes reflected red in firelight and while the demonbroc wasn't a rodent, their eyes shone red as well.

Whatever the creatures were, they stared at him without making a move to run away or attack, so he decided to continue his search for the stairs. The lighter quickly got hot on his thumb and he had to release the button, plunging the lobby into darkness once more. He used the memory of the open space that the light had showed him to navigate towards one of the walls as the lighter cooled. Once he got there, he turned towards the interior of the building and began walking along the wall until he came to a doorway.

He struck the lighter and the dark blue and white pictogram of a male shone back at him. Aeric definitively did not want to go in there. Since the building was off-limits, the bathroom was likely used by street people or workers in an emergency. No one would have cleaned it in decades. Yeah, not a pretty picture.

Aeric continued along the wall, stopping at each doorway he came across. Ladies' restroom, supply, concierge, vending, finally he came to the doorway labeled stairs. He opened the door cautiously and examined the stairwell. Once he determined that it was safe, he began to climb.

TWELVE

"Ahh, what a lovely morning for a war," Starr purred as she strapped a pistol belt around her slim waist.

Kendrick smirked at her choice of wording. "Yes, it is. We're going to wipe those clowns off the face of the earth and then the Vultures will rule all of the remaining parts of Texas."

She picked up one of her knives and then stopped. "How long did you say it was gonna take?"

He sighed; the girl couldn't remember details about anything to save her life. "It's about 160 miles, so we'll be there in a week."

"A week? That's *so* far away!" She flopped dramatically onto the couch at the end of their bed. "Can't we make them walk faster?"

"Not if we want the army in any condition to fight when they get there," Kendrick answered. "The tanks can't go that fast either, their engines are cobbled together from the other vehicles and the fuel has so much stabilizer in it that it's damn-near worthless. I think twenty, twenty-five miles a day is about right."

Starr held her knife out for him to see, waving it lazily in front of him. There were dried streaks of blood on the blade and he felt himself stiffen against the restraining fabric of his pants. "I need some entertainment then," she stated. "We need to bring some of the inmates along. Maybe we could have a tournament or something each night, like a gladiator ring or a marksmanship competition where we start at the feet and work our way up to the head."

"Sure, we can bring a few of them along." He changed his tone and asked, "Don't you think it'd be better to allow your frustration to build during the march? Then, when we get to San Angelo, you can take it out on Traxx and his band of rejects. Wouldn't that be more satisfying?"

Her eyes flashed from their normal dark brown to almost black. "You can't expect me to go an entire week without torturing someone. I'll go insane! The longest I've gone was three days that time I had the flu. When I got better, I didn't even torture that bastard; I just killed him and bathed in his blood. No," she stamped her foot like a child. "A week is too long."

Sometimes Kendrick did indeed question her sanity. He liked to torture people too; it was cathartic to hear their screams and know that he held their very lives in his hands, but Starr took it to a whole new level. Her tastes ran towards long-term torture so she usually got a month or two out of each of her victims before they died. He'd already planned on bringing several hundred prisoners back with him. They could use them as slaves in the fields until they were called to the palace.

"We'll take a couple of inmates with us, then. It will be good entertainment for the troops," he said, warming to the idea. "It'll help to increase their blood lust. They'll be foaming at the mouth by the time we get there, and when the walls explode, they'll rush in and murder everything in sight."

"How many of them do I get?"

"Hmm… Three? Four? What do you think you'll need for the trip? It's not *that* far away."

"No, my lord," she replied, her dark eyes practically glittering in the light from the windows. "How many of the slaves from San Antonio do I get?"

"The ones that we keep, we have to feed," he reminded her.

"Not all of them. Starvation is an exquisite form of mental and physical torture. Of course, I'll need to keep some of them healthy so they can survive the cutting—" she stopped suddenly. "I want women. Lots and lots of women. I'm tired of the same things. Cutting off testicles and ramming things up men's asses has gotten stale."

Kendrick nodded. Besides the occasional woman, most were kept safely away from Starr since they needed good breeding stock to replenish their population. If it came to it, one male could get every woman pregnant, so they were much more expendable. He reached out to his lover and pulled her close to him. "Then you will have one hundred women to experiment on."

"And little boys?"

"Of course, my dear. Whatever you desire."

She pushed herself away from his embrace and whirled around to face him. "Oh my god. I am so turned on right now."

He grinned even wider than he had before. "Me too. We need to get going, though."

Starr didn't pay any attention to what he said. Instead, she turned and picked up one of her homemade sex toys off the table beside the couch. A mischievous smile made her dimples appear and she tossed the object to him. He caught it and wondered how much longer the toy would be good for, they usually only lasted a week or so before they began to rot and the smell became a turn-off.

The first time he used one of her toys on her, he'd been horrified. The implement had brought her to orgasm quickly and her level of passion afterward had been unmatched. Now, they rarely went more than a few days without one of them. She left her pistol belt on, sliding her pants down around her ankles and bent over the couch, presenting him with an ample view of her. Kendrick unbuttoned his own pants and adjusted his grip on the severed human arm. He knew what she needed.

*****

Aeric glanced at the sky. The early morning sun was still low on the horizon, but they'd lost about two hours of daylight. Given all the activity around the palace, the army should have left hours ago. It seemed like everyone was ready to go and something had caused them to delay. The Vultures didn't seem concerned with how long they could march before they needed to make camp.

A man walked into his line of sight from the south leading two horses. He stopped by the center door and waited for whoever was coming out. *This is probably the moment I've been waiting for,* he told himself. The horses were likely for Kendrick and his second in charge. The doors opened and he peered through the rifle's scope.

The old man had been telling the truth. It was Kendrick; the man he'd called his son. He'd filled out since he disappeared, much more muscular than before. Now that he was older, he looked like the man that raped his beloved Kate and impregnated her. He wore a sneer openly. Aeric remembered that it had begun to appear when he thought no one was looking during those last few years in San Angelo. Traxx wondered if it was his dissatisfaction at something that was happening on the ground or if he always wore the expression.

He continued to watch him as he walked down the steps, arm in arm with a scantily-clad Hispanic or Asian woman; he couldn't really tell at this distance. He wondered if she was Kendrick's wife. What if she was pregnant with his child, would that only perpetuate the cycle of hate as another child grew up fatherless? Then, he thought of something entirely different, *Why in the hell would anyone go into the wastes wearing a skirt and halter top?* All of these thoughts jumbled through his mind until one question surged to the forefront.

Could he do it? This was his best opportunity to kill Kendrick.

The man who'd led the horses held out a stirrup for the leader of the Vultures so he could mount the horse. Of course he could kill him; he planned to murder everyone that Aeric knew in a few days. The thought of the death of his children and grandchildren, Veronica and Tyler, Lorelei and other friends galvanized him into action. He flipped the safety on the silenced 30.06 to fire and centered the crosshairs on Kendrick's head.

He'd already thought that the man was dead; what would a confirmation of all those years of wondering matter? The meaty part of his finger rested against the trigger and he exhaled his breath, pausing afterward like the Shooters had taught him. The flesh on his index finger spread slowly as he gently applied pressure on the rifle's trigger.

*****

"I'm so ready to get on the road," Starr sighed.

Kendrick threw his head back and laughed, "You're anticipating the—"

A scream of pain erupted from the page who'd brought his horse. The man fell to the ground, writhing in pain as a crimson smear spread slowly across his shoulder. Kendrick's mind went through several instantaneous calculations to determine what had happened.

After the page helped him into the saddle, he stood off to the side respectfully out of the way. Someone had been aiming a weapon at his head; when he'd laughed at Starr's impatience to be on the road towards San Angelo it caused his head to move. The bullet traveled past his face and into the unfortunate man standing beside the horse.

"Go!" Kendrick screamed, kicking the animal hard in the flank as he grabbed its mane and held on tightly.

The horse took off like a rocket and then stumbled as another bullet slammed into its rump. Kendrick hadn't been prepared for the movement and flew over the horse's head, falling hard against one of the concrete-topped stone retaining walls near the second set of stairs. His shoulder impacted against the low wall with bone-jarring force. He didn't wait for another shot and had enough presence of mind to decide that they were coming from somewhere in the city. He scrambled behind the stone, lying flat on his stomach.

His shoulder was on fire. The sound of running horse hooves echoed in the morning; his horse lay on its side, back legs groping for traction on the cement. Kendrick recognized that the noise had come from Starr's horse, which was upright and making its escape from the kill zone. Was she still in the saddle or had she fallen as well?

He quickly forgot about the horse as men all across the palace lawn began to scream in panic. The Vultures were under attack! Several men already lay sprawled at odd angles on the ground, their blood puddling underneath them.

"The city! The attack is coming from the city!" he shouted to the Vultures huddled behind whatever cover they could find.

"My lord!" someone shouted from around the corner of the palace.

Kendrick turned towards the voice and the bones in his shoulder grated together. He screamed in pain. His arm was definitely fucked up. He saw Quellan, the captain of the palace guard peeking around the corner.

"My lord! Come this way!" Quellan called.

"The attack is coming from the city!" Kendrick grimaced.

Quellan looked out beyond the long-dead trees that lined the palace walk. His eyes drifted upward towards the remaining high-rises. "The hotel, my lord! They must be shooting from the hotel."

Kendrick peeked up over the retaining wall and was rewarded with a massive cut from flying cement chips. He ducked his head down and ordered, "Have the buildings searched and anyone found inside killed."

"Yes, sir!" Quellan replied before he disappeared back behind the building.

Kendrick adjusted his position behind the wall and probed his shoulder with his fingers. He winced in pain, the damn thing was dislocated.

*****

"Fuck!" Joseph muttered. "Goddamned prideful old bastard missed."

He peered through his scope and acquired another target. Then he squeezed the trigger, punching a hole through the chest of a Vulture standing near the steps that the man and woman had walked down before they mounted their horses. The Shooter assumed the man that Aeric had shot at was Kendrick.

Joseph adjusted his aim and picked out another target, firing again before swiveling to a third person. He was on what Captain Griffith called "autopilot." Apparently, before the war, the military could tell one of those computer-things what to do and then leave it alone to complete the task it was given. That was what they called autopilot.

Aeric had stopped trying to shoot at the man behind the stone wall by the time Joseph had killed his fifth Vulture. Now the mayor was helping to pick off anyone who was still in the open. Joseph fired once more and then dropped the magazine on the M-2010 sniper rifle that he used. It had a five-round magazine. He'd been able to cheat on the first one by having a round already chambered to give him six shots. He rapidly went through the second magazine and replaced that one as well.

Then it was time to move. He'd shot—and likely killed— eleven of the Vultures in under four minutes. He threw the sniper rifle over his shoulder and picked up the shorter M-4 carbine. The stairs flew under his feet as he raced down from the sixth floor of an old building of some kind. The layout had confused him when he first entered because he'd been expecting an apartment building like the ones in San Angelo. This was strange, though. Each floor was a wide-open area with pieces of old desks and chairs. It didn't seem all that comfortable, making him wonder what the old timers meant when they talked about how nice the old world had been.

Joseph's upper body started to pitch forward as his momentum carried him faster than his feet could go. He grabbed the metal handrail to right himself and forced his legs to go slower. If he fell in the dark stairwell, he could easily break a leg and then it was over.

He burst through the door into the office building's lobby. Three men stared back at him in shock. Their eyes were impossibly wide as Joseph flipped the safety on the carbine off and fired four rounds from the hip into the two men on the right. The rapid crack of the rifle echoed across the lobby and out the broken windows to the street. There was no hiding his location now.

His momentum carried him into the third attacker and Joseph dropped his shoulder. He hit with the force of a demonbroc attacking a child and the man went flying backwards. The Shooter fell forward onto his stomach, the rifle skittering away across the concrete floor.

He was out of time. He couldn't afford a long, protracted fight, so he pulled the pistol from the holster on his hip and fired a round into the man. The *pop* of the military M-4 rifle had been nothing compared to the explosion of the .45 handgun in the confined space. The rifle had been designed to be as quiet as possible to help conceal a soldier shooting the weapon; the .45 on the other hand was an up-close-and-personal killing machine with zero considerations for sound dampening.

Joseph didn't wait to see if the third Vulture was down for good; he couldn't afford to waste the time. He pushed himself up awkwardly as the large rifle across his back threatened to off-balance him. He ran bent over at the waist to where his M-4 lay and scooped it up before straightening up and dashing through the doorway onto the street.

He'd taken the time to rehearse his escape route, so he didn't hesitate when he came out. The alley was off to his left and he darted into the gloom as chips of masonry from the wall on the corner flew towards him. More of his pursuers had found him.

He sprinted down the alley, making minor adjustments to his path because he had no way of knowing if they were at the head of the alley, aiming rifles down on him. Behind, the rough coughs of several guns echoed down the alley. Somehow, they missed and he was spared.

Up ahead, the narrow space ended at another street and Joseph darted around the corner. He paused to catch his breath, pulling a grenade from his pouch. He took a deep breath and pulled the pin, then spun back into the mouth of the alley. Several men were about halfway down and he threw the explosive with everything he had.

He didn't wait to see where the grenade went. Instead, he turned and ran along his pre-planned escape route back towards the school. The sound of the explosion in the alley only lasted for a second. The clamor of the screaming men, maimed and dying, carried across the Austin morning for a long time.

THIRTEEN

"It has begun."

"I'm sorry, what was that, sweetie?"

Maria turned towards Veronica, scaring her. The little girl's eyes were rolled back in her head, exposing only the whites of her eyes. "The war has started."

Veronica dropped her rolling pin, knocking coarse grains of wheat and oat in every direction from her cutting board. "Here? Now?" she asked in a panic.

"The birds hunt for carrion. Soon, they'll take flight from the nest. Then nothing can stop them."

Veronica had been privy to enough of the girl's visions now to realize that she was talking about the Vultures. The "nest" was surely Austin where they lived; what did she mean by "carrion"? It was a word that she'd heard before, long ago when she was a teenager, the meaning lost to the years now. She stared at the little girl without seeing her as she tried to remember what the word meant. Finally, she dredged a definition from her memory. Her father had used the word to describe dead deer on the highway as they drove to Odessa.

Dead deer? Did she mean animals or people? Who were the Vultures hunting? The realization settled in her stomach and she leaned backwards against the counter by the old stove. They weren't hunting *dead* animals, that wouldn't make any sense. Her vision must have told her that Aeric was already dead. Even if he was alive and being hunted, the end result was already decided.

Had Lorelei Griffith's bid to provide Aeric protection failed, then? The captain stopped by the day Aeric left on his fool's errand to Austin and told her about Joseph. Had he been unable to protect Aeric and her husband was dead, murdered like some animal and left as roadkill for creatures to eat?

A moan of despair escaped her lips as the visual of dogs picking at Aeric's remains hit her. She screamed at the freak standing across the room from her, "You get out of my house! This is your fault, you did this to us!"

Maria stared blankly at her, water dripping unheeded from her hands where she'd had them in the dish water. The girl was still in some sort of trance, which infuriated Veronica even more.

She picked up the rolling pin and charged towards the girl. Veronica raised the weapon high above her head. "You little bitch," she hissed through clenched teeth. "It's not fair that you get to destroy our lives and act like nothing happened afterwards. If it wasn't for you, Aeric would have never left and he'd be here with me."

The rolling pin went higher as she prepared to bring it crashing down on the girl's face. Slowly, the blue of her eyes began to roll back down and she blinked several times before realizing that Veronica stood in front of her with an implement of death in her hand. She screamed and threw her hands above her head.

Her scream, the scream of a scared little girl, was enough to shake whatever craziness had taken hold of Veronica. She dropped the rolling pin behind her, the thud of the heavy wood on the tile echoed across the kitchen. "Oh my. Oh my goodness. I'm so sorry, Maria." She pulled the girl into her arms and hugged her tightly. "I don't know what I was thinking."

"Did I have another vision?" Maria asked. "I was washing the dishes and then the next thing I see is you with the rolling pin. Were you going to hit me?"

Veronica's cheeks flushed and she felt a flash of heat rise up from the open collar of her shirt. The embarrassment that she felt at losing control of her emotions was palpable—and inexcusable. "I... I don't know what happened, Maria. I wasn't thinking clearly."

She squeezed the girl tighter than before. "I'm sorry. I'm so sorry," she repeated.

Maria's arms slowly made their way up from her sides and she hugged Veronica back. "I don't mean to make things worse," she sobbed. "I can't help it. When the vision hits me, it just takes over and I don't know what I'm saying."

"I know, sweetheart, I know." The tears traced lines down her burning cheeks. The embarrassment of what she'd almost done hadn't let up; she still felt terrible. "I promise you that I will protect you if your vision comes true."

She pulled back from Veronica and stared up at her. "What did I say?"

Veronica wiped the tears from her cheek and used the back of her hand to wipe her nose. "You said that the war had started and the Vultures were hunting Aeric."

"I used his name?" Maria asked in surprise. "I've been told that I never use names."

"Well... Maybe you didn't use his name," Veronica admitted. "But you said they were hunting carrion and that they'd leave their nest soon."

"What's carrion?"

"It's dead meat. The Vultures are hunting dead meat."

"Oh..." her voice trailed off, clearly not wanting to think about it.

"Maybe you were mistaken," Veronica said hopefully.

"Um, yeah. Maybe."

*****

"Shit, I think they've found us again," Joseph whispered.

Aeric sat up and listened. It *did* sound like someone was moving in the darkness. They'd been in a constant run and gun since Austin and were almost out of ammo. They were exhausted and still pursued at every step along the way.

After their initial fight in the city, each of them made their way separately to Vandegrift High School where they'd stashed their bicycles along with the articles from their backpacks that they didn't need for the attack on the Vulture headquarters. Once there, they compared notes about what had happened.

Aeric didn't know why he'd missed the shot on Kendrick until Joseph told him about the man's laughter. He'd been at a different angle and watching through his scope when it happened, whereas Aeric had fired and then had to readjust his sight picture after the recoil from the rifle took the crosshairs off of his son.

They'd expected to get rest and then leave the next morning. Unfortunately, they saw men leading dogs up the hillside from the east towards the school almost immediately upon their reunion. It had been impossible to hide from the city's residents as they fled, so they hadn't bothered to try. The presence of dogs, tracking them added to the likelihood that they were on a one-way trip.

The initial firefight at the school was over quickly as they used their longer-range rifles to decimate the Vultures. The school's location at the top of a hill would have been easy to flank and attack from their blind side, so they fled quickly once a lull in the fight allowed them an opportunity. They'd been harried ever since, often getting only two or three hours of sleep before their tireless pursuers reappeared.

In an effort to confuse the Vultures, they'd gone north towards the old Buchanan Lake Dam. They'd crossed the slime-crusted Colorado River to the north bank, thinking that would throw off the dogs and camped in the shadow of one of the dam's arches near the spillway. It was a good spot to hide, accessible only by crossing over the hard rock after wading through the water.

Aeric cocked his head in the darkness to try and get a better angle for his ear. The scrape of boots against the exposed rock told him all that he needed to know. The Vultures all seemed to wear tough-soled hiking boots—which were great against the reptiles and insects of the wastes, but poor for disguising their movement. Far below, they could hear the dogs snuffling on the far bank where their trail had gone cold into the filth.

"We gotta go," he whispered.

Joseph looked up at the dark clouds above, replying, "I can't see a damn thing. If the cloud cover would clear, we could try and shoot some of them."

Aeric shook his head uselessly in the darkness. "Nah, not worth it. Right now, they don't know if we went down river and tried to double-back on them or if we kept going straight. If we shoot at them in this darkness, we wouldn't hit any of them. All we'd do is let them know that we were still here."

They picked up their packs and slid their arms through the straps as quietly as they could and then pushed their bikes northward towards the spillway. They reached the top and ran into a concrete barrier that marked the side of the spillway. There wasn't an easy way to go over it, so they had to go back down the hill until they could skirt around near the bottom and back up the dam's side.

It was a painstakingly slow process as they moved across the awkward angle of the concrete spillway, pushing their bikes. Aeric no longer heard the Vultures searching below; he didn't need to hear them to know that they were still there. Those dogs had pursued them for a long time. They had their quarry's smell imprinted on their brains and the river trick wouldn't deter them for long.

"We need to cross the lake," he said flatly. "They're gonna find us soon if we stay on this side of the water."

"If we cross the lake, we lose the bikes," Joseph pointed out.

"Maybe we could steal a boat big enough for the bikes, too." Finding a usable boat was unlikely. The few that they'd seen since they arrived at the lake were nothing but washed-up wreckage. The larger bodies of water like Old Fisher Lake at San Angelo had fared better than the streams and ponds, so if the water was drinkable there were probably people living around the lake, which meant the potential for usable boats. However, anyone they ran into wouldn't give up their boat easily and they'd likely have another fight on their hands.

The baying of the hounds behind them tore through the night as they rediscovered the trail on the near side of the river. They had to make a decision quickly. Once they made it off the spillway, they either had to keep riding around the edge of the lake until they found a boat or they could swim for it. More than twenty men pursued them, so staying for a fight wasn't an option and the idea of swimming across the lake in the darkness wasn't appealing either. If they didn't drown or get attacked by some type of mutated animal in the water, they'd probably lose their weapons and backpacks. In reality, they only had the one choice. They had to continue around the lake until they found a usable boat.

At the bottom of the spillway, an old weed-choked gravel path led northeast along the edge of the lake. The path made for faster riding as they pedaled as hard as they could to put some distance between them and the Vultures, but they had to swerve to avoid the creeping grasses and cacti that could easily puncture their tires, which slowed them down significantly.

Chunks of gravel began to fly up all around them and then reports from the gunfire reached their ears. The long stretch of relatively open trail provided excellent fields of fire for their pursuers. Aeric whipped his bike back and forth erratically, trying to avoid the whizzing bullets and the thorns.

Seconds after the firing began, Joseph cried out in pain and jerked his handlebars too hard, causing the front tire to turn completely sideways. His momentum carried the back half of the bike up and over the front and the Shooter went flying through the air. Joseph landed hard and Aeric hit his bike, unable to avoid the wreckage. He crashed sideways, skidding several feet across the gravel.

The stars above him were fuzzy and his head throbbed. Aeric wondered where he was and then the sound of the Vultures shooting at him reminded him quickly. "Joseph! We gotta go," he screamed as he scrambled on hands and knees toward the safety of the bushes along the path. The M-4, hanging loosely from its strap across his shoulder slammed repeatedly into him, alternating between his knee and elbow as it swung.

Aeric wasn't watching where he placed his hands as he crawled and the spike from a cactus impaled him. He grunted in pain and fell to his side. In the darkness, he could barely make out the dark gray tip of a thorn protruding from the back side of his hand. The base of the thorn rested against his palm, it had gone completely through his hand. The wound in his palm wasn't bleeding like the back side yet, so he left it in place and pushed himself up, running at a crouch towards the concealment of the bushes. He reached them a half-second before Joseph did.

"The lake is this way," Aeric shouted as he pushed his way through the spine-covered vines and razor-sharp grass. He winced as a hundred small cuts and pricks opened his skin, causing blood to flow freely and mingle with the massive wound in his hand.

The weeds gave way and his feet plunged into the muddy water at the edge of the lake. Joseph emerged behind him, favoring his left leg. "This way," Aeric called over his shoulder as he splashed in the open water towards the north.

They'd gone only twenty feet before providence smiled on them and Aeric's shins banged into the rough metal of an old upside down flat-bottomed fishing boat. "Ugh," he grunted as the boat caused him to stop.

"Flip it over!" Joseph said as he pulled his carbine off his shoulder. Aeric bent to the task while the Shooter covered him, prepared to deal with whatever had taken up residence underneath the boat's hull.

He pulled hard on the small boat, flipping it up on its side and the night's darkness gave way to brilliant light and sound as Joseph fired his M-4 into something underneath. He allowed the boat to fall over onto its bottom and fumbled for his own rifle.

"Don't bother. I got it," Joseph winced as he stepped around a dark form on the ground and gripped the side of the boat. Aeric stared at the hairy mass of teeth and claws for a moment before rushing into the water beside his companion. He held the boat steady, while Joseph clamored awkwardly over the side and then pulled himself up while the other man leaned against the opposite gunwale.

"What was that thing? I couldn't see clearly after the flash from your rifle."

"Either a demonbroc or a dog," Joseph replied calmly. He looked around at the boat and asked, "How do we make this thing go?"

"I uh…" Aeric trailed off. There weren't any oars and even if there were a motor, it probably would have been useless along with every other mechanical engine that used spark plugs for ignition. They could use long poles to push themselves off for a few feet, but wouldn't be able to touch as they got farther out into the lake. They'd be sitting ducks for the Vultures to pick off.

"The rifles! We can use the stocks on the rifles as paddles," Aeric whispered excitedly.

Joseph had never been in a boat before and Aeric hadn't been in one since he was a teenager, so it took a few tries, wasting time that they didn't have, to make their longer, full-stocked sniper rifles work as paddles. The M-4s had a narrow stock without the larger surface area the two rifles had and were useless for the task.

They'd gone a couple hundred feet when the water around them began to plink. The Vultures had found where they went into the lake. They both paddled for everything they were worth, learning quickly to work in unison instead of fighting against each other. The boat slid across the surface of the water and the shore disappeared into the darkness behind them.

*****

"What do you mean they got away?" Kendrick hissed into the Humvee's radio.

"*I mean, they got away and we can't find them, sir,*" the imbecile on the other radio answered. "*We tracked them all the way to a giant lake and they got away in a boat. We shot one of them before they got in the boat, though. There was a lot of blood on the ground.*"

Kendrick wanted to throw the handset into the wastes. Doing so would be pointless, though. The damn thing was connected by a cord running from the receiver to the radio. He wondered for the hundredth time who'd taken a shot at him. It *had* to be the San Angelians. First they showed up in Eden after a decade of abandonment and then, just days later, the old man stopped answering the radio.

Of course, that could have been because the battery died, he reminded himself. His father had seized a large stockpile of them from Camp Mabry, the old National Guard base in Austin. The batteries weren't designed to hold their charge for years, so the Vulture engineers had jury-rigged a solar panel to act as a power supply for the battery charging case that had kept their military radios working, even if it was basically on life support. The battery that he'd given the watcher had been new in the factory packaging, so it probably hadn't held much juice.

The most damning evidence that it was the San Angelians, in Kendrick's mind, was that the assassins fled towards the northwest. They'd made a beeline towards the setting sun until they were forced to go north to avoid a small force that he'd sent on horseback to sweep around in front of them. Somehow Aeric and his idealistic rejects had gotten word that he was coming to destroy their city and they'd attempted a preemptive strike.

While he hated the man for what he'd done to Justin Rustwood, Kendrick had to respect Aeric's move. Traxx didn't know about the explosives that he'd set in the walls or about his surprise in the sewers, but he knew that Kendrick would eventually be able to find a way in, so he tried to end it before it began. Aeric probably thought that if he assassinated the Vulture's leader, they'd once again fall into the power struggle that had decimated the Vultures during the twenty years that Greg Sanders had been in control.

He pulled the receiver back towards his face and pressed the button on the side. "Okay, if you can't swim or take a boat across, go to the far side. The dogs will pick up their scent."

"Yes, sir."

Kendrick thought about it for a moment and continued, "I want them caught before they get back to San Angelo. If they escape, I will give you to Starr."

"*We'll get them, sir. They lost their bicycles and at least one of them has a bullet hole or two in —*"

Kendrick didn't bother to listen to the rest of his lackey's excuse. He dropped the receiver into the front seat of the Humvee and walked over to the large tent that made up his command post. He admired his Vultures' quick work; the tent had been a pile of fabric when he started the radio conversation with Hobbes, now it was already up and they were carrying bedding inside.

He smiled at Starr as she came skipping through the camp towards him. Three men dragged a screaming captive several yards behind her. "Hiya, Kendrick!" she gushed as she kissed him quickly on the cheek. "It's been two days. You said on the second night that I'd get to have one."

"You're right. I was on the radio with Hobbes, is the cage set up yet?"

"Almost, or at least it will be by the time we get over there," she replied. Starr rubbed at the bandage on her hand where she'd cut herself jumping from the horse. "Did they kill them yet?"

"No, the idiots let them escape across a lake…in a boat. How the hell did they find a boat that wasn't rotted through or in someone's possession?"

She stared blankly at him and he said, "It means a boat that nobody owned."

"Oh, maybe that's how they got there in the first place and were running to where they'd left the boat."

Kendrick hadn't thought of that possibility. If that were true, then maybe the shooters hadn't been from San Angelo. If they came by boat, they could have been from anywhere on the Colorado River that wasn't cut off by a dam. "Hmm... Maybe."

He decided to change the subject and asked, "What are you planning for tonight's entertainment?"

She grinned mischievously at him. "I want to cut off his eyelids so he suffers the entire dusty trip. And I'll pull out his fingernails slowly with some needle-nosed pliers. You know the men enjoy getting an entire, intact nail as a reward. I've even heard that they trade them as currency!"

Kendrick nodded his head, he'd heard that too. "Seems a little mild for you, my dear."

"I want him to last," she deadpanned. "Maybe I'll take a few other body parts that will hurt like hell, but won't kill him."

Kendrick thought for a moment before answering, "Nipples?"

"Sure."

"Ears?"

"Maybe one."

"Testicles?"

"Dammit, Kendrick! I didn't want to ruin the surprise, but you're too good," she answered, practically bouncing in anticipation. "I'm gonna nail his nut sack to a piece of long wood that'll rest across his thighs. I glued sandpaper to the back side, so as he walks the wood will pull against his balls while it rubs away the skin on his legs. Everything will be made even worse by the dust and salt in his sweat. Doesn't that sound exciting?"

He pulled his enthusiastic little torturer into an embrace. "Yes, sweetie. The men will love it."

"Oh, maybe I'll put a hot poker up his ass too. That's always a crowd pleaser."

*****

The boat finally ran aground on the far shore of the lake and the men stepped wearily from it as the sun peeked over the eastern horizon. Aeric's arms, back and shoulders ached from the effort of rowing the boat across the lake using only the stocks on their rifles as oars and his hand throbbed uncontrollably where the thorn was still embedded.

He was better off than Joseph, though. The Shooter was leaking blood from his thigh and every time he'd shifted on the fishing boat's seat, it tore away any scab that had tried to form. It was still dark out and difficult to see, but the man looked much paler in the moonlight than he had before they bedded down for the evening at the dam.

"How you holding up, buddy?" he asked in concern.

"We need some time to get a good pressure bandage applied to both the entry and exit wound," he muttered. "And I need food. So hungry."

They'd cut miles and miles of shoreline off of their route by rowing straight across the lake. He wanted to take advantage of their lead and couldn't. There was simply no way that Joseph would be able to make a run for it with his leg bleeding the way it was. Aeric glanced around the area where they'd landed. It looked like as good a place as any to try and make camp. There was a small square shape not too far inland that looked like it might have been a house of some kind.

"Alright, let's see about that house over there. Maybe we'll get lucky and nobody will be living there."

He helped Joseph hobble along, which was harder than he thought it would be with both of them wearing backpacks and carrying two rifles. They'd walked fifty feet before he spoke again, "I changed my mind. Maybe we'll get lucky and somebody *will* be living there. We need supplies that we don't have."

As they neared the squat, one story building, he realized that it had been a store of some kind. Fifties-style gas pumps, considered old before the end of the world, rusted in the parking lot along with various pieces of trash and abandoned material. Everything seemed intact except for the front door, which had a large hole bashed through the glass.

"Wait here and cover me," Aeric ordered as he shifted Joseph's weight off of his shoulders and leaned him up against the gas pumps.

He slid the carbine off his shoulder and pressed the stock deep into his shoulder with the barrel pointing slightly down in front of him like the Shooters had taught him. They called it the low-ready position. He could easily lift the barrel up and fire an aimed shot, which was much more sensible in a potential encounter than carrying the rifle at his side or on his shoulder. The damned spike in his hand felt odd against the pistol grip. He couldn't risk removing it until he had a place to perform the minor surgery that it would require. They *needed* that gas station.

Aeric stepped forward cautiously towards the gas station. The hole in the glass meant that the store had been raided at some point. He had no way of knowing if that was last week or if it had happened twenty years ago. The morning had lightened up enough that he could make out vague, indistinct shapes behind the grime-encrusted windows and he didn't see any movement.

He picked out his path among the refuse in the parking lot and stared hard at the space in front of him, watching for tripwires or any type of movement. He didn't want to set off some paramilitary nut-job's grenade booby-trap and end up maimed—or worse. As he walked, his mind drifted to the possibilities of how someone could have set up a trap, to defend themselves or to catch something for food. Lord knows they'd heard plenty of stories about cannibals in the wastes as the resources dwindled during those lean years where virtually nothing would grow.

If he'd been setting the trap, he would have rigged it to blow the gasoline pumps as well. That way, he'd have been guaranteed to get most of the raiding party in the explosion. The rain of body parts wouldn't have been a pretty sight. It was every man for himself first, then family and friends. Nobody else mattered.

Glass crunched under his boot, shattering the early morning stillness. Aeric paused and waited for some type of reaction from inside the gas station. He waited for several seconds before finally continuing on. It was nerve-wracking to be outside the walls of San Angelo again. He'd done it often enough on the Gathering Squad as a young man, but hadn't been on any type of clearing operation since Veronica's father died and he became the mayor in his place. And he'd never cleared anyplace by himself before. Even immediately after the war, he always had Tyler right by his side or providing backup from a few feet away.

His mind wandered again to his earlier thought that nobody else mattered. He still remembered those innocent days of his youth when he thought that human beings cared for each other. He'd even engaged in a debate that freshman semester at UT that mankind ultimately wanted the get along and become a community. One of his arguments had been that if mankind was so evil, as they were portrayed in movies and literature, then the first societies would have never been formed. He used to think that mankind ultimately was good and wanted to be together in some type of society.

He still felt that way, to an extent, but he'd been wrong in his argument about the good intentions of humanity. People wanted to be together when there was enough food to go around. When there wasn't, they were violent, petty and mean. The ancients knew how to farm, how to hunt and how to preserve food from going bad, the people that survived here in Texas did not know how to do any of that at first—and people died by the thousands.

Aeric reached the door without incident. There hadn't been any traps in the parking lot; now he had to contend with the door itself. An easy trick would have been to tie fishing line to the door handle and the other end to a grenade pin, then when he pulled the door open, the pin would come out, the spoon would fly and *boom*, no more Aeric Traxx.

Then the logical part of his mind took over. The average American, even the average Texan, didn't have grenades lying around. It was unlikely that they had anything like that. They could have set up some type of ram to come down from the ceiling into the doorway like in that movie with the alien headhunter in South America.

Something like that would be fairly easy to set up and far more likely to happen than a grenade. Even so, he pulled gently on the door to see if it was locked. It wasn't. He pulled hard on the door and swung down to the side, crouching beside the brick exterior. If there was some kind of booby-trap the brick should keep him safe, he reasoned.

No explosion rocked the morning and there wasn't a giant wooden log smashed through the now-closed front door. There hadn't been a trap after all. He stood and proceeded cautiously through the store, checking behind the counter and along each of the pilfered shelving units. Surprisingly, some things still sat on the shelves, including what looked like some canned food. He left things where they were so he could continue clearing the building. The back storeroom was dark and empty, cleaned out of most of the supplies like the front had been. The store was vacant and most of the useful stuff had been taken long ago. It would serve them well as a place to get cleaned up if the locals thought it was empty.

Aeric walked rapidly across the parking lot to where Joseph stood. The man's eyes fluttered against the exhaustion that blood loss and their escape had caused him. "Come on, buddy. The inside is clear and pretty clean. We'll see what we can do to get you patched up."

Joseph's exhaustion was apparent as all of his bodyweight slumped onto Aeric's shoulders and his feet dragged awkwardly as they walked from the pumps to the store's front door. Once they were inside, Aeric pulled him deeper into the store between the shelving units and began searching for a first aid kit. There was probably one in the back near the receiving door, so he went there first. It didn't take him long to find the rusted white box strapped to the wall.

The inside of the first aid kit still held bandages, their paper wrappers brittle with age. As a bonus, inside was a little brown bottle of hydrogen peroxide that he could use to help disinfect their wounds. There was nothing that he could do about the peroxide's expiration date. It was more than thirty years past when the manufacturer recommended it being replaced. Oh well. They'd discovered over time that the medicines and canned goods were still usable long after the date stamped on their packaging. He hoped the same could be said about the bottle of disinfectant.

"Okay, Joe. I'm back," he said hoarsely. There was a lot of work to get done before he could get any rest.

Joseph muttered something that he couldn't understand. He knelt beside him and grasped his belt, reminding him of the time, long ago, when Veronica forced his clothes off of him and threw him in the shower after he'd killed his first man. He'd been covered in blood then as well. It seemed to happen much too often in his life.

"This is gonna hurt, Joe," he said while he unbuckled the belt and pulled the Shooter's pants down. The scabs once again ripped away and blood began to trickle out. Joseph didn't cry or attempt to fight him, making his job easier. Surprisingly, the peroxide still bubbled up as he poured it over the wound. It looked like the bullet had passed clean-through without hitting the bone. They were lucky.

He finished cleaning Joseph's wounds then used wadded up pieces of cloth, torn from a collection of old touristy t-shirts from the back room, and tape from the first aid kit to put a pressure dressing on the back and front of his leg where the entry and exit points were. Once Aeric was finished, Joseph turned over to sleep, leaving him to his thoughts and the task of doctoring his own hand.

He held his hand up to examine it closely in the morning light. The thorn had entered through his palm and exited the back side of his hand before breaking off from the cactus or vine that it had grown from. It had been in his hand for more than an hour—probably closer to two—and while it throbbed, the intense pain had subsided. Aeric guess that his endorphins had suppressed the pain while he and Joseph fled for their lives across the lake and that thrill was gone now, leaving him feeling miserable.

"This is gonna suck," he muttered as he grasped the thorn.

"Mmm?" Joseph mumbled.

"Nothing, just talking out loud to myself. Sorry. Go to sleep, Joe."

He made a mental note to be quieter and pulled the spike from his hand. The endorphins that had helped numb the pain apparently weren't strong enough to deal with a large gaping hole in his hand. Pain exploded across his enflamed flesh and his entire hand felt like he'd stuck it into a fire.

The wound, which was blocked by the thorn before, bled profusely. The older, darker blood that had been trapped mingled with new deep crimson to pour down on his lap. He cursed silently and leaned forward in an effort to keep from being covered in blood. There were creatures in the wastes that could smell blood from a long distance away and bring them running. The pain was intense, so decided to use the disinfectant while he was already in pain. He picked up the bottle with his uninjured hand and poured the liquid into the large hole in his palm.

The white bubbles from the hydrogen peroxide turned rust brown immediately as the blood mingled with them and began to drip off onto the floor. Once the bubbles began to dissipate and turn red once again, he poured more of the peroxide on the wound. He did that a few times on his palm and the back of his hand until the bubbles stopped appearing. He remembered his mother telling him as a kid that once the bubbles went away, the injury was as clean as it could be at that moment so he put the bottle down and wrapped his hand in one of the old t-shirts.

Once he'd exhausted his limited first aid capabilities, he grabbed one of the cans off the shelf and positioned himself so he could see the door while still being hidden from anyone observing from a distance. He pulled the can opener from his bag and then wiped the dust off the can.

"Heh," he grunted when he saw the contents of the can. It was the same gas station brand of ravioli that he and Tyler had survived on for the first week after they left Austin. He hadn't touched the stuff since then. "Ain't that a kick in the nuts."

FOURTEEN

"Come on, Traxx! They're getting closer. We're not gonna make it."

Aeric gritted his teeth and pedaled harder. Sweat poured from his forehead and pooled along his lower back as he stood on the pedals, giving it everything he had. Up ahead, less than three miles away, the walls of San Angelo rose up out of the haze. While he couldn't quite make out the Eastern Gate complex, he knew it was there—and they were in danger of being cut off from it.

Aeric had been able to find a bicycle that had a pump for the nearly dry-rotted tires. A little more searching in the area around the gas station had yielded the mangled remains of two bodies, each with a single bullet hole in their head. The smaller of the two had a small hole in the back of the skull and a gaping vacant space on the front. That one had been shot in the back of the head. The second, larger skeleton, was the opposite and still clutched the rusted rifle that he'd used to take his own life. The two people had died beside a small grave that had a pile of rocks laid over the top to deter the scavengers that had eaten their bodies.

Further investigation of the home confirmed his belief that it had been a family. Their home had been picked through by scavengers who'd left the old photos on the walls. The short bed in the child's playroom sealed the scenario in Aeric's mind. The child had died and the parents committed suicide—take that back, the father had shot the mother and then himself. It was a sad, often repeated event during those lean years after the war.

He found an old Radio Flyer wagon in the carport and had been able to lash that to the bike's frame. Bedding and old clothing from inside the family's home went into the wagon for cushioning and he'd used that contraption to haul Joseph all the way back to San Angelo. It had been a long, tiring, and uneventful trip until this morning.

The two of them were on a smaller, less-used road traveling almost due west towards the city. The main road from Austin went northwest to southeast and then split off west and north around the outside of the city's walls. Aeric didn't notice the dust as he pedaled, focused on the road in front of him, but Joseph saw the massive dust cloud of the Vulture army traveling on the main route behind them.

The road the Vultures were on was much better than the one they traveled. Before the war, Farm Road Seven Sixty-Five had barely qualified as more than a two-lane track; years of disuse and lack of maintenance had turned it downright treacherous for Aeric and Joseph as they flew down the road. They didn't have any choice. The city's defensive protocol was clear. If sentries saw raiders of any kind, they were to lock the gates down and prepare to repel them. If they didn't beat the army, which traveled on a better road, then they'd be permanently locked out until the fighting ended and the Vultures went back to Austin.

He pedaled as hard as he could for a few minutes in silence and then threw his head to the side to check their progress. They'd pulled out in front of the slower-moving army. They must not have noticed Aeric and Joseph yet, otherwise he was sure that they would have surged forward with some type of response force. They had horses that could have easily run them down, but for some reason, the Vultures continued at their steady pace, which allowed him to pull away.

"I...think...we're...gonna make it," Aeric panted. He was exhausted; the headlong flight had taken everything out of him.

"I hope you're right, Traxx. There's no way that they haven't seen us yet. You can bet if we don't make it through those gates, we're done for."

The thought of the gates slamming shut, locking them outside with the Vulture army caused Aeric to dig deeper into himself and push harder. They were less than a half a mile from the gates. That meant only two or three minutes more of the maximum effort and then he'd be able to stop to get some water.

Two minutes. He could do anything for two minutes. He willed his legs to pump harder. Veronica was inside the walls. His sons, Mason, Anthony and John, their children, his grandchildren, Tyler and Nicole, Kayla and Lorelei; everyone that he knew and cared about lived in San Angelo. They had to make it back inside so he could be with them and defend his home alongside the Shooters and the other defenders like he'd done hundreds of times over the years. He'd failed to stop the attack; he couldn't fail to be there with them for it as well.

The gates loomed before him. They were closing. He heard Joseph shouting behind him and he glanced back, the Shooter was waving a small neon pink piece of fabric over his head. It was an old VS-17 panel that ground troops used to signal pilots back in the old world. Since they were virtually indestructible and folded up to the size of a deck of playing cards, the Shooters had adopted them as way of signaling each other from long distances to avoid accidentally shooting one another.

Joseph's signal worked. The gates stopped closing and Aeric heard the shouts of encouragement from the defenders. The cinderblock, brick and metal walls came and went as they raced through the gate. His chest hurt and his lungs heaved as he tried to catch his breath. The bike skidded to a halt a few feet beyond the walls and he heard the clang of the gates as they closed.

His chest seized, spread pain across his left side. He vaguely heard the metal crossbeams inserted into place behind the gates. It sounded like he was underwater. Aeric was dimly aware of people thumping him on the back in congratulations before he collapsed.

*****

"Oh! He's waking up," Veronica said.

Aeric blinked against the bright light and looked around blearily. He recognized the dresser and the useless ceiling fan above. He was in his bedroom and sunlight streamed in through the windows on the west side of the house. He didn't remember going to his house. The last thing he remembered was making it through the gate and then pain. So much pain in his chest; it was more than from exhaustion or the exertion of their narrow escape, something had happened.

Veronica leaned across him and held onto him. Her gentle shuddering told him that she was crying. He let her get it out and after a moment, she pushed herself up. She had red-rimmed eyes and her face was puffy from crying. He wondered how long she'd been at it. "How do you feel?" she asked.

"Ugh," he replied. "I feel like crap. What happened?"

"You beat the Vulture army inside the walls and then collapsed," Mason stated from the other side of the bed.

He turned to see his oldest child grinning at him. Beside him, little Aiden reached out and grabbed Aeric's shirt, using the fabric to pull himself up. "I'm glad that you're okay, Grandad!" the little boy whimpered as he hugged Aeric.

Aeric hugged him back, feeling like he'd been run over by a truck and then backed over again for good measure. "Thanks, little buddy. I'm alright, just tired."

He lolled his head over to the side and Veronica's lovely face came into view. "Hey, baby," Aeric muttered.

She fell forward onto the bed beside him and hugged him around his grandson. "I was so worried about you, Aeric," she sobbed.

He hugged her back awkwardly and said, "It'll take more than a bike ride to do me in."

Veronica pulled back and touched him lightly on his chest, "Aeric, you were writhing on the ground and clutching your chest. Then you stopped. We think you had a heart attack. If it hadn't been for Joseph's quick reaction in giving you CPR, then you probably would have died."

"A heart attack?" he asked. That must be why he felt like crap. He'd chalked it up to his bad back and the overwhelming exertion from trying to race the Vultures while hauling Joseph in a wagon behind the bike. "What about the Vultures?"

"They're sitting outside the walls," Mason answered. "They're outside of rifle range and they haven't tried to attack; it's like they're sitting there waiting for something."

Aeric tried to sit up. His son placed a restraining hand across his chest. "Sorry, Dad. You've gotta get some rest."

"Bullshit, Mason. I have to oversee the defense of the city."

"Captain Griffith has it under control. You're not in any shape to go anywhere. Mr. Winston and his engineers have done an outstanding job on those walls. The Vultures are gonna sit out there until they starve to death or go home because they aren't getting through those walls."

Aeric's exhaustion overcame his desire to micromanage the city's forces. He nodded his head reluctantly and lay back against the pillows. "You're right. I'll stay here and get some rest."

Mason smiled and reached over to gently pull Aiden off of his grandfather. "Maybe you could tell Aiden a story. I haven't ever gotten around to telling him the story about how you met mom. He'd really like to hear about all those toys from the old world."

He looked past his son to the little boy. There wasn't any way for the new generation to avoid making the same mistakes in the future without learning about those in their past. "Okay, Aiden. Get comfortable by your old grandad."

The boy eased himself into a position on the bed where he could see Aeric's face. "Let's see. I guess the story starts a few weeks before I graduated from high school—that was the first time that I saw the evidence of a terrorist attack. I was walking to school in the rain and this strange gray sludge fell out of the sky and hit me right on the head."

"What's strange about that, Grandad?" Aiden asked innocently.

Mason grinned down at the two of them. "Alright, Dad. Mom and I are gonna go downstairs and then I've got to check on the defenders on the walls."

"Goodbye, Son," Aeric answered. "We'll have Aiden stay here tonight. The Traxx family story will take a long time if I'm going to tell it properly."

Veronica leaned down and kissed him once again. "Don't scare him, Aeric. And you still need to get some rest."

"I'm not going to scare him. I'm just going to tell him the truth."

She straightened at the waist and stared down at her husband. "That's what I'm afraid of."

Mason and Veronica left Aeric and Aiden alone in the bedroom. Aeric had planned on simply telling the boy the story about his journey to Springfield with Tyler, but felt compelled to expand the story.

The hours ticked away and the tale continued past Kate's death and by the time he was finished, he'd told Aiden about his latest adventure to Austin and how he and Joseph had escaped all the way back to San Angelo. The boy's innocent questions carried the story along and by the time he was done, the sun had fallen below the horizon.

For the first time in years, Aeric felt totally relaxed. He felt as if his soul had been cleansed.

*****

"We've been here for days, Kendrick. Are you sure that your man on the inside is even still alive?"

"Patience, Starr," the leader of the Vultures admonished. "He's probably waiting until the moment is right. I would have received a notice if he'd died."

"How?"

"I have my ways," he replied. "That old fool in Eden told Aeric Traxx that I was coming after him, so we've lost the element of surprise, but I have other resources in and around this city. Razing San Angelo has been on my to-do list for as long as I can remember."

"I wish you'd have let me play with him at least before you beat him to death," she pouted.

"In spite of what you think, everything on this planet is not a plaything for you, my dear. I regret killing Judd. I acted out of haste and anger. To think, the assassin that my men let escape was Aeric Traxx. Imagine how demoralizing it would have been for them if we'd been able to capture him and nailed him to a cross outside their city walls. Tyler probably would have challenged me to a fight right then and there; kill two birds with one stone and all that."

Starr looked at him skeptically, "Didn't you say that he was a giant? Like almost seven feet tall and muscled like a god?"

Kendrick's eyes flashed in anger, "Do you doubt me?" He had never approved of the almost godlike worshiping that the people of Austin had heaped upon his father, but he did allow himself to believe that he was nearly indestructible. Along with that came the feeling that his word was the law and he was always correct.

"No, of course not, Kendrick. You've made him seem like a monster that could break a man's spine with his bare hands. I didn't think you'd be capable of winning in hand-to-hand combat against someone like that."

He glanced over at Quellan. The captain of the palace guard caught his eye and quickly found a spot on the wall of the tent to study. Kendrick turned back to Starr and said, "You'd do well to remember your place, woman. I am the master of the Vultures and will not be talked to like that. I will show you the amount of pain that *I* can inflict during a torture. Do you understand me?"

She fell to her knees in front of him and pretended to apologize. "I'm sorry, my lord. I didn't mean anything by it. I'm just a silly girl and didn't think about what I was saying."

Her patronizing tone infuriated him and he grabbed a handful of her hair, jerking her upright. "You little fucking whore!" He held her at arm's length and threw a vicious punch into her stomach, releasing her hair as he did so. She collapsed into a ball at his feet with her hands clutching her stomach. The anger at her words threatened to overwhelm him and he pulled his leg back, intent on smashing her beautiful face into a pulp with his boot.

The fucking bitch saw his leg and threw her arms up over her head, screeching that she was truly sorry. The leader of the Vultures thought about finishing her anyways, he could always find another woman willing to share in the power that he could offer.

Instead, he slowly lowered his boot to the ground. Starr was the only woman that he'd allowed to see his true self and he cared for her. If it had been anyone else under his boot, he would have killed them without any warning. He actually cared for her.

"Stand up," Kendrick ordered.

She stood shakily and wouldn't meet his gaze. The salty lines that ran in multiple directions across her face made a slight lump form in his throat. He swallowed it and said, "You will never speak to me like that again. Do you understand?"

"Yes, my lord," she muttered.

"What was that?"

She looked up at him and replied, "I will never talk to you like that again, my lord. You are the master of the Vultures. You are invincible."

"Good. Quellan, leave us and fire the flares. If that idiot Huerta is waiting for a signal, let's give him one."

"Yes, sir," the captain replied and left the tent. Kendrick heard him tell the men outside the tent flap that he was not to be disturbed.

"You must realize, Starr, that I could never let you show insubordination towards me—especially in front of a subordinate like Quellan. That kind of atmosphere becomes ripe for a coup and I like being in charge."

"Yes, my lord. I understand." A strange smile played across her face and she clapped her hands. "I'll make it up to you. I'll find a way to help you defeat their giant. I promise it!"

He sighed, "I don't need any help. I'll just shoot him."

His words didn't seem to have any impact on her. Instead, she began pacing, her arms wrapped tightly around her midsection. She muttered something about blood and souls being the key to victory. Her mind seemed to be slipping further towards the brink; maybe he should have crushed her skull when he had the opportunity to do so. He could have blamed it on his rage and he would have forgiven himself.

Starr stopped and turned her backside towards him, "Do you want me?"

Kendrick unbuckled his pistol belt and tossed it on a desk. Her strange behavior could be analyzed later. He picked up a knife and handed it hilt-first to her. "You know what I like."

She took the weapon enthusiastically and unsnapped his pants. Yes, she knew exactly what he liked.

*****

Red explosives burst in the air, signaling the traitor that it was time. Edward Huerta looked around the assembled group of boys. The Vulture army had sat outside the gate for almost a week now. He'd taken it upon himself to reunite the two gangs that Kendrick had started all those years ago.

Huerta, a legend among the youth of the Barrio as a symbol of resistance against the collective groupthink of the city leaders, had brought the gangs together by killing Bull and Fish in front of them. Now both gangs had adopted the green square on their chest—Kendrick's symbol—to help identify them as Vultures to the invading army and protect them during the upcoming bloodbath. He'd effectively sealed off the Barrio to keep away intruders and instructed the boys of their mission to bring down the walls. All they needed was the signal.

He took the flares to be that bastard Kendrick's go-ahead signal. It had taken him long enough to decide to attack, maybe there were preparations that had to be made that he knew nothing about. Whatever the reason, they were finally ready.

"Right, *men*," he began, choosing to call them men instead of boys to strengthen their courage. "We have a mission. For more than twenty-five years I've worked in those stinking sewers. I refused to let that self-righteous fuck, Traxx, or his lackeys make me part of their system. Then, Kendrick Rustwood—the man in charge of that giant army outside the city walls—came to me. I worked closely with him to devise the plan to bring down these walls."

He took a breath and jabbed a finger towards the city's perimeter. "Those walls have cut across our city, causing your families to be homeless and they forced us into filthy places like the Barrio. Before men like Traxx and Delgado, the old mayor, our families owned homes, had a steady supply of food and weren't looked down upon by the other residents of San Angelo. After those walls were built, they became a symbol of power for those in charge, those who've made us their slaves. This morning, we're going to bring them down!"

Huerta paused as the assembled gang members cheered him on. They were eating it up. The stupid fucks didn't realize that he'd turn on them the moment he had the chance. Kendrick had promised *him* a position in the Vulture's hierarchy; he hadn't said anything about the Barrio trash that helped him destabilize the city. Bull's gang had been releasing demonbrocs for weeks, causing widespread panic and even a few deaths while Fish's gang had been stealing and stockpiling supplies, causing neighbors to turn on one another in accusations of theft. Now, they'd destroy the walls and the frightened, untrusting defenders wouldn't be able to put together a coordinated response. The Vultures would walk in, virtually unscathed.

He raised his arms to quiet the boys down. Better to not bring attention to themselves just yet. "Alright, men. Settle down. As some of you know, instead of disposing of the shit like I've told the City Council I was doing, I've stockpiled it. Yes, I've been saving the feces of every man, woman and child in this city for years. Do you know why?"

"For fertilizer?" one of the boys in the back asked.

"That would be a good reason, but no," Huerta acknowledged. "Shit, especially dried shit, burns very hot for a long time. I've lined the sewer system that runs underneath the city with that dried shit. Once we light it, the fire will rage uncontrolled beneath their feet. The heat will set off the explosives in the walls and the city will fall to the Vultures."

Once again the cheering reminded him of why he'd spent most of his adult life in those sewers, toiling away in the stink and the filth. Traxx would pay for creating the Barrio. The conditions inside the slum had allowed diseases to spread, killing thousands of people, including Huerta's family. He allowed his mind to manipulate the timeline since he knew that his wife and child had died of some type of flu years before the walls had been relocated for the third time, when the Barrio was created. Whether it was the creation of the walls or the lack of proper sanitation without the appropriate nutrition and medication, it didn't matter to him anymore. He'd allowed his hatred to fester under the gently massaged timelines.

It was the only thing that had kept him sane down in those tunnels for so long.

FIFTEEN

Aeric glanced sidelong at his friend. Tyler had miraculously appeared at the city hall this morning proclaiming that he wasn't about to die at home alone of some bullshit disease while everyone he knew got to fight one more final, epic battle. Clearly he remembered video games and movies far too well.

"Are you sure that you're ready to go out on the wall, buddy? I mean, a few weeks ago, you were coughing up blood and couldn't stand."

Tyler stopped him with a massive hand across his chest. Even though the cancer had eaten away at him, Tyler was still an intimidating subject. "What's your hang-up, Aeric? I've fought and bled for this city—for you. If I was one to point fingers, then I'd come back at you with something about you needing CPR just a couple of days ago." He shrugged and gently took his hand off of Aeric's chest, "It's a good thing for you that I *don't* go around pointing fingers."

"You're right, man. I'm sorry. I didn't mean to—"

"Yes, you did," he replied through a grin. "I can take it, though. So, now that we've got that settled, what's the plan?"

"We don't know what they're waiting for. That old man in the prison had said that the Vultures had a nasty surprise for us. He refused to elaborate, though. He was insane, so there's no telling if they actually have something planned or if his demented mind created it."

Tyler glanced down at Aiden, who'd become Aeric's shadow over the past week, raising his eyebrows in a silent question. "It's okay," Aeric confirmed. "I've told him everything about the

Vultures and their wicked ways. Sure, he's young, but this world has a way of eating up the innocence of youth."

The big man nodded his head, his shaggy blond hair becoming more disheveled as he did so. "We should attack them," he stated simply.

That was the last thing Aeric thought he'd hear from the mouth of his lifelong friend. "What do you mean? San Angelo's strength is in our walls. We've trained to defend from above, not to conduct offensive, open warfare in front of the gates."

"Exactly. It's the last thing Kendrick would expect. He trained with us and knows our tactics. He helped to build those walls, so he knows how formidable they are. There's nothing that—"

Aeric held up his hand and then slid his open palm down across his face. "How could I have been so stupid? Kendrick helped to *build* the walls. He knows their weaknesses; that's what he's counting on."

"You think those flares this morning were some sort of signal?" Tyler asked.

"You can count on it…" He trailed off as one of the hoodrats from the Barrio walked across his line of sight. He recognized him as one of the boys who'd been outside the grocery store where Maria lived before she moved into the Traxx house. He wore raggedy clothing like most of the other residents of the Barrio, seemingly oblivious to the fact that there were rips in the fabric. He was also covered in mud and what looked like smears of black ash from a fire.

Tyler followed his gaze toward the gang member. "What is it?"

The boy was one of hundreds that Aeric saw on a daily basis; what stood out and caused him to stop was the green square of fabric above his left breast. "We've been infiltrated!" he shouted. "The Vultures are inside the walls."

The gang member in question took off at a dead sprint towards the Barrio. "Prepare for an attack!" Aeric yelled towards the defenders above them on the wall.

One of them began ringing a bell loudly in warning. Men and women streamed out of houses near the walls where they'd been resting and went up the ladders to the top of the wall. The defenders crouched down behind the ramparts, staring out into the wastes for the pending attack. They were ready to repel the Vultures, as they'd done time and again against raiders and bands of scavengers.

Aeric clutched Aiden to his side and spun in circles in the open assembly area behind the walls. He knew what he saw. The Vultures in Austin wore the green square to indicate that they were part of the gang and one of the gangs in the Barrio had worn the same symbol. The fuckers had been here all along.

The surprise attack was revealed across the northern end of the city as thick black smoke began pouring into the sky, followed by more in the west. They'd started fires inside the city. They planned to burn it and force the residents out in the open to be slaughtered. Aeric would never allow that to happen on his watch.

Then the explosives hidden in the walls detonated and the world descended into chaos.

Defenders that didn't die instantly in the explosion were thrown thirty feet into the air, only to fall back to the earth, twisted and broken. Scores died from secondary effects of the blast. Some who'd been standing near the explosion had their insides liquefied from the overpressure. Others suffocated on their own blood as their lungs were punctured in a hundred places by shattered bone fragments. Still more of them had limbs which bent at grotesque angles. Even if they survived, they'd never walk again. The force defending the walls of San Angelo was decimated and a large, gaping hole more than forty feet across stood open to the attackers.

Even though Aeric's body had shielded Aiden from the worst of the damage, the boy bled from multiple cuts and stood looking at the mayhem in a daze. "Go, Aiden! Run to your grandmother. Tell her the city has fallen and to evacuate the family through the Northern Gate!" Aeric ordered with a hard shove from behind, sending the boy off towards the old campus where the secondary line of defense had been established.

"We'll meet you in Tennyson," he called after the retreating boy, telling him to move the family to the ruins of a small town about fifteen miles beyond the gate. Tennyson had been set up as a known evacuation point for the city's residents if the walls were ever breached. As a former resident, Kendrick would know about the escape route to the north. So far, there hadn't been any reports of Vulture activity on that side of the perimeter and Aeric wondered if Rustwood had forgotten about the rally point.

"We need to prepare to fight," Tyler bellowed. "Here they come!"

Aeric turned from his grandchild's fleeing form towards the smoldering hole in the wall. Dimly, as if from a distance, through the ringing in his ears, he heard hundreds of small pops as the remaining defenders near the Eastern Gate began firing at the advancing Vulture army.

A quick glance through the walls told him that they were still out of range. "Save your ammo!" he yelled hoarsely. His throat felt like it was on fire, probably from the dust and choking black smoke in the air. The fires from the north and western side of the city had spread at an alarming rate, covering everything. Not far from where he stood, bright orange and green flames poured from an open manhole cover, sending the greasy blackness skyward to once again blot out the sun. Fires burned unchecked across the city as homes and supply depots burned.

The fires had their intended effect on the defenders as residents raced away from their positions along the remaining portion of the wall back towards their homes where family members had been left. While not everyone fled to save their families, the damage had already been done.

Aeric stared in shock at the large empty spaces along the parapets. Less than a third of the force that he'd seen at their positions before the blast remained. "The city is lost," he muttered.

Two large hands gripped his shoulders on either side and shook him violently enough to make him think there'd been another explosion. When the shaking stopped, Tyler stared hard at him. "You're this city's leader, now act like a leader and organize this defense," he ordered.

Tyler's words shook him from the dark place that he'd entered. His friend was right; they could fight and delay the attackers long enough for people to come from the other sectors to defend the city. He picked up the old cheerleader's megaphone and yelled instructions through it. "Even out those gaps! We still have a chance to stop them. They've used up their surprise, now it's time to show them that we won't just roll over! Use aimed shots to take out anybody who's in the open. Don't waste your time shooting at the armored vehicles; we have specially trained soldiers for that."

The last part was at least partially true. Lorelei had taken forty of her Shooters off to begin developing weapons capable of stopping the hodge-podge collection of armored cars, and the two old world tanks that the Vultures brought with them. She was a realist and knew that they had little chance of killing the vehicle itself. However, if they could knock the tracks off of the tanks and blow out the tires on the armored trucks, they wouldn't be able to move. Then the defenders had a chance to wipe out the crew in more traditional ways.

Aeric's words of encouragement heartened the defenders. They spread out like he'd ordered and the amount of outgoing fire lessoned dramatically as men and women took their time to aim at individual targets, instead of spraying bullets in the general direction of the enemy, hoping that one would find its way into the flesh of something.

He rushed behind the rusting hulk of an old pickup truck and unslung the 30.06 rifle from his back. It was the same weapon that he'd used as a paddle to escape across the lake. His body protested as he knelt, but he willed his mind to be quiet, to accept the pain since there was nothing that he could do about it. He pulled the bolt back and chambered a round, then settled the butt against his shoulder while he rested his cheek on the stock.

Aeric began the methodical work of shooting unsuspecting men and women as they charged towards the city across the killing field. The armored vehicles hung back and he wondered what the hell was going on. "Why aren't they shooting back or attacking with the trucks? They know we don't have anything capable of penetrating their armor."

Tyler held out his hand and said, "Wait a minute. Give me your binoculars."

Aeric lifted them off of his neck and passed them to his friend. After a few moments of adjusting the focus and then sweeping back and forth, he muttered, "They're decoys; unarmed men and women, probably prisoners. They're making us use up our ammo."

"And to demoralize us," Aeric said before calling for a cease fire through the megaphone.

Within minutes, the ragged cries and pleas for mercy drifted towards the defenders and a handful of the original prisoners who'd charged across the open came stumbling through the hole in the wall. They all wore long-sleeved shirts, with their arms pulled out of the sleeves and tied behind their backs. Black wooden sticks had been tied at the ends of their shirtsleeves to give them the appearance of soldiers charging with weapons as they ran.

Aeric pulled one of them behind the truck and forced him to his knees. "Who are you?"

"Javier, my lord. Please, don't kill us. We were just tending our crops with our families. None of us want any part of this."

"You're from Austin?"

Javier smiled, "That's what it used to be called, yes. Now they just call it The Nest. The Vulture Nest."

Chills ran down his spine as Aeric recalled the conversation that he had with Veronica regarding Maria's latest vision. She'd said that once the birds left the nest, nothing could stop them. Bullshit. His survival after being hunted all the way to the lake and then his escape had proven that her visions were just one possibility in an ever-changing future. He'd make sure that this one about the nest didn't come true either. He *would* stop them.

Shouts along the wall warned defenders to look out. The Vulture army was moving forward slowly. Once again, Kendrick's tactics proved to be effective as they gained well over three hundred yards before anyone began to fire at the real enemy. The defenders didn't want to risk shooting any more innocents and had allowed valuable stand-off range to be lost.

"Shoot!" Tyler yelled and then grabbed the megaphone from Aeric. "Shoot! This is the real attack!"

His words seemed to galvanize the defenders as first a few fired down at the advancing army, then several more joined in until finally the entire line was firing at the exposed enemy. That's when Kendrick ordered the two tanks to open fire.

They didn't target the individual soldiers on the line; they fired through the hole in the wall deeper into the city. Behind him, thousands of feet away, the shells exploded against buildings, killing and maiming people by the dozens. Then, the tanks stopped firing their high-explosive rounds through the holes and crewmen popped out of the hatches to fire the mounted machine guns. They raked the parapet. The smaller caliber 7.62 millimeter bullets of the loader and the coaxial gun sent shards of white-hot metal in every direction as they disintegrated against the brick defenses, while the larger .50 caliber that the tank commander fired punched holes through the masonry. It was a bloodbath.

Aeric took the opportunity to snipe one of the commanders. The bullet threw his head backwards and then he fell forward causing the barrel of the fifty-cal to aim skyward. The gun continued to fire as the weight of his body pressed against his hands, pouring rounds from the end of the barrel until the tube became so hot that it warped and rounds began to bounce from side to side down the tube. The end of the barrel exploded as one of the outgoing rounds impacted against another round that hadn't exited the tube yet.

The second tank commander noticed that his partner was dead and dropped inside the tank, immediately ceasing his own gunfire while the tank continued onward. Aeric smiled and called for a general withdrawal into the city. "Fall back! Fall back and fight them for every block. This is our home! We know where we can hide and shoot these bastards. We know where to go where they can't reach us. Your family's lives depend on the next couple of hours. Go, and make history!"

He and Tyler took a few more shots at the advancing Vultures before he heeded his own words and melted into the smoke-filled streets.

*****

Random sounds of gunfire echoed behind them and off to the east as they ran towards the Barrio. Aeric knew the gangs had started the fires that raged across the city and somehow, they'd rigged the wall to blow. The signs had been so obvious that they were up to no good. But he hadn't thought that anyone in San Angelo would have done something so foolish as to allow the Vultures inside the walls.

Hell, the gangs from the Barrio had been bold enough to wear the symbol of the Vultures openly and he'd been so focused on Maria's prophecy that he didn't catch it. He told himself that it was understandable since the green square hadn't been the Vulture's symbol when he'd been their captive and that no one had heard from them in the recent past. Ultimately, though, when it came down to it, he still blamed himself for the attack.

Kendrick had led the Vultures here because of his hatred for Aeric and his role in Justin's death. If it hadn't been for Aeric Traxx, the people of San Angelo wouldn't be facing certain death. They would have continued on with their lives, scraping out a meager survival on the edge of the wastes.

In the back of his mind, another voice countered his assessment. If it hadn't been for him, San Angelo might not have survived the first year. He'd been the one to send Lorelei and her platoon here. They'd been key in the city's defense and were responsible for training everyone in marksmanship and patrol techniques. He and Tyler had led the Gathering Squad into Garden City where they found Ted Winston. Ted had engineered the walls that protected the city for three decades and converted the engines of the trucks and heavy equipment from gasoline to steam. The Gathering Squad had been responsible for finding the seeds that grew the crops and bringing the goats from the wasteland into the city for milk, butter and meat. No, Aeric Traxx may be why the Vultures were here now, but he wasn't the reason for the city's demise.

"It's right up here," he huffed, pointing towards a hole in the makeshift wall that the residents had constructed around the Barrio.

Tyler glanced at him pointedly and said, "It's my body that's failing, not my mind."

"Sorry," Aeric replied. He'd forgotten that Tyler was one of the people who helped establish the grocery store as a temporary housing area when they'd moved the walls for the third time; the residents had refused to relocate any more after that.

"Hold up," Tyler whispered as he grabbed the meat of Aeric's upper arm.

Aeric slowed to a walk, and then quietly stalked forward, mimicking Tyler's movements until they were at the gate, hidden from view of the other side. The big man reached out and grabbed the end of a rifle, yanking a startled boy off his feet into the street. He clamped a hand over the youth's mouth and then wrestled to subdue him. Aeric could see that even the little bit of fight that the boy put up was wearing down the big man.

He pulled out his knife and waved it in front of the boy's eyes, causing him to go limp and stop fighting. "Thanks," Tyler panted. "I just don't have the energy anymore."

Aeric ducked his chin in acknowledgement. The cancer was eating away at Tyler. "Listen here, kid," he added a menacing tone to his voice. "I'm going to give you one chance to tell me how many Vultures there are in the Barrio."

"I... I don't know," the boy stammered.

"Not good enough," Aeric hissed and plunged the knife deep into the teen's shoulder. Tyler reacted too slowly in replacing his hand and the boy's strangled cries of pain echoed briefly across the gloom.

"I'm going to ask you again. Look at me." Aeric poked him hard in the ribs with the tip of the knife, "Look at me, dammit! You see these scars on my face? I know how to torture someone for days without killing them. Is that what you want?"

The boy shook his head violently from side to side. "You have an opportunity here. If you tell me what I need to know, I'll kill you quickly, painlessly. If you don't, you'll be strung along, wishing for a death that won't come. Do you understand?"

Hot tears fell against Tyler's hand as the Vulture realized the consequences of his choice to join the gang. Aeric couldn't risk leaving the kid alive when he went into the Barrio—or allow him to grow up to be a man who hated Traxx and his family like the other Vultures.

"We have a deal?" Aeric asked.

Tyler uncovered his mouth and he sputtered, "Please! Please, let me go! I leave. I never come back. I—"

Aeric shut him up with a punch to his stomach. "Not the deal, kid. You made your bed, now you've gotta lie in it. The choice is yours how you go out though. Quick or slow?"

The youth thought about it for a moment and then nodded his head slowly, accepting his fate. "Ten soldiers and Mr. Huerta. He leader here."

Aeric cursed under his breath, "Huerta. I should have known that he was mixed up with this too. Ten including you or are you number eleven?" He couldn't risk allowing any of them to survive and escape to shoot him in the back.

"I the ten one," he replied in the strange dialect that had developed in the Barrio.

"Okay, the fires, how many did you guys light?"

"All 'dem. Sewers filled with years of shit, burns hot. City will burn. No help now."

"God damn it!" he muttered, enunciating each syllable. "Where are the other Vultures?"

"Everywhere."

Aeric stabbed downward into his thigh, eliciting a screech that Tyler quickly cut off. "Sorry, wasn't expecting that," he said sheepishly.

"Where are the Vultures from the Barrio?" Aeric asked, clarifying his question.

The boy sobbed in pain and replied, "Inside. All back from starting fires."

"Where is Huerta?"

"At demonbroc nest. Gonna let them go."

Aeric thought for a minute about what to ask next. "Explain to me how to get to the nest."

The boy gave him directions to the secret entrance into an unused labyrinth of tunnels, blocked off from the rest of the sewer system. The entryway was in the old supermarket through the back of the store. "Anything else you want to say?" he asked in contempt of the Vulture who'd helped to engineer the collapse of his city and condemned the residents who survived to more hardship.

"I sorry, Traxx. I never want to hurt people."

Aeric nodded to Tyler who wrapped one hand firmly around the youth's chest and the other at the top of his head, pulling it backwards to expose his throat. "You brought this on yourself, kid. May God have mercy on your soul."

The blood sprayed from the teenager's throat like water from a fire hydrant when firefighters used to open them to let off the pressure. The initial burst of arterial blood covered Aeric and then bubbled down his chest, over Tyler's arm, pooling in the gravel around the big man's pants. Once the muscle contractions stopped, Tyler gently lowered the Vulture to the ground and reached up for Aeric's hand to pull himself up.

"Did you have to do that," he asked sadly.

Aeric stared hard up into his friend's eyes. "Do you want Kayla and Anna to survive? These people are the reason our city is burning down. They don't care about anyone except for themselves. We have to wipe them off the face of the earth. Otherwise, they're just going to continue attacking us until we're all dead."

Tyler nodded. *He didn't have to like it,* Aeric thought; *he just had to do it*. For their families' safety, this nest of Vultures had to be cleared out. They were exceptionally dangerous to the city's residents because they lived here and were known by everyone. They could easily infiltrate a group of defenders or refugees in Tennyson and murder every one of them while they slept.

It didn't take long for them to find two more of the Vultures in the Barrio. A woman's screams directed Aeric and Tyler towards the shadows less than a block from the gate where they brutalized her. Tyler's inhibitions at killing the teenagers disappeared as he swung his old baseball bat into the back of one of their heads, caving it inwards several inches as the skull shattered and drove the sharp fragments into his brain. Aeric had to break their silent approach and shoot the second when he pulled his own rifle up to his shoulder.

"Three," Tyler stated quietly as he watched the naked woman run towards the supermarket where she probably lived.

Luckily, the sounds of gunfire all around the city drowned out the sound of Aeric's rifle and no one came to investigate the disturbance. Neither of them liked being out in the open as they planned out their next steps but they had no choice. It didn't make any sense to search the entire compound. They didn't have much time to get to Huerta before the city would be completely overrun by the Vultures and their families' escape route to Tennyson was cut off. If he released those damned brocs, it would be a bloodbath.

"Let's go," Aeric muttered as more screams filled the night.

They found numbers four and five giving the same woman a hard time outside of the supermarket. She fought to pull herself away from one of them as the other held a pistol at his side, laughing at his fellow gang member's struggle.

"Fuck! What is it with these assholes?" Tyler whispered.

"They target people who can't fight back," Aeric stated calmly as he centered the crosshairs of his rifle on the head of the thug holding the pistol. "The Barrio hoodrats are weak, pathetic creatures who prey on those who are weaker than them."

He stopped talking and squeezed the trigger. The side of the supermarket became painted in a mixture of red, white and pink as blood, skull fragments and brain matter splattered against the dingy walls. The one holding the woman released her and began screaming in unison with the woman as he watched his friend's insides ooze down the wall. The Vulture turned to run back inside and Aeric took him low in the back then chambered another round.

"Come on. They know we're here now."

Tyler chased after Aeric as fast as he could, but even crossing the old parking lot was too much exertion for him, causing him to fall behind. Aeric glanced backwards and waved his friend forward.

The pain in his back and the overall exhaustion that he'd felt for the past several days—years, honestly—melted away. His body's endorphins had kicked in, giving him a short-term rush of energy that caused the aches and pains of his everyday life to dull. He had to wipe these people out, expunge them from San Angelo's record.

He slowed as he got nearer to the front door. The teen that he'd shot in the back clawed his way towards the entrance, both of his legs dragging uselessly behind him in a trail of blood and viscera. He'd hit the thug's spine. Aeric slammed the butt of his rifle into the base of his skull, causing his forehead to hit the cement and bounce back up comically. The blood that began to ooze slowly from his ear canal told Aeric that he'd successfully incapacitated the youth.

He flattened against the wall near the wailing woman and Tyler came huffing up. "Get out of here," Aeric ordered. "It's not safe."

"My babies are inside," she cried.

He stood rooted in indecision for a moment and then said, "Do you want to see your children again?"

She didn't answer so he asked again, louder. Terrorizing some poor woman wasn't how he wanted to be remembered, so he held up his hands to calm her down. "Look, I'm sorry this happened to you. We need to get inside if we're going to stop Huerta before he does anything else to sabotage the city. Can you get us past the door?"

"Huh?" she asked dumbly.

"Inside. We need to get inside. Edward Huerta is the cause of all of this. He's the leader of all these gangs. They started the fires."

"Huerta?"

"Geez… We're gonna go in and get those gang members. I need you to be our decoy." She stared blankly at him and finally, he said, "We're going to save your children. I need you to take us inside."

The mention of her children spurred her mind from wherever it had taken flight and she nodded her head roughly. "We'll follow behind you and stay off to the side until you clear the doorway. Do you understand?"

"What about my children?"

"Miss… I'm sorry, what's your name?"

"Megan. Megan West," she replied.

"Megan, as soon as the other Vultures dismiss you as a non-threat, go to them. I don't care what you do after that." He amended his harsh tone once again, "Sorry. I don't mean that. Once we get inside, there's going to be shooting. You need to get to your family and keep them safe. Then, when you can, you need to leave the city, Megan. Go to our back up location in Tennyson. San Angelo has fallen and it's Huerta's fault."

Megan accepted his apology and steeled herself to walk into the supermarket. Aeric rested the heavier 30.06 rifle on the side of the building and unslung the compact M-4 that was designed for fighting in an enclosed space. Tyler followed his lead and slid the baseball bat into the converted arrow quiver on his back in exchange for a pistol. He'd been out of the game so long because of his illness that he didn't even have a rifle anymore; those had all gone to the defenders on the wall.

Aeric was amazed to see the way Megan was able to calmly walk to the building, open the door and then quickly cover her private areas. Smoke flowed in through the doorway and they used it to help disguise their entrance behind her.

Rough-sounding words came from the mouths of the young gang members inside. Smoky torches burned along the top of several of the aisle-dividing, shelving units causing the Vultures to be silhouetted against the light, further helping to disguise Aeric and Tyler's movements. They quickly crouched behind one of the old cash register stations near the doorway and listened to the exchange between the woman and the boys who'd doomed his city.

"Hey, bitch. Rat and Poncho done with you already?"

"Yeah, they finished quickly," Megan replied, her voice shaky. "They said they had to get ready for a fight or something."

"We can have a turn, den."

"I have to take a shit," she countered.

"Eww. You nasty," a different young voice stated.

"Sorry, gang rape does that to me." Aeric grinned at her choice of words. She was a feisty one. Maybe he'd been wrong about her being a victim. Maybe she put on whatever mask helped to keep her and her family alive.

"Go on. Get outta here, gross-ass bitch."

He saw her shadow march resolutely across the wall behind him and risked a quick peek around the conveyor belt. He counted four boys, all holding rifles, sitting in old folding chairs facing the door. They'd exchanged their homemade spears somewhere along the line for the rifles—either they'd had them all along and kept them hidden or they'd taken them off of dead defenders at the walls.

There wasn't a sign of the fifth Vulture, but Aeric decided to risk it. They'd be unlikely to get a juicier target than four of them all together, not paying attention. He whispered to Tyler the setup of the boys and told him that he had the responsibility of taking out the one on the far left and he'd deal with the other three since he had the semi-automatic rifle.

Aeric held up three fingers and said, "On the count of three. One... Two... THREE!"

They both stood and began firing. The *pop* of Tyler's 9-millimeter pistol sounded loud in the confined space compared to the relatively quiet M-4. Two of the boys went down without ever knowing what happened. Aeric nailed the third as he lay on the ground where he'd dived, not quite making it behind a pile of wood that sat near an old grill.

There wasn't any sign of the fourth Vulture who'd been there a moment before. After a brief pause, a squeaky voice yelled out that he surrendered, trying to make himself heard over the terrified screams of the other supermarket residents.

"Come on out—and keep your hands where I can see them," Aeric ordered.

A pair of grubby hands extended from behind the wood pile followed by the body of a thirteen year-old boy. Aeric squinted in the dim light and recognized him as the gang member that he'd punched when he came to see Maria for the first time.

"Nice and easy, Flame," Aeric said.

The boy flinched and said, "Mr. Traxx? That you?"

"Yeah. How many of you are there, Flame? How many of you became Vultures?"

He thought about it for a minute and replied, "Ten. Plus, Mr. Edward. He always been Vulture."

"Shit," Aeric muttered. He'd *always* been a Vulture. "Do you know where your other friend is? You, your friend and Huerta are all that's left."

The boy's shoulders slumped. He hadn't expected to hear that everyone else was dead. "Claw with Mr. Edward in tunnels," Flame replied.

"Claw? I thought he died," Aeric asked in confusion.

"No. He okay. No dick, but he alive."

"The entrance to the tunnels are in the back of the store, right? Are there any secret traps or anything?"

"Why should I tell you, Traxx?"

"Because if you tell me the truth, I'll forgive you for getting mixed up with the Vultures."

The boy's shadow nodded and he said, "No traps. Tunnels start in big metal box floor."

"There's a trap door or something?" Tyler asked.

"Uh, sure. Door in floor." He laughed nervously at his own choice of rhyming words.

"Anything else we should know?"

"No. I told you everything. You let me go now?"

Aeric shifted his feet, brought his M-4 up rapidly like he'd been taught. He fired two quick rounds into Flame's chest and followed the boy's falling body with the muzzle until he was sure he was dead. The screams that had quieted down to a collective whimper erupted once again and several people ran towards the storeroom in the back. It was going to be a lot more difficult to find Huerta and Claw if they were intermingled with a bunch of supermarket residents.

Tyler glanced over at him with his one good eye and said accusingly, "You told that boy you'd forgive him for what he'd done if he told you the truth."

"What?" Aeric shrugged. "I forgave him... I forgave him for condemning thousands of people to their death. I can't let someone like that stay alive, though. Imagine if he made it to Tennyson and people knew that he'd been one of the people to blow up the wall and start the fires."

"You've lost your way, Aeric," Tyler accused. He gestured vaguely towards the eastern border of the city where the Vultures had attacked. "Somewhere along this journey, you've become one of them."

"Ty, that's not—"

"No. I don't want to hear it, Aeric. You've lost it, man. You've done things in the heat of the moment before that I was able to look past or make excuses for. Remember that Wal-Mart where you shot that man in the back and then we walked by his family like nothing was wrong? Or what about Sterling City and that music hall?"

"I did those things to survive. The guy at the Wal-Mart was to protect you, Tyler."

The big man nodded his head. "We've both done some fucked up shit, Aeric. And I acknowledge that fact, but you murdered that boy in cold blood." Tyler paused, making Aeric think that he was organizing his thoughts. "When this is over, if we survive, I'm going to the council. You're not fit to lead this city anymore. You've become just like the Vultures. We're through after this."

His words hit Aeric harder than any punch he'd ever taken. They felt worse than when Justin had tortured him and paraded around with Kate on his arm. The sting of his words hurt more than when she'd died and even more than Judd's information about his stepson's hatred of him. The feeling of emptiness welled up inside him and threatened to overtake him.

Like Veronica, Tyler had been with him from the beginning. He'd been his roommate and teammate in college before the war and had been with him every step of the way since then, with the exception of his assassination attempt in Austin a week ago. The man had been there for the birth of all of his and Veronica's children, even several of his grandchildren; he never thought it would come to this. Sure, their relationship had deteriorated slightly over time as Tyler and Aeric became more involved with their own families, but they'd always been there for each other.

"Okay, Ty. If that's how you feel, then so be it," Aeric conceded. He swallowed hard and continued, "I viewed Flame as a legitimate threat to the safety of this community and was in a position to put an end to that threat. I took that opportunity and I'd do it again if it meant keeping my wife and kids—and your family—safe for another day."

Tyler sighed heavily and ejected the magazine on his pistol. He dug around in his pocket and pulled out a few more bullets and crammed them on top of the others in the magazine until it reached capacity. He pushed it back into place and mumbled, "Let's just get this over with and put an end to Huerta."

Aeric followed his lead and swapped out magazines as well before walking towards the back of the store where the entrance to the demonbroc breeding tunnels were supposedly located. He'd just started down one of the aisles when Megan appeared, clothed, and thanked them for helping her. She gave each of them a hug and promised that she'd see them in Tennyson as she herded two little kids towards the exit.

They continued once she was gone and had to step over cowering residents, while also avoiding those who ran, screaming at the sight of their weapons. Aeric eased his way through the door when they arrived at the back of the store. It was dark and there were heaps and heaps of clothing and pilfered goods piled haphazardly. It didn't help that they had no idea what Claw looked like, but either he or Huerta could have easily been hiding behind any one of the piles.

"Now we know where all the stolen goods are going," Aeric muttered, which Tyler ignored as he scanned the room.

Screams of panic and fear echoed around the storeroom. They were muffled and didn't sound like they were on the same level of the building. "Those must be coming from the tunnels," Aeric surmised.

"This way," Tyler answered, walking rapidly towards an old cardboard crushing machine. The sounds seemed to be coming from inside.

"Big metal box," Aeric shrugged and indicated a door in the side of the machine with his chin. "Kid wasn't lying."

They found the door's release lever and it swung outward to reveal an enclosed, vacant space inside the crusher where the banded cardboard used to sit, ready to be sent to the recycling center in the old days. Centered in the floor of the storage area, a wooden door fit roughly over what appeared to be a hand-hewn hole in the cement floor.

"I'll move the door, you cover the hole," Tyler stated.

"Okay. I'm ready," he replied as he bent his knees slightly and aimed his weapon at the hole.

The moment Tyler pulled the cover away all hell broke loose. People, covered in gashes and bleeding profusely, tumbled up the stairs. Several held long, glistening ropes of intestines in their hands, uselessly trying to keep them from dragging on the ground or getting trampled by the crush of bodies behind them. Aeric was practically bowled over by the press of bodies and he slid up against the side of the cage as they rushed out.

Below, a strange mixture of mewling and harsh, angry growls floated through the opening. As the flow of humanity ebbed, the screams coming from the tunnel had stopped, replaced by grunts of pain and the wet, sickening sound of tearing flesh.

"Cover it up! Cover it up!" he shouted to Tyler, who stared dumbly at the bloody mass of fleeing residents making their way out of the storeroom.

"Huh? Oh, the door." He bent and picked up the heavy wooden slab, and slid it back into place. A dark gray paw thrust through the opening right before it closed. Three six-inch, razor-sharp claws unsheathed and the paw batted uselessly at empty space until the wood crushed its leg. What sounded like the screech of a banshee in some campy horror movie reverberated through the small space inside the crusher.

The door started to move slightly as it was hit from underneath. Something was clearly trying to get out. "We need to move, now!" Aeric ordered before racing out of the machine. He slammed the locks into place the moment Tyler cleared the doorway.

"That'll hold them for a second. We are in some really deep shit."

"Was that what I think it was?"

"Yeah. Fucking Huerta has been breeding them for meat. No telling how many of them are down there. Now they're loose, we've got to get out of here now."

They burst into the sleeping area of the supermarket and Aeric began waving his arms above his head, shouting, "Everyone needs to leave now! The demonbrocs have escaped from the tunnels!"

Several of the residents looked up from where they crouched, attempting to render aid to the injured who'd emerged from the tunnels below the supermarket. "Leave them! They're going to die anyways," he yelled as he shoved a woman away from a teenager covered with lacerations, including a cut on his thigh deep enough to see the quivering muscle beneath the skin. His femoral artery whipped back and forth, spraying blood everywhere. The kid was a goner and wouldn't survive more than a few minutes at best, Aeric thought. That's when he noticed the blood-soaked square of cloth on his shirt.

The ear-shattering screech of bone claws raking against the cardboard crushing machine's metal walls tore his eyes from the identification marking to the back room. The fucking beasts had made it out of the tunnels. It wouldn't be long before they ripped their way through the thin steel side of the holding area.

Aeric bent over, heedless of the blood spraying across his face and hands, and grasped the boy's shirt, pulling his upper body up off of the ground. "Claw! Claw, look at me. Where is Huerta?"

The boy's eyes refused to focus on him as he answered, "Told me…let brocs out. Went to…"

Aeric shook the kid violently, the rough fabric of his shirt causing the wound from the thorn in his hand to reopen. His blood mingled with the gore that cascaded out of the Vulture as he asked through clenched teeth, "Dammit, Claw! Where did Huerta go?"

"North… northern gate," Claw answered breathlessly, his head lolling backwards, stretching to the limit his skin allowed.

"Goddammit, Claw! What about the Northern Gate?" he asked as he shook him again. Aeric set him down and then pulled his head up by the hair so the boy could see his ruined face. "What's he doing up there? Claw! Is he going to Tennyson?"

The Vulture's eyes stared off towards the light of one of the torches. He was too far gone to form words. Aeric released his grip on the shock of hair and his head dropped heavily to the ground. He stood up and turned to Tyler, "Huerta escaped. He's going to the Northern Gate. I don't know if he's trying to block off our escape route or if he's trying to leave before the demonbrocs kill everything they see. We need to stop him."

Tyler looked at Claw's blood streaming down Aeric's face in disgust. "We can warn the residents about the evacuation on the way there. Let's go."

They ran as fast as their tired, broken bodies would carry them from the supermarket. Behind them, the piercing shrieks of the people who'd chosen to ignore their warnings about the demonbrocs echoed across the Barrio and they died by the hundreds.

SIXTEEN

"Where is he, dammit?" Kendrick screamed in frustration while his men turned over the mangled bodies near the wall so he could see their faces.

He'd allowed the bulk of his army to move forward and continue the attack while he held back to find Traxx's body. That arrogant bastard would have surely been at the gate, prepared to fight. Except for the fact that there was no proof, Kendrick was certain that he was dead. There was simply no way that he had survived the explosion. They'd searched for his body among the hundred or so bodies at the breach point and none of them belonged to his stepfather. It was maddening.

"Perhaps we should consider that he wasn't here at the gate, or that he somehow survived the explosion, my lord," Quellan offered.

Kendrick whirled on the man and then checked his temper; Quellan had done nothing to him and had been a loyal right-hand man. "Eh, maybe you're right, old friend. You don't know him like I do, though. He's one of those 'lead from the front' kind of guys that you read about in stories. You know the type, the do-gooders who can do no wrong and their people would follow them to Hell and back."

"Didn't that *do-gooder* assassinate eighteen of our men in cold blood? I would hardly call him a hero."

"He's no hero," Kendrick agreed. "The people love him because he's a natural leader who does what has to be done, regardless of the damage. I'd have expected him here at the gate, getting himself shot at instead of running the defense of the city like he should have been doing."

"Well, he's not here, maybe he's learned a thing or two since you left fifteen years ago... My lord," he amended quickly.

Kendrick, too lost in his own thoughts, didn't notice Quellan's insubordinate statement. Instead, he wondered where the bastard could have gone. It wasn't like he'd be able to escape from the city. Where else could they go?

"Oh my god," Kendrick said. "There's a town, north of here. It's called..." he trailed off as he attempted to dredge the name from his memory. After a few seconds, he grasped it and pulled it to the surface of his murky thoughts. "Tennyson."

"My lord?" Quellan asked.

"They have a fallback location in Tennyson," he answered. "It's an abandoned town fifteen or twenty miles past the Northern Gate. When I left, they were planning to build fortifications there that would allow for someplace secure in the event of a problem in San Angelo."

"Should we move against this place?"

Kendrick banged his open palm against the hood of an old pickup truck that sat near the gate. "We can't split our forces now. We should have blocked off the Northern Gate before we attacked. I forgot about it."

"It's okay, my lord, we'll—"

"Forgot about what?" Starr asked as she walked up to the two men from wherever she'd been in the wastes. She was naked and smiling, covered head to toe in gore; clearly she'd enjoyed whatever she'd been doing.

"What is all over you? Is that blood?" Kendrick asked.

Her grin widened maniacally and she responded, "Mmm...hmm. I've been bathing in the blood of our enemies. You're supposed to do it too."

"Why on earth would you do that?" he questioned.

"The blood sacrifice will grant us access to their souls. With their souls, we can gain control of their confidence. Then, after I consume a few special parts, you're assured a victory against the giant!"

"This again? I told you, I'll just kill Tyler with my gun or have somebody shoot him. I'm not stupid enough to I'd fight him hand-to-hand." He thought about what she'd said and then asked, "Wait, did you say *consume*?"

Starr ignored him and continued on, "He told me this will work. I just have to eat some of their muscles for strength and a heart or two, for courage. Then—"

"What?" he choked. "Who told you those things?"

She clapped her hands and hopped slightly in an annoying gesture that she'd recently adopted. Partially-dried clusters of filth fell from her, landing on the pavement with tiny plops as the blood splattered against her bare feet. "*He* told me."

Kendrick looked towards the area where he'd last seen her fifteen minutes ago. She'd been examining bodies like he'd been doing, except she didn't know what Traxx looked like. "He, who?"

"You know..." she tapped her forefinger on the side of her head. "I heard Him. He spoke to me! Isn't that wonderful?"

Kendrick frowned. Out of the corner of his eye, he saw Quellan shift closer from where he'd stood apart at a respectful distance away, edging closer to the two of them. "The Vultures don't need help from some voice in your head, Starr, and we don't need to steal the souls of these people. We'll assure our own victory."

She scowled at him, placing her hands on her hips. "I thought you'd like that I took an interest in your war."

"An interest?"

"Yeah, this silly little fight you have going on over the murder of someone that you never even met."

He didn't understand her thought process. One minute she was talking about a voice telling her to wallow around in blood and intestines of their enemies, then the next she was saying she did it to show some type of common interest with him. She'd always been more than a little off in the head and he'd thought that it kept things exciting and interesting with her. But now, he legitimately wasn't sure of her sanity.

Starr had always exhibited an overzealous fondness for torture, and she liked being fist-fucked by severed appendages—which was odd until it became an exciting part of their sex life. And, truth be told, Kendrick had heard the voices whispering in his own head, urging him to avenge his father's death. Oftentimes, those voices threatened to overwhelm him and drive him mad, but he'd been able to keep them in check so far.

He'd felt that she was slipping for a long time and it caused an internal conflict within him. He enjoyed her company because she was just as crazy as he was. The difference was that he walked a razor's edge between sanity and madness; it was clear to him that Starr had lost the battle against her inner demons. It was time to let her go.

"Starr, I need you to go back to Austin."

Her eyes narrowed. "What?"

"You are relieved of your duties to me. Go back to Austin and remove your things from the palace."

Her face contorted in rage and she lunged at him. A burst of speed from Quellan brought him between the two of them and he clotheslined her, knocking her backwards.

Starr sat on the ground, staring daggers at them and clutching her throat where Quellan's arm had impacted. "You. You son of a bitch!" she spat. "I have done everything for you! Murdered, lied, fucked...murdered some more. Everything I've ever done has been for you!"

"Starr, leave now or I will have Quellan shoot you like the pathetic dog that you are." The captain placed the muzzle of his rifle on the bridge of her nose to emphasize Kendrick's point.

"You wouldn't shoot me. You're *mine*," she hissed.

"I was never yours, you crazy fucking whore," he stated. "You were a useful distraction while I prepared for this 'silly little war' as you called it."

"A distraction? You're calling me a distraction?"

Quellan stabbed the rifle forward into her cheek, knocking her head back slightly. She scrambled backwards on her ass out of the way. "You'll pay for this, you little-dicked asshole. I'll kill you and eat your testicles!"

Kendrick shuddered. "I already regret it. I should kill you right now and be rid of you. We've shared so much over the years that it wouldn't feel right, though." He smiled sadly down at her, "I do care for you, Starr; otherwise, you'd already be dead. Please, leave before I change my mind."

He turned and strode deeper into the city of San Angelo towards the sound of gunfire, away from her screeches of promised pain and death. Kendrick put her out of his mind and thought about Traxx. If he wasn't killed at the breach, he'd surely be leading the defense, giving the residents more time to escape out the Northern Gate. He'd catch him and there would be no mercy given to *that* one.

*****

"Leave me!" Joseph screamed to his squad mate.

"No way, buddy," Gloria answered. "I spent too much time patching up that leg. I'm not gonna let you lie down and die now."

She didn't allow him to argue; instead she looped her hand through the back of his equipment suspenders and pulled him towards the second barricade around the Provisions Warehouse. Somehow, the two of them had gotten left behind at the first earthwork when the Shooters repositioned to the other barrier.

Joseph cursed his fucked up leg. He knew how they'd 'accidentally' been left behind. He was a liability. Without the ability to move around, anyone who stayed with him ran the risk of being surrounded and then dispatched at the Vultures' leisure.

He ejected the magazine from his M-4 and slapped a new one into place as Gloria drug him on his ass back towards the rest of the defenders. He pulled the charging handle back on the rifle to chamber a round and pushed with his right leg, attempting to help Gloria.

They were still twenty feet from the second barricade when the Vultures swarmed over the top of the first line of defense. The Shooters behind him began firing and he jerked up his rifle, shooting while still moving in the opposite direction. He saw two of the attackers fall from his aimed fire and he silently thanked Captain Griffith for all the seemingly pointless training that she'd put the Shooters through.

Far across the dead space between the two earthworks, the sound of a revving engine filled the air. Vultures scattered sideways and then the brick wall exploded. The front deck of one of the Vultures' tanks burst through the barricade, pausing half-way through the obstacle. Oily black smoke belched from the engine as whatever they'd used for fuel propelled the monstrosity forward. The exhaust combined with the clouds of filth from the burning city to create an effective screening smoke for the Vultures on the ground, who used the cover to advance.

When they'd rammed the wall, the tank crew had turned the gun around over the back deck to keep it from getting damaged when they demolished the earthworks. The tank pushed the rest of the way through the wall and began to rotate the main gun back towards the front once they'd cleared the debris. Although he'd never seen a tank before today, he'd seen enough to know plenty about their capabilities. If they got the turret around before he and Gloria had made it to the safety of the barricade, there would be nothing left of them.

He screamed at her to hurry and risked a glance over his shoulder. Gloria had dragged him to within ten feet of the second set of earthworks. Joseph allowed the hope to blossom in his chest that they'd make it behind the wall.

And then his hope was shattered.

The rapid reports of a heavy machine gun hit him moments after Gloria's blood cascaded down onto his helmet into his eyes.

She slumped forward, dead before she hit the ground. Joseph abandoned his attempts to fire his weapon; his little rifle couldn't do anything against the armor of a tank. He flipped over onto his stomach and pulled himself towards the barricade, fleeing in terror from the beast that had punched ten, fist-sized holes through his friend in two seconds.

He heard the tank surge forward behind him. The metal treads clanked across what used to be a parking lot thirty years ago. Now it was a killing field. He'd almost made it to the base of the wall when his eardrums shattered and he was thrown against the brick. Debris and pieces of earthwork fell down on him from a large hole in the barricade. They'd fired the main gun from less than a hundred feet away.

Blood poured in thick streams from his ears and nose. He kept crawling as best as his shattered body would allow through the hole that the tank had created in the wall. He barely made it through when his right let went white-hot. He rolled to the side up over chunks of rock and lay on his back behind the faulty protection of the barricade. Men and women ran towards the north, no longer bothering to defend their supplies or the city against the onslaught of the Vultures.

Joseph looked down at his ruined body through a haze of blood and sweat. He was seeing double, maybe triple and couldn't focus. He'd been shot through his uninjured leg. *It must have been a small caliber bullet*, he thought, detached from his current situation. The round had entered below his calf and exited from his abdomen near his belly button. He was done for.

Through the ringing in his ears, the clanking of the tank echoed like it was in a tunnel. Joseph knew that he was dying.

He could accept death in battle, but not getting crushed by the tank's treads; where was the dignity in that? He turned back onto his stomach and clawed his way up the dirt of the earthworks to gain elevation, out of the path of the armored vehicle.

Once again, the barricade exploded inwards when they rammed the second wall. He cried out hoarsely as his body slowly slid down the rampart towards the tank. He tried uselessly to gain a handhold in the dirt, but couldn't stop his momentum. The slide turned into a full-on fall and he rolled downwards. The fall ended with him thudding roughly on top of the vehicle's turret.

He felt the beast surge forward underneath him as the tank crew pushed completely through the second wall. He was dizzy and the edges of his vision started to go black. He fought against the feeling, begging the God of his forefathers for a little more time on Earth.

He was rolled gently from his back onto his stomach when the tank's turret turned, bringing the gun back to the front. Close by his head, the sound of metal scraping against metal caused him to turn slightly towards the noise. He stared at a round metal door of some kind and beyond the door, a man had emerged. The man leaned forward to fire the large machine gun mounted in front of the opening towards the fleeing Shooters.

He giggled slightly to himself and pulled the last two grenades from his suspenders. They'd given him an opportunity to avenge Gloria's senseless death. The pull-rings fit perfectly into the cuts in the joints of his fingers and he jerked them out.

With the last of his strength, Joseph pulled himself to the hatch and dropped both grenades inside.

*****

"Ah, fuck! I've gotta slow down, Traxx."

He turned and regarded Tyler. Why should he care what he felt like? He'd made it evident that their friendship was over after this, so what did it matter? He slowed to a walk. It *did* matter to him. They'd been friends and helped each other out more than he could have ever imagined in ten lifetimes. He hadn't stopped caring about the big guy, even if Tyler had given up on him.

"Okay. We can walk a couple of blocks, but no more."

Tyler nodded and then started coughing. He bent over double, hacking violently. The pavement turned dark underneath him as fluid expelled from his lungs. It was more than a simple reaction to the acrid smoke that hung low across the city; it was his body failing him.

Aeric gave him a few moments before asking, "Are you gonna make it?"

Tyler straightened out and gave him a bloody grin. The dark red fluid ran from his nose, over his lips and dripped from his chin to land on his barrel chest. "Won't be long now. This has taken too much out of me."

"The cancer?"

"Yeah. I ain't got long before I'm done." He took several deep breaths and smeared the bloody mucus across his face with the back of his hands. "Okay, I'm ready."

They started walking towards the north again, darting between shadows and hiding in patches of low-hanging smoke when they could. Aeric had decided to skip the Provisions Warehouse and head directly for the Northern Gate. Veronica would have gathered the family and gone there after Aiden passed his message that the city had fallen. Maybe she'd already taken it upon herself to lead them to Tennyson.

The old Air Force base passed by on their right and Aeric wondered about Lorelei and Joseph, the Shooter whom he'd grown fond of after their mission to Austin. Far to the western side of the city, probably near the Provisions Warehouse, a massive firefight still raged. They could hear the tanks firing and he hoped the Shooters would heed protocol. Their primary duty was to ensure the safety of the residents, not the supplies.

Several loud explosions reverberated from the west. It sounded like buildings crashed to the ground. The defenses around the Provisions Warehouse had surely fallen and the Vultures were destroying everything in their path. His city was gone.

"Aeric!" Tyler hissed. "We need to hide."

"Huh?"

Tyler jerked him sideways into an alley and put his finger to his lips. Aeric nodded in understanding. Several people walked by in the street. He couldn't make out who they were through the haze and ash. They all seemed to be armed, walking haphazardly without checking their surroundings; definitely *not* Shooters. It could have been residents of San Angelo who were going to the rally point or they could be Vultures, confident that they were in charge of the city.

A strangled noise came from Tyler and Aeric whipped his head around to see what was happening. The big man had his hand pressed against his mouth and covering his nose. He was trying to hold back another cough. If he let it out, whoever it was that had passed by would surely hear him and come down the alley to investigate. Aeric willed his friend to stop and keep it inside.

The group disappeared and Tyler allowed himself to cough. More blood flew outward between his fingers and ran down his arm. They waited for the inevitable return, weapons pointed at the head of the alley.

No one else appeared through the smoke, so they cautiously emerged from the alley onto the sidewalk. Tyler looked both ways. "I can't see anyone else," he said.

"Alright, let's go."

They passed several bodies, twisted grotesquely in death. Most of them had been shot in the back, gunned down as they fled. "The Vultures are heading towards the Northern Gate," Aeric surmised.

"Are we too late?"

"I don't know. The only thing we can do is keep going."

A small shadow appeared in the darkness and a whispered voice drifted towards them, "Grandad? Grandad, are you here?"

"Aiden? Aiden? Is that you?"

"Grandad!" The little boy materialized through the smoke and ran up to Aeric, who knelt down and hugged him.

He finally broke away from the embrace and held Aiden at arms' length. "What are you doing here, boy?"

"I came back to find you."

Aeric's lipped thinned as he pressed them together. "Did you get the message to your father and grandmother to evacuate the city?"

He nodded, "I told Grandma. She had all the grandkids with her. Dad and Mom were with Uncle John fighting against the Vultures."

It made sense. Every healthy person who wasn't charged with watching children was supposed to defend the city. "Did she listen? Did they get out of San Angelo?"

"Yes, sir. They left through the Northern Gate towards the town they're supposed to go to."

"Tennyson?"

"Yeah, that one. I ran back when they were leaving through the gate. I had to find you and Dad."

Aeric hugged him again. "It's not safe in the city, Aiden. You should have left with them."

"Well, we can leave together now," the boy reasoned. "Have you seen Dad?"

"No, I haven't, sorry. Let's keep moving. Maybe we'll find him on the way to the gate."

The three of them continued towards the Northern Gate. There was some type of temporary lull in the fighting, gunfire no longer sounded in the distance. They were only about half a mile from the exit and hadn't seen anyone else besides the group that passed them before they reunited with Aiden. Aeric began to wonder if Huerta had escaped along with everyone else.

If he'd escaped, he probably went to Tennyson with the refugees. No one knew that he was responsible for destroying the walls or burning the city. He could infiltrate with the rest of the residents and betray them again. Aeric had to put a stop to Huerta if his people were ever going to be safe.

They turned onto one of the paths through the old golf course towards the gates. The fairways had been turned into farmland in places where there'd been grass before the fall of the old world. He was lost in his thoughts when the haze erupted into flashes of light from the corn fields on the southern side of the path. They'd walked right into an ambush. Aeric was hit three times before he fell to the ground.

"Grandad!" Aiden screamed.

"Aeric, hold on!" Tyler shouted as he threw Aiden to the ground.

Bullets chewed up the cart path around him, carving out long, linear grooves into the pavement. Another round slammed into Aeric's ankle, shattering the bones. He cried out in pain, the other bullets had hit soft tissue and hadn't been nearly as painful.

He felt himself jerked backwards as Tyler yanked his arm to pull him behind an old stone park bench. "Hang in there, buddy," the big man grunted.

Aeric's head lolled to the side. He was quickly losing consciousness. He must have been hit worse than he thought. *How long has it been since was shot?* he wondered. He had so much more to do; he didn't have time to recover from an injury. He had to go to Austin...wait, that wasn't right, he'd already done that. He needed to stop the birds from attacking people in the park, right?

His eyes focused for a moment on the dark green leaves of the sweet potato plants beside the path. *Wait, why are the bushes so tall?* He realized that he was looking *up* at them. Was he on the ground? He remembered working to plant the crops, but couldn't recall the time since then when they grew to their current height. He tried to wipe his hand across his face. Nothing happened. What was wrong with him?

Small thuds of rounds impacting against the opposite side of the bench and someone returning fire nearby reminded him that he was in a fight. He had to help!

A little boy's face appeared over him. *Who?* It was Aiden, his grandson. "Hey, little buddy," Aeric murmured, his tongue thick in his mouth.

"Grandad! Are you okay?"

"Mmm…hmm. Sleepy," he replied.

Tyler, his lifelong friend, the man whom he would give his own life for, showed up. *Where did he come from?* "Aeric, I'm sorry."

"It's okay, bro." Something was wrong with his mouth; it didn't sound anything like what he'd expected it to.

"Aeric, I'm sorry. I didn't mean what I said about our friendship being through. You're the strongest person that I've ever met," Tyler blubbered.

Is it raining? Why is Tyler's face wet? he asked himself in confusion. *Oh no! Acid rain is going to ruin the crops.* They had to harvest what they could before it was too late.

"Everything you've ever done to help our city has been selfless. You've made those decisions that I wasn't strong enough to make myself."

Aeric grinned, "It's okay, Big Guy. You don't need to be sorry."

"I promise you that I'll keep your family safe, the Vultures won't get to them," Tyler continued.

"Vultures?" he muttered. *Of course, the gang from Austin!* They were under attack, he had to fight. He couldn't feel his weapon, had he lost it somehow?

A shock of black hair spread across his face as Aiden fell over him and hugged his torso tightly. Aeric's body lifted up slightly, then again as Tyler pulled the boy away from him. Aiden was covered in blood. It spread over one side of his face and across his chest. *Oh no! Was his grandson injured?*

"Grandad, you're gonna be okay," the boy sobbed.

Once again, Aeric tried to raise his hand so he could check Aiden for injuries, without success. *Why won't my body respond?*

"Aiden, we need to go," Tyler said. "There's nothing we can do for him. He's gone."

"No!" Aiden screamed. "We can't leave him."

"We can't take him. We need to go."

From far away, Aeric heard Tyler say something about lungs and intestines. *What did that mean?*

There wasn't any light calling him home. He didn't feel himself floating upwards or any of the other clichés that he'd heard about dying when he was a kid. The darkness simply closed in around him and he knew no more.

SEVENTEEN

"They've stopped firing my lord," Quellan stated.

Kendrick turned to the captain of his palace guard and regarded him silently. The man had proven himself time and again to be particularly adroit, however he also had a tendency to state the obvious, which was getting as tiresome as Starr's lunacy had become. *Was it time to make a change in his position as well?* he wondered.

"I know they've stopped firing. I can hear that for myself, Captain. Send out a few men to see if there's anyone who's going to shoot us when we get back on the path."

Quellan nodded and gestured three men forward. Kendrick watched as they broke the corn stalks, making a rough path from where they'd hidden to ambush the family who'd came up behind them in the darkness. His small force was on the only direct route to the Northern Gate. If they had any chance of snaring Traxx before he ran away to another stronghold, they had to take the paths through the northern crop fields.

He'd been told via the radio his men carried that one of their two remaining operational tanks had been destroyed by grenades. The inside firing controls were demolished and the breech had somehow been damaged beyond repair as well. The second tank had been immobilized by some sneaky sonsofbitches who'd blown the tracks off and damaged the road wheels. For the moment, both tanks were out of the fight. His men would have to cannibalize the first tank for parts to repair the other before they went to Tennyson.

"The way is clear, my lord," Quellan said, gesturing to the men he'd sent to investigate the path.

Kendrick stood and walked cautiously to the spot where the family had hidden behind a bench. Several of his men stared at something on the ground. As he got closer, he determined it was a body. The smoke and haze made it difficult to see clearly until he got within a few feet of the scene.

"Oh my God," he muttered.

"What is it, my lord?" Quellan asked in concern.

It was unmistakable. The man's build was as he'd remembered it, tall and muscular, yet not nearly as tall as that freak he kept near him at all times. Patches of short-cropped dark hair poked their way through the layers upon layers of scars that crisscrossed the body's ruined face. They'd gotten him. In a stroke of pure, blind luck, they'd killed the one reason for this war.

"It's him."

"Him?" Quellan asked. He examined the body at his feet and gasped. "Is that Traxx?"

Kendrick nodded his head confidently, "Yes, Captain. This is Aeric Traxx, the man who murdered my father and then tried to raise me as his own along with those three whelps of his."

Tears threatened to pour forth from Kendrick's eyes. He couldn't believe that it was over. It had finally come to an end. He knelt beside the body and pressed his fingers roughly against Traxx's jugular. No pulse, he was truly dead.

Kendrick pulled his knife from its sheath and turned the body over. If there was still pressure in his veins, he didn't want to be covered too badly in blood. Without any hair or loose skin, he did the only thing he could and crammed his fingers in above the eyes, using the sockets to control the head as he sawed.

He'd never cut the head off of a body before and it took him longer than he thought it would. When he finished, he stood with the severed head and held it up for all of the members of his guard to see.

Out in the crops on the opposite side, a girl screamed. Harsh words drifted across the murk; someone was trying to keep the girl quiet. "Go," he told Quellan, who dispatched the same three men to search the fields on the opposite side of the path.

"It is finished, Quellan."

"I'm sorry, sir?"

"Call off the army. We travel back to Austin immediately."

"I... Sir, the people of this city are on the run. They're fleeing through this Northern Gate that you had us headed towards. We can keep this place and take all of the supplies. I—"

"Don't you dare speak to me in such a tone, Quellan! I am the master of the Vultures. I wanted to see Traxx's head on a spike outside of the palace and I have it now. We are through here."

"Forgive me, my lord. We need their supplies in Austin. Your father's warehouses are almost empty. You'd be a fool to leave anything useful here."

"What did you call me?"

Quellan's hand dropped to the pistol on his belt and he drew it. "I said you'd be a fool to leave the supplies."

Kendrick backed away a step, dropping Aeric's head. "What are you doing? Guards, kill him!"

Quellan shook his head slowly. "No. They understand that we've wasted hundreds, if not thousands, of lives and destroyed the last remaining armored vehicles that we had to come here for your personal vendetta against that man. The food supply is perilously low in Austin. More people, these men's families, will starve to death unless we bring back this food."

"You treacherous snake!" Kendrick bellowed. Behind him in the direction where the girl had screamed, grunts of surprise and then pain sounded across the night. "There. Your men have met something that they weren't expecting. I'd be willing to bet that Traxx's pet giant showed them the dangers of overconfidence."

"You're not fit to lead the Vultures any longer, Rustwood. When you started this war, you told of the unlimited wealth of supplies that these people had amassed and I believed you. I sold your plan to the men. They wanted to mutiny before we even left." He paused and then smiled, "Oh, you didn't know that? Your heavy-handed, bizarre and sick practices with your whore were the butt of every joke among the men. You only stayed in command as a figurehead; I was the one who truly pulled the strings, you imbecile."

Kendrick felt his insides boiling over to the point of madness. He was the leader of the Vultures, not the idiot Captain of the Guard. "How dare you—"

A small hand appeared and passed quickly in front of Quellan's throat several times. He gurgled a response to Kendrick, not yet aware that he was dying and fired the pistol several times as he fell to the ground. In his place was a grinning, nude Starr.

She'd come back and saved him. "I'm not a whore," she stated and stalked seductively towards him. He glanced at the remaining members of his personal guard. They had stood by, watching the interaction between him and Quellan without doing anything. They would pay for that later, but for now, he'd keep them around to make sure that he made it out of the walls safely with his prize.

Starr nudged Aeric's head with her toe, "Who's this?"

"This." He bent and picked it up, "This is the reason we came to San Angelo. Starr, meet Aeric Traxx."

"Ugly motherfucker."

"Yeah, well. My father did that to him."

Starr grunted in acknowledgement and said, "Do you forgive me yet?"

Forgive her? his mind scoffed. *Forgive her for what, being a psychotic bitch or the part where she threatened to castrate him?* He suppressed his anger and replied, "I... Yes, I forgive you, Starr."

She smiled and threw her arms wide. He hesitantly opened his and she dived in, wrapping her arms around his midsection and grabbing hold of his shirt as if she wanted to hold him close and never let him go. She snuggled up close to him, rubbing her nose into the space between his pec muscles and then stabbed him in the kidney.

He screamed in pain as she held him close and plunged her knife repeatedly into his right side. Kendrick couldn't escape her tight grasp on his clothes and was already rapidly losing his strength. "Help!" he called out to the few remaining guards. They'd wandered away, no longer interested in what happened to him.

Starr's right arm unwrapped from around him and came to the front. "I am not a whore!" she shouted into his chest as she gouged the knife into his stomach. "Do you hear me? I am not a whore!"

He leaned away and tried to head-butt her in the face. Starr anticipated it and pulled her head back. "I'm not as innocent as I pretended to be," she hissed into his face through gritted teeth and bit down onto his nose. She jerked back hard, separating the soft tissue and stabbed him in the arm.

Finally, she let go and he collapsed to the ground. His arm didn't work and he was starting to go into shock. He felt her hands unbuckle his belt and then jerk his pants down roughly. "Oh God. Please don't," he moaned, unable to stop her.

A few seconds later she held up two pale, bloody lumps of flesh and swung them back and forth above his face. "Lookie at what I've got!" she squealed and then popped one of them in her mouth.

She gagged and continued chewing until she swallowed. "Ugh, they could use some salt. Here, you try the other one." She pulled his jaw down and crammed his second testicle into his mouth. Then she slammed his mouth shut on the soft tissue.

"How's it taste, honey?"

She waited for his answer and then slammed the knife into his chest, leaving it in. "Okay, this is boring. See ya."

Starr pushed up off of his stomach and wiped her bloody hands on his pant leg before wandering off into the corn field.

Kendrick realized the irony that he lay beside his stepfather's body, bleeding to death. The one man who only two weeks prior would have done anything for him. Instead, the son had attacked his home, destroyed everything that he'd worked for and orchestrated the man's death. Kendrick wanted to beg the corpse for an apology, but his pride wouldn't allow him to do it.

Instead, he turned his head, choosing to stare at the green fields that he'd worked as a child. He tried to conjure up fond memories. The only ones that would come were of the shame and humiliation he felt from being lied to by Traxx, who pretended to be his father.

Kendrick watched the gently swaying corn stalks, feeding on his hatred of Traxx, until he died.

*****

They ran as soon as the girl appeared and provided the needed distraction. Aiden's legs were bruised, probably bleeding underneath his jeans. He'd never given any thought to how tough sweet potato plants were before now.

What are you doing, you selfish turd? his mind screamed at him. His grandfather was dead and that madman had cut his head off. *Why had he cut the head off of a dead man? What purpose did that serve?*

He'd been the one who cried out when that happened and made those men come to investigate the noise. Tyler had made quick and quiet work of them and now he was covered in the blood of his grandfather *and* the three strangers.

Aiden had learned a great deal about Tyler from his grandfather over the last week when the man was bedridden after his heart attack. To the boy, he'd always been the big, goofy uncle who was clumsy and knocked things over because he couldn't see well, especially in the dark. Aiden had been around him almost every day of his life until he got sick about a year ago and until last week, he thought he knew all that there was to know about him.

Further proof that he didn't really know his uncle was the way that Tyler had flipped the switch from sorrow to mind-numbing violence when those three men entered the field and scared Aiden. He'd never witnessed anything like it before and he was in awe of the man's capability to kill so effortlessly.

They'd run for a good ten minutes, jumping over old golf cart paths into new types of crops, never daring to run down the path itself, when Tyler called for a halt. "I'm sorry, Aiden," he said between great, heaving coughs that spewed blood in all directions. "I need to walk. I can't keep going like this... Just need a break."

"It's okay, Uncle Tyler. I know that you're sick."

He coughed into his clinched fist again and then craned his neck far to the side so he could see Aiden around his eye patch. "You know I'm not your real uncle, right?"

Aiden took an exaggerated step over a large watermelon. "Yeah, I know. Grandad told me all about you and him last week while he was resting."

"Did he? Only the good parts, I hope."

The boy shrugged, "I don't know. He might have left out parts of the story, but I don't think so. He seemed to think it was pretty important that I know the Traxx family history."

Tyler nodded, "Your grandfather was a smart man—way smarter than me—and honest. Good Lord, was he honest." He laughed and that turned into another coughing fit.

When that passed him by, he pointed to his eye patch and said, "We didn't always see eye-to-eye, no pun intended."

Aiden rolled his eyes and replied, "Ha ha, Uncle Tyler."

A massive hand landed on his shoulder. "Look, son. I'm having a hard time dealing with Aeric's loss as well. We've been almost inseparable for more than thirty years and now he's gone. It's... It's tough.

"I told him..." he sniffled, causing Aiden to look up at him. Was he *crying*? "Only a few hours ago, I told him that our friendship was over. I'd disagreed with something that he did. Looking back on it, he was right. Those kids would have caused further damage to the survivors of the battle. It had to be done."

"I'm confused. What had to be done?" Aiden asked.

"We had to kill them," he replied. Over the next several minutes, Tyler related the events that had occurred in the Barrio after Aiden went to warn his grandmother.

Gunshots rang out occasionally while Tyler told the rest of their story. When it was complete, Aiden took a deep breath and let it out. "I knew those kids. They weren't much older than me. I can't believe that Grandad killed them like that."

"I felt the same way at the time. I know now that it had to be done. Look at what they did to the city with the fires and all the death that they caused by blowing a hole in the wall. They were evil."

Aiden nodded. "Most of 'em were, but not all. Flame was a good guy when the rest of them weren't around. He was just scared and tried to join whatever team gave him the best chance at survival."

"You're probably right," Tyler agreed. "Thankfully, your Grandad took that option away from me and didn't let me vote.

He eliminated any chance at further betrayal. He was exactly the strong, confident leader that this city needed."

They traveled in silence after that until they came to the end of the fields. The Northern Gate was on the other side of the darkened medical supply factory that seemed to absorb the darkness around it. They could hear the murmur of a large crowd of people. The survivors of San Angelo had remembered the fallback point in Tennyson and were trying to escape.

"I wonder how many people made it out," Aiden contemplated aloud.

They rounded the corner of the building and saw hundreds of people holding backpacks and suitcases. Some people had carts and wheelbarrows loaded with their possessions. Tyler clapped him lightly across the back, "I bet most everyone did. That's why there's so many of them."

The crowd seemed to be milling about, not exiting as they should, so Tyler asked a woman in the back who was trying hard to keep six children together. "Hey, why aren't people leaving? We can't stay here any longer."

She looked him up and down. Her eyes went wide at the blood covering him. She put her hands over the eyes of a young boy, replying, "The Shooters only have two trucks; they're taking as many at a time as they can."

"What? Everyone is waiting for a *ride*? The Vultures are all over the city, we need to leave. Now!"

"Don't bark at me, soldier. I already have two other families' children to watch because they went off to fight. We're doing what we can."

Aiden watched the interaction and the expression that passed across Tyler's face. The big man was about to explode. He reached out and tapped him on the arm. "Uncle Tyler, you've gotta get up high where everyone can see you and tell them. Talking to one lady isn't gonna help."

He ruffled Aiden's hair and he felt several strands stick to the mess on Tyler's hand. "Sorry, Aiden," he apologized and wiped his hands on his pants. "You're right. Come on, stay with me."

They shoved their way through the crowd until they came to an old car that had been modified to act as the gate. Giant pieces of metal were bolted to one side and a team of men would roll it into position when the gate was closed. Tyler climbed on the car's hood and shouted for the crowd to listen to him. Even Aiden, who was only a few feet away, had a hard time hearing him over the murmur.

Emotions played across his uncle's face, the scar that disappeared under the eye patch where his eye had been poked out by the Vultures stood out stark white against the deepening red of his face. Tyler pulled his pistol from the holster on his shoulder and fired two rounds into the air.

Several people screamed while others raised weapons towards him. Once most people had quieted down, he yelled, "Listen up! I'm Tyler Nordgren, a lot of y'all know me. Until I got sick I was in charge of the Gathering Squad. We have to leave, *now*! We can't wait for the Shooters to come back with their trucks. It's an hour round-trip up to Tennyson. The Vultures are inside the city and getting closer every second."

"Where is anyone who's still in charge of anything, Tyler?" a man yelled.

Aiden recognized him as Christian Santos, one of the engineers who helped Mr. Winston maintain the walls before he died. "To be honest with you, I don't know where Captain Griffith or Nicole Martin are."

"What about Traxx? Nobody's seen him since the explosion down south."

"Aeric..." Tyler took a breath and then coughed. "Aeric is dead. The Vultures killed him when we were making our way across the old golf course fields."

Several people gasped and looked to the southwest in alarm. "That's what I mean," Tyler shouted them down. "The Vultures aren't far; we need to leave. Take what you can and start walking. Hopefully they'll be satisfied with sacking the city and taking our supplies and just let us escape."

"How do we know that you're telling the truth? Maybe you and the other Gatherers just want us to leave so you can have everything to yourself."

Several people shouted encouragement for the dissenter and the crowd began to become rowdy. Aiden scrambled up the hood and stood beside Tyler. "My Grandad died right over there," he said as he pointed towards the fields. "I watched one of them cut his head off with a knife."

The crowd slowly began to quiet down at his words and Aiden continued, "Aeric Traxx was trying to make it to the Northern Gate to make sure people got out of the city. San Angelo is lost. The Vultures own it now. They were the ones who set the fires; Aeric killed them. He killed all of the infiltrators except Edward Huerta. He's the leader of the Vultures in San Angelo and he's the reason that the wall exploded."

A commotion in the center of the crowd caught his attention. The scuffle lasted for a full minute before several men dragged a bruised and battered Huerta through the press of bodies. They dropped him heavily to the ground and Tyler eased off the hood of the car, and then walked over to the traitor.

"Why did you do it, Ed?" Tyler asked between wheezing breaths.

"Because you people are so simple. None of you understand that the Vultures are the only power that matters anymore. We were the creators of the Reset and we'll be here long after you pathetic worms are gone. The Christian bible was wrong. The *mighty* shall inherit the earth; the meek are just fodder to be trampled upon under the soles of our boots!"

Tyler shook his head and muttered, "I haven't heard that shit since I was a prisoner in Austin. Is that where you were before all of this? Did you come from Austin?"

Huerta's eyes shone brightly in the moonlight. "I was one of Justin's original disciples. I knew the man and was there when you people killed him. I followed you and Traxx here all those years ago to keep an eye on you until the Vultures could reestablish control after you'd cut off our head. Kendrick offered to make me his second in command once every one of you was dead."

"Is that why you're trying to sneak up to Tennyson? Were you planning to betray us there as well?"

Huerta shrugged, "The offer was plain that all of the city's leadership had to be dead. I'm simply following through on my investment."

"In fact, as soon as I can, I will kill all of you, just like that bastard Traxx—"

Aiden jumped backwards and almost fell off the car. The impossibly long blade of a sword pushed its way through Huerta's chest from behind. The Vulture gurgled and slapped ineffectively at the blade before falling. When he fell, Aiden saw his grandmother, Veronica, standing in the front of the crowd. She held Aeric's old sword that he used to spend hours training with in case the ammunition ever ran out.

"Grandma!" Aiden shouted and jumped from the car. He dodged around the body and hugged her tightly. "I thought you'd gone."

"We tried to, but got stuck in this crowd."

Aiden looked expectantly behind her. He saw his brother Alex and a few of his cousins. There wasn't any sign of his parents. "Dad?" Aiden asked expectantly.

Veronica shook her head. "He was stationed out on the western perimeter along with your mother and uncles. I haven't seen any of them since they left John and Anthony with me."

Aiden suppressed the urge to cry. His grandfather had been a great man, the leader of everyone here. He could hold it together for a little while longer if it meant that they'd be able to help save everyone. "Alright," he said loudly so others could hear him. "My father and mother know where Tennyson is. It's our duty to escape so we can survive. If they make it out of the city, they'll meet us there."

Several people murmured approval at his words and he was clapped on the back and hugged more times than he could count. Words of encouragement and sympathy passed over him from friends and strangers on their way towards the gate. His grandfather had been well-respected and most people seemed to genuinely like him because he was willing to make the hard choices when others wouldn't. Aiden grasped his grandmother's hand and shuffled his feet along with everyone else.

The press of the bodies began to lessen as the crowd streamed out of the open gates into the wasteland beyond. Most of them, Aiden included, had never been beyond the walls once they were built. It was simply too dangerous in the outside world. That way of thinking would have to change for the time being...at least until they found a new home.

Aiden knew that Tennyson was only a temporary solution. They couldn't stay there forever. The Vultures were a plague. They'd use up the resources in San Antonio and move to the next place. At best, they could only stay a few days before it became prudent to leave once again and get ahead of their enemies.

He kicked his foot at a fresh pile of ash, the remnant of a home near the gate that had burned quickly when the Vultures started the fires earlier in the day. The gray flakes flew outward in all directions, a few of them landing on his nose and causing him to cough.

The only place that he'd ever lived disappeared slowly behind him, one step at a time.

EPILOGUE

"That's how we came here, Grandad?" Tanya asked.

"Hmm? Yes, dear. Tyler led our group to Tennyson. Out of the five thousand or so who'd started the day in San Angelo, less than a thousand made it to Tennyson."

"Were *all* of them killed?" she asked.

"Nobody knows for sure about the residents who didn't make it to Tennyson because the Vultures occupied the city after that. We know that most of the Shooters and Gathering Squad were killed in the morning when they blew the wall and during the stand at the Provisions Warehouse. People continued to trickle in for weeks after the city fell..." he trailed off. It had been a lifetime since he'd thought about most of the people whom he'd known as a child that died in San Angelo.

"My father and mother were in Tennyson when we got there. Both of my real uncles were dead, along with one of my aunts who'd been killed by a stray demonbroc when they fell back from the walls on the western side of the city.

"Kayla was there with Anna, your grandma, when we arrived at the stronghold as well, but Tyler died a few days after he convinced everyone to take a chance in the wasteland and led the group to Tennyson. We never heard anything about what happened to Nicole. They may not have been lovers, but Tyler and Nicole were absolutely in love. Her loss tore him up more than the cancer ever could have and he lost his battle."

"So, Maria's vision that Tyler would save everyone was true?"

Aiden grinned at her. "I never believed that looney old bird could predict the future, but yes, in a sense, all of her visions came to pass, more or less. The funny thing is that my grandmother never had any more visions after the city was destroyed. She lived to be almost ninety years old, even with all the radiation and poor diet that we were subjected to on the journey here."

"Wow, she lived a long time," the little girl said solemnly.

He nodded. "Veronica Traxx is the matriarch of our family. She brought Aeric to San Angelo and she was the one who made the decision about where to go from Tennyson. She even convinced several other families to go into the wilds with us. Without her, we probably would have stayed in Tennyson."

"Did you leave the new place because of the Vultures?"

He shrugged, the girl lifting into the air as his stomach muscles contracted. "That's one of the reasons. There were rumors that Starr became the leader of the Vultures and enslaved everyone who'd chosen to stay in San Angelo. We thought it best to leave and take our chances far away from them."

He chuckled, trying to lighten the girl's mood. "You know, Maria survived too."

"She did?"

"Yeah. She married my brother Alex."

"Aunt Mary was *Maria*? Is that why you called her a looney old bird?"

Aiden nodded his head. "She changed her name after we left Tennyson. The name Maria had been given to her by people who abandoned her and reminded her too much of the harshness of the Barrio, so she altered it slightly. When she married...."

He swiped angrily at his eyes, muttering, "Damn, must be some flies in here or something."

"It's okay to cry about Uncle Alex."

Aiden smiled sadly at his granddaughter and wiped at his eyes again. "Thank you, sweetie, I'm better now. When Mary and Alex got married, the one thing that she wanted most in life was beyond them. They tried for years to have a family. Unfortunately, she never became pregnant and died without any children.

"Now that Alex is dead, I'm the only person alive who knew Aeric Traxx."

Tanya lay against him and rested her head on his chest. "Grandad, I know the story of our family now and I won't forget about Aeric," she stated solemnly. "Or Tyler or Veronica. We're alive because of them."

The front door opened and closed. He looked up expectantly towards the study door. Aiden's two remaining sons appeared and Blake shook his head slightly. They hadn't found the boys.

The old man frowned and then nodded his chin in acceptance. He looked down at his sleepy granddaughter and continued where he'd left off before Blake and Garrett had returned. "It's more important than ever that you know the story of our family. You'll need to pass on everything that I've told you to your children so the memory of Aeric's sacrifice will never be forgotten."

She sat up suddenly, "Do you think I'll have children one day, Grandad?"

"Of course you will! You're a caring and well-mannered girl. You'll make a wonderful mother." He patted her leg affectionately, "In fact, you'll be just as strong and compassionate as Veronica Traxx was. I bet you'll be the greatest leader that our family has ever known."

To be continued in
Dark Embers, Book 3 of *The Path of Ashes*

If you enjoyed this book, please leave a review! It sounds trivial. However, the number of reviews helps other readers discover my work and adds to the chances that the book will be recommended in online searches. Thank you for your support!

<u>ABOUT THE AUTHOR</u>

A veteran of the wars in Iraq and Afghanistan, Brian Parker was born and raised as an Army brat. He's currently an Active Duty Army soldier who enjoys spending time with his family in Texas, hiking, obstacle course racing, writing and Texas Longhorns football. He's an unashamed Star Wars fan, but prefers to disregard the entire Episode I and II debacle.

Brian is both a traditionally- and self-published author with an ever-growing collection of works across multiple genres, including sci-fi, post-apocalyptic, horror, paranormal thriller, military fiction, self-publishing how-to and even a children's picture book, Zombie in the Basement, which he wrote to help children overcome the perceived stigma of being different from others.

He is also the founder of Muddy Boots Press, an independent publishing company that focuses on quality genre fiction over mass-produced books.

FOLLOW BRIAN ON SOCIAL MEDIA!

Facebook: www.facebook.com/BrianParkerAuthor

Twitter: www.twitter.com/BParker_Author

Enjoy this exciting free preview of
Dark Embers, **Book 3 of** *The Path of Ashes*

The Keep's hallways were cold and dark. *It shouldn't be this cold*, Tanya thought, pulling her robe tighter around her small frame. She clutched the hilt of the dagger that rested in its sheath inside her pocket. She always had a weapon of some type with her these days; the threat from the Vulture army outside the walls was too great to risk being unarmed. She'd found that the small knife was especially useful if she had to fight in close quarters, like the building's hallway.

She walked from her private chambers toward the nursery where her baby, Michael, slept. She'd been woken by a nightmare, a dream of her children being murdered when the Vultures attacked the city. The princess knew that her imagination tended to run into overdrive this time of year. It had been twenty years since slavers attacked the old Traxx compound in the middle of the night. In the attack, her cousins, Caleb and Varan, were abducted, her uncle Luke was killed and her grandfather's brother was killed by a demonbroc. It'd been a traumatic night for a seven year old girl.

Tanya arrived at the nursery. The heavy steel door was closed, as it should have been, and she contemplated not disturbing her children since the Guard was in place, but the feeling that something was amiss wouldn't leave her. She nodded to the man sitting beside the entrance and tried the handle. *Locked.*

A slight sigh of relief passed over her lips. The baby was still secure inside. She tapped gently on the doorframe, rewarded with the sounds of the nursemaid stirring inside.

Clarissa followed the protocols and asked, "Who is it? The prince is sleeping." She sounded annoyed at the late intrusion on her own sleep.

"Clarissa, it's Tanya. Something felt wrong, so I wanted to check on Michael."

"He's sleeping, My Lady. You're the only visitor that we've had tonight."

"No one has come to see you? Not even his brother or sister?" she clarified.

"No. Once we locked the door for the evening, there have been no disturbances. Do you want me to remove the locks?"

"No, thank you. Go back to sleep, my mind is just playing tricks on me."

"Yes, My Lady," Clarissa responded.

Tanya waited for a few more seconds and then turned down the hallway to go to the twins' room. They were six, which meant that they were loud at night as they protested their bedtime, so they'd been moved from the nursery once Michael was born. Otherwise, the baby would have never slept.

She peeked around the corner and saw the two Guards sitting attentively beside the door to the adjoining bedchambers.

"M'Lady!" the older of the two Guards whispered, jumping to his feet when he noticed her.

She placed a hand on his arm. "Good evening, Frederick. I had a strange feeling, so I wanted to check on our babies."

"They are secure inside. I wouldn't let anything happen to them."

"I know." *Am I being paranoid?* She hesitated, then after a moment's pause she said, "I wish to check on them."

"Of course," Frederick replied. "James, can you watch the doorway? Secure it behind us."

"Yes, Sergeant. Tap the code when you're ready to leave." Tanya nodded her approval of the Guard's protocol. Since the attacks by the

Vultures, security of the Traxx family had increased even more than it had before. The Keep felt like a true fortress these days.

Once the door was secure behind them, Tanya grasped Frederick's hand and they walked side-by-side through the entryway to the twins' bedchambers. "What do you think is wrong?" Frederick asked.

"I don't know. I just have a feeling that something is."

He squeezed her hand lightly. "It's been twenty years, right?"

She nodded and wrinkled her nose at the sour smell in the twins' suite. She'd have to have the maintenance man examine their bathroom. The toilets in the building were still operational, flushed by pouring water into the reservoir behind the seat, but it was far from a perfect system. The refuse went into a gigantic underground tank far from The Keep that had overflowed before, causing a disgusting, smelly mess inside the building and out in the field. It had taken a crew of ten men several weeks to clean the filth out of the tank, using buckets and hauling the night soil off in carts to be used as fertilizer.

"Yes," she acknowledged, making a note to have the septic tank examined. "Twenty years ago today, my cousins were abducted and we've never known their fate. They're dead, in all likelihood, but I wish we knew for certain."

"It's just your mind playing tricks on you, then, dredging up memories of the past. The Keep is secure. See?" He gestured to the bricked-over window in Jensen's room. The small space at the top that wasn't sealed to allow in fresh air was firmly locked for the night. The boy slept soundly on the old, worn mattress, small noises escaping his lips when he breathed out.

She nodded in the darkness. "Looks like you're right. I guess I'm feeling nostalgic."

"It's okay; you're allowed to, Tanya."

Tanya bumped her shoulder into him, "Sorry to make you leave your card game."

"Mmm...hmm," he murmured, turning toward Jade's room "What's that smell?"

"I noticed it too," she answered, relieved that at least one of her senses wasn't going crazy. *Maybe I'm pregnant again*, she thought in a panic. Michael was only three months old. It was much too soon for her to have another child.

A thump in the next room made her jump. Frederick slowly drew his sword so as not to make more noise than necessary. "What is it?" she asked.

"Stay here," he ordered, taking charge of the situation as a trained Traxx Guard.

"I'm not staying here if something's the matter with my daughter," she hissed back at him, pulling the dagger from her pocket.

He sighed and his shadow moved away from her toward the shared bathroom that led into Jade's room. The smell of stale sweat, assaulted her nose when he opened the door. Frederick glanced back at her and motioned for her to stay once again. She shook her head furiously at his suggestion.

He pushed open the door into the second bedroom slowly, peeking around the corner. Tanya jumped when he yelled and charged into the room, sword lifted above his head. Tanya didn't understand what was happening. She heard the sound of metal hitting against something hard, like wood and then a loud crash.

She rushed into the room and stopped. The room was much too bright. Moonlight shone through the *open* window. Frederick lay bleeding from a wound to his head amongst the bricks that had once sealed the room from the outside world. A tall man with an oversized backpack stood with one leg on the windowsill, preparing to jump. In his arms, he held her daughter.

Tanya screamed, running at him with her own weapon held in front of her. He turned toward her and hissed.

What looked like scales of some type covered the man's face and he wore a type of close-fitting armor that was nothing like the Vultures wore. She had a moment to think that his yellow eyes looked much more snakelike than human, and then she was upon him.

Tanya thrust outward, attempting to come in low with the knife, under his guard, but he easily batted her arm away. She allowed the momentum from his defense to turn her around and crouched as she spun. He swung a brick at her head and she ducked under it, stepping inside his defense and burying her dagger deep into the man's leg.

He cried out in pain and almost dropped Jade, who somehow remained asleep through the ordeal.

Tanya's weapon was gone, stuck in the kidnapper's leg, so she dove to where Frederick's unconscious form lay, grabbing his sword before standing up. She wasn't as well trained with a sword as she was the dagger, but she was decent and could hold her own against most of the Guard.

"Put my daughter down."

He pulled the knife from his leg and it clattered to the floor. "You are doomed, but Gaia will protect this child from your war," he rasped, the words misshapen in his mouth.

The kidnapper pulled himself completely up on the windowsill and leapt into the night.

Tanya screamed and rushed to the window. They were six floors up; the fall would kill them. Far below, a set of triangular wings appeared above the man's back and the contraption caught the wind current, lifting them higher into the air.

The princess watched helplessly as her daughter disappeared into the night.

Near the walls, the alarms began to sound and her heart dropped in her chest. The Vultures surrounding the city had finally chosen to attack.